Red Equinox

By
Douglas Wynne

JournalStone
San Francisco

JOURNALSTONE
YOUR LINK TO ARTISTIC TALENT

JournalStone books may be ordered through booksellers or by contacting:

JournalStone

www.journalstone.com

ISBN: 978-1-940161-45-7   (sc)
ISBN: 978-1-940161-46-4   (ebook)

JournalStone rev. date: January 16, 2015

Library of Congress Control Number: 2014960074

Printed in the United States of America

Cover Art & Design: Chuck Killorin
A derivative of "Boston skyline from the Atlantic Ocean" by Willem van Bergen. CC BY-SA 2.0
A derivative of "Octopus vulgaris 02.JPG" by H. Zell. CC BY-SA 3.0
Author Photo: Jen Salt
Edited by: Dr. Michael Collings

For Jennifer

8/18/17

Red Equinox

Happy 30th Birthday Jay!

Best,

Douglas Wynne

That time of year thou may'st in me behold

When yellow leaves, or none, or few, do hang

Upon those boughs which shake against the cold,

Bare ruin'd choirs, where late the sweet birds sang.

—Shakespeare, Sonnet 73

There was a demoniac alteration in the sequence of the seasons—the autumn heat lingered fearsomely, and everyone felt that the world and perhaps the universe had passed from the control of known gods or forces to that of gods or forces which were unknown.

—H.P. Lovecraft, "Nyarlathotep"

Chapter I

Death has a way of calling us home, and when it does we put on our best. Becca Philips hadn't been to Arkham in years, hadn't worn a dress in almost as long, and now here she was, stepping off the train and feeling out of place in both.

Water Street looked just the same as it had the last time she'd been here. The same shops struggling to net a few of the North Shore tourist dollars that tended to flow around Arkham before continuing up the coast to Newburyport and Portsmouth.

She took the Garrison Street Bridge on foot. It was a cool day and overcast. The updraft off the river chilled her through, and she pulled her coat tight around her chest, hair flailing in the wind and whipping across her eyes. Gulls wheeled high above, and the last boats of the season trolled the dark water below. Both avoided the stark little island of standing stones upriver from the bridge. Same as it ever was.

The dress was a simple black thing, knee-length with little red roses, and she wondered now why she'd bothered with it. Her usual mode of dress had mostly been inherited from the woman she was here to honor anyway. Catherine Philips, her late grandmother, had only ever worn dresses to university fundraisers, never in the classroom or the field. Thinking of her, Becca longed for her cargo pants and leather jacket—the sort of attire Catherine would have been wearing in some sepia-toned photo taken in front of a pyramid back when her hair had been as dark as Becca's was now.

From the bridge she could see the white steeple, her destination and another reminder of the dissonance between a life well lived and a proper burial. Catherine had set foot inside churches less often than dresses.

The service was already underway when Becca arrived. She settled quietly into one of the empty pews at the back of the nave and let the sonorous words of the minister wash over her as she searched the sparsely peopled rows for a mane of sun-bleached hair combined with an inherent restlessness of form. Finding him nowhere, she realized she'd dressed up the little bit she was capable of just to highlight his inevitable shabbiness, his disrespect for his own mother—he who would arrive on the back of a Harley in oil-stained jeans if he arrived at all. But of course he hadn't. He'd blown them both off to the bitter end.

A man in a brown suit stepped out of the shadows of the narthex and sat down beside her. Her heart jumped into her throat for a second, but it wasn't the grizzled hand of her hard-living father patting her knee, and she found herself looking into the empathetic eyes of her surrogate uncle, Neil Hafner.

She was surprised at how much he had aged since she'd last seen him: his doggish face now even more hound-like in its sagging, his fading freckles framed by thinning pale hair. Becca gave his hand a squeeze and let it go.

The rows in front of them appeared to be mostly occupied by Catherine's colleagues and students, with the family underrepresented. She spotted her Uncle Alan with Michelle and the girls, but Becca had always been closer to Neil, who was neither family nor faculty and who had always been more of a friend to Catherine than either. They had met in the nineties when the folklore professor needed photographs of bas-reliefs for a book she was writing. Later, when Becca had shown an interest in photography, Catherine had enlisted Neil as a mentor.

He reached into his jacket pocket and produced a small wooden box, hinged and redolent of cedar, which he held above her lap until she took it. Now he was the one scanning the rows and aisles, but somehow she doubted he was looking for her father. He folded his hand over hers just as she was about to pop the lid on the little box, leaned in and whispered, "Not here. And don't let anyone see. It belonged to Catherine."

Becca slipped the box into her purse and glanced around the church, trying not to appear too furtive, but all eyes were on the altar. "Who are we keeping it from?"

"The university might make a claim on it if they knew it wasn't lost, but she wanted you to have it."

A birdlike man with dandruff on his black suit collar glanced over his shoulder at them from a few rows up and Neil settled back against the hard wood beside her. When the man faced forward again, he whispered, "Tell you later."

The open coffin lid glowed in the dusty autumnal light, the white silk lining catching the lowering sun through the tall windows. She couldn't see Catherine's face from this distance but knew she would need to see it before leaving, before she could even begin to process the reality of her death. It seemed impossible that a personality as bold as her Gran's could simply be extinguished without a struggle. The woman had been a force of nature: fearing nothing, seeking out the darkest corners of the globe and of the human psyche for her scrutiny.

Becca believed it was that intrepid spirit that had caused her students and children to fear her. But Catherine had softened with age and had never demanded as much of Becca as she had of her own children, all of whom had fled from her sphere as soon as they could. Becca had come to believe that given a second chance at parenting, Catherine had deliberately chosen a different approach. Or maybe the woman had felt to some degree responsible for the circumstances that had landed Becca in her care.

Despite the years they had spent together in the house on Crane Street, there were still sleeping tigers they had never dared disturb, and now Becca had to find a way to accept that they never would.

The service ended as she brooded and she felt a little jolt at the realization that the front rows were now rising and lining up to approach the casket. Becca numbly found her feet and wondered if she would cry when she saw the embalmed body. She hoped she would. She'd been ruminating on the loss in an effort to break down some intangible barrier in her own heart, but the tears remained stubbornly frozen by the dream-like distance the roomful of strangers, formal clothes, and ill-fitting religious trappings imposed upon the primal loss of the woman who had raised her.

Maybe the increased dosage of Zoloft that her therapist had put her on to gird her against the fading light and impending threat of winter was keeping grief at arm's length. Maybe it was the past two years away, years in which she had finally left Arkham without looking back and had immersed herself in her art and the city and ill-chosen men. She should have called more often, should have visited, should have been less self-absorbed, knowing that she was the last in a long line to abandon Dr. Catherine Philips.

Her children don't see it that way. You know the narrative. She drove her husband to the asylum, her daughter-in-law to suicide, and the rest of the family to mass exodus. She and the dark things she couldn't stop poking and prodding.

When Becca's turn came, she knelt and looked down at the body that somehow was and was not her grandmother, and wondered if the stroke had delivered that which a lifetime of inquiry had not: knowledge of the other side.

* * *

The tears finally came at the graveside. Something about the smell of wet grass from the morning rain and the mound of clodded earth beneath the tarp made it possible for her to feel in a way that had eluded her within the dark wood confines of the church.

They had given her a rose to place on the coffin, and she watched the petals fracture into red shards through the water in her eyes. Neil, beside her, handed her a handkerchief, and wiping her nose she found an odd comfort in this evidence that she could still feel what you were supposed to at a funeral, despite her efforts to protect herself from feeling too much.

As Neil led her back to the car with a pair of ladies he had promised a ride to the campus, she let her eyes linger on the tree line, but her father still wasn't there, wasn't leaning on his bike and watching from a distance because no distance from his mother, not even in death, would ever be safe enough. She regretted dressing up; it felt weird to be carrying a purse instead of a camera bag, and now all she wanted to do was get home and out of the dress and the scratchy black hose.

Neil appeared beside her and patted her shoulder to draw her distant gaze back to him. "You're not alone in this," he said. "You might expect a death in the family to change people or bring them around, but…. If you'll let me give you one last photo lesson: it's the shadows that define things. Okay, *two* last lessons: sometimes you have to alter the focus to see what's right in front of you. Right? Promise me you'll call me if you need to talk."

Becca said she would. It wasn't until after he'd dropped her at the station on his way to the university and the train was pulling out that she remembered the cedar box.

She wondered if he'd set it up that way, offering the ladies a ride so that she couldn't react to the contents of the box, couldn't ask questions he didn't have answers to, or questions he didn't *want* to answer—like, *is this a family heirloom or a stolen antiquity?*

Becca hadn't seen the object for many years, had forgotten all about it. But now, seeing it again, she remembered.

* * *

"What's a myth, Gran?"

"It's a kind of story. Like a fairy tale."

"Why not just call it a story then?"

"Well…a myth is a special sort of story. A story that endures and explains the world."

"Indoors?"

"**Endures.** *It lasts a long time. So long that people eventually forget it was made up. They begin to believe it was first told by a god, when in fact it had probably been a shaman.*"

Becca knew about shamans. She had seen pictures of them in Gran's crazy books. Bones through the nose and death in their eyes. "Where does a shaman get the story from?"

"That's a good question. One I've spilled a lot of ink on. Some of them climb trees to the stars." Gran's smile told Becca that she was being challenged to question this.

"Where else?"

"Some go to the underworld. And some might find a myth hiding behind ordinary things, using them as masks: animals and insects, lightning and hail.... Anything in the world can be the seed of a story if you plant it deep enough."

"Tell me one. Make me a myth, Gran."

The bedroom was dark except for the muted gold glow of the nightlight. They had finished one book but hadn't started another yet and didn't need the bedside lamp to read by. Becca liked the spaces between bedtime books, the times when they just talked and mused while her eyes grew heavy. "Make me a myth about something in this room."

Gran sighed and smiled. She searched the shadow-drenched corners for inspiration, ran her hand over the comforter, and then produced a golden scarab beetle pendant from the neckline of her cotton nightgown. The metal glowed in the dark as she turned it on its chain, and Becca felt almost hypnotized by its beauty.

"Once upon a time in Egypt, there came a black pharaoh on the wings of a sandstorm out of the desolate wastes."

Chapter 2

Something had moved in the room. The scarab beetle pendant swung from side to side like a pendulum from the chain draped over the mirror where Becca had hung it before falling asleep. Just the slightest motion, as if the tail of a cat leaping out of bed had struck it. But Becca didn't live with a cat anymore, not since Josh had moved out, taking Ftang with him. And yet, as her sleep-heavy eyes blinked and focused on the golden shine of the thing, it swung, and she thought of her grandmother swinging a pendulum once, a ring on a string, to answer a question *yes* or *no*, and she'd almost fallen asleep again when the explanation came to her: she must have brushed it with her arm while rolling over, or jostled the peach crate which served as a bookshelf and nightstand with her elbow. The recently dreaming part of her mind told her that the beetle had opened its shell for a second and fluttered its metallic wings; that it had stirred at first light. But that was nonsense.

She untangled her body from the sheets and touched the scarab. Her finger found the bezel where the gem was missing between the pinchers and probed the hole like a tongue exploring a cavity where a filling had come loose. She wondered what kind of stone it had been. Diamond? Ruby? Emerald? Her memory of the thing from the few times she'd seen it on Catherine was dim. The bezel looked a little too big to have held a diamond.

The shapes of her room were slowly coming into focus now, softly delineated by the watery gray light of an overcast September morning. There were still days in September when she would awaken to a blaze of stark light and shadow, but not this one. Even with all of the windows that came with a warehouse loft, and even as late as 9 AM, the effect on a gloomy day was of shapes emerging from murk, her furniture appearing like the mossy, barnacle-encrusted features of a shipwreck at five-hundred fathoms.

Becca stared at the high ceiling and pondered the meaning of the missing stone. Scarabs were dung beetles. They pushed balls of shit through the sand. But she remembered Gran taking her to the Boston MFA when she was a girl, remembered seeing paintings and carvings depicting the beetle pushing the solar disc. She wished a beetle would push the sun out of the clouds today so she could think right. It was hard enough getting out of bed on a good day, but without the vitamin D, without the light, without someone to push her out of bed anymore...everything was harder. And yet she knew she had to do it, had to get up and get dressed and push her own ball of shit through the day. Her army bag, leather jacket, and boots beckoned. Her urban uniform. *Get up, soldier, you can do it.* She swept the sheets aside and rolled out of bed.

Everything was harder this time of year when the light was dying, when the year was dying, when she was reminded of her mother dying, and now Gran had gone and laid a new painful association on the cycle by also dying in the fall. It was a season of death, even had a holiday to acknowledge the fact. Only rather than lighting fires against the shadows on All Hallows Eve, her culture warded off depression with sugar. Nowhere near as effective as the Lamictal and Zoloft she was now washing down with a warm glass of water from the tap, standing in her underwear and a black tank top and gazing out at the tin-type print of a day that lay stretched out wet below her through the warped glass.

Rent was cheap at the edges of the flood zones, and the view could be oddly beautiful in a semi-apocalyptic sort of way. On recent afternoons when the autumn sun slanted down and sliced the limpid surface of the shallow water at the base of the building, casting undulating lattices of light over the bricks, sine waves of amber fire, she could almost feel blessed to be alive in such a time. But today there was none of that. Only a stew of fallen leaves and plastic bottles floating on black water. Boston was a city built on marshland, raised up on fill less than three centuries ago. The Back Bay neighborhood had actually been a bay not that long ago, and now it was going that way again. The people on TV were finally admitting that this was no temporary state of affairs. Glacial melt and Hurricane Sonia had reminded Boston of her true level, her humble origins beneath the water line, and that dirty water was here to stay.

She picked her phone off of the kitchen counter, checked the time on it, then carried it back to bed, setting it down on the crate beside the paper square she'd fallen asleep pondering: the note from her grandmother which had lain underneath the beetle in the fragrant box.

Looking at the scarab, she let her hand fumble over the detritus atop the crate (a stack of paperbacks and dusty photo magazines partially obstructing an antique brass-framed mirror, a couple of prescription bottles, and a nest of worn-out hair elastics) and plucked up the paper square. It was a simple, yet elegant missive, only about the size of a Post-it note, but inked in Catherine's handwriting on heavy cream-colored stock with a linen texture. Becca felt a desperate sadness claw unexpectedly at her heart as she noticed now on closer inspection how the carefully inscribed lines wavered ever so slightly, betraying a tremor in the woman's hands. The note read: *May Kephra, guardian and guide, light your way in dark places.*

Kephra. No idea. Typical Gran to be dropping obscure references even from the grave. But Becca had no doubt that a search for the name would lead her to some wiki of mythological figures. Her throat thickened as she thought of the countless fairy tales and legends they had read together. Gran had taught her that every object was a story, and Becca had applied the lesson to her own art: if every shard of pottery anyone had ever unearthed could tell a story, then so could every photograph.

So what was the story of the beetle that had for so long hung around Gran's neck, and which now hung from her mirror?

She tilted the mirror toward her. Her reflection betrayed trepidation in her ice-blue eyes, a furrow in her brow she wasn't awake enough yet to be aware of. It was fear, she knew, now that she saw it written plainly in the glass.

Mirrors are windows, mirrors are doors.

Where had she heard that?

Catherine had been found dead on her bedroom carpet, spilled out of the chair in front of her vanity when the stroke hit.

Becca touched the metal scarab, lifted it in the crook of her finger for a moment, then let it swing back against the mirror with a sigh. She wasn't sure if she was ready to wear it yet, knowing that it would always remind her of how she had failed the woman who had been more of a mother to her than her own. Failed to call when the darkness was upon her, and failed to get her ass on a train before it was too late because she'd been absorbed in the perspective-wrecking drama that came with being fucked up about a boy. Josh, who hadn't even bothered to check and see how she was doing, never mind accompany her to the funeral. True colors, that's what that was.

The scarab, released from her hand, rocked on its chain. She caught a glimpse of its reverse side in the mirror and remembered the markings. Yesterday she had done little more than glance at it and hang it where she could contemplate it while she drifted off to sleep. Now she turned it over and ran her thumb across the inscription: finely etched hieroglyphics she couldn't read. Another mystery. Even the metal was a mystery. It looked too lustrous to be anything less than the purest gold, but there was no karat marking or jeweler's hallmark to tell.

She picked up her phone. The thought of going to work at the gallery and falling back into the mundane rhythms of her life felt wrong. It felt like a betrayal of her Gran's memory to let the world sweep her along without a moment's contemplation. With a twinge of guilt, she called in sick and was relieved when Glen didn't pick up. She left a voicemail, then called Rafael and asked him to spot her on a trip to the asylum.

He was waiting with a hot tea in a Styrofoam cup from a donut shop when she stepped off the Green Line T at Harvard Ave and Commonwealth. She took the cup with a wince when he offered it. "You know this stuff takes like a billion years to break down in a landfill, right?"

Rafael stuffed his hands in the back pockets of his torn-at-the-knees, paint-encrusted jeans, hunched his shoulders so that the hood of his sweatshirt drooped over his eyes. Even in baggy clothes with shoulders slouched like a reprimanded dog, his toned and wiry physique showed through like titanium tent poles propping up shabby canvas. He'd spent his teens climbing building scaffoldings in San Paulo, emblazoning the city's back alleys with street art before coming to Boston to attend the Museum school on a scholarship after a vacationing faculty member had seen his work. One city's graffiti had been another's entrance exam.

"Sorry," she said. "I mean, thanks." She gave him a peck on the cheek and regretted the gesture as soon as she saw the way it lit up his face, his full lips spreading into a heart-shaped smile that was equal parts surprise and delight.

He nodded toward the hill. "We goin' somewhere new in there, or are you shooting stuff you've seen before?"

Becca shrugged, hiked the heavy camera bag higher onto her shoulder.

"Here," he said, "Let me. Looks heavy."

"I got it. Maybe when we get to the top of the hill."

Rafael swung his arms at his sides, then punched his left palm. He had no gear of his own to carry, didn't need any for a site as familiar as this one. He claimed to have been over every square foot of Allston State Hospital and had proven himself a reliable guide to Becca, who was taking her time, exploring the place methodically, absorbing the site one room at a time.

Together they walked through a parking lot and onto Brainerd Road, passing the ramshackle three-story apartment houses of the college ghetto—houses that leaned at odd angles, veering off their foundations, cheaply painted by the students who inhabited them, cats slinking nonchalantly around the eaves, ghostly traces of stale beer and pot smoke clinging to the moldy fabric of porch furniture. The natty suburb had an almost feudal geography, the houses becoming steadily more upscale as one ascended the hill, the rundown Victorians giving way to red brick apartment buildings, then to handsome if modest Town Houses and bi-level homes with vinyl siding and flower boxes in the windows.

Rafael was in better shape, his breathing less labored than Becca's when the incline grew steep. He shortened his stride to match her pace and took the army bag that held her camera and lenses from her shoulder to no protest this time. Relieved of the weight, and no longer feeling like she was hiking in the White Mountains, she turned and walked backwards for a few paces, taking in the view of the hazy blue buildings and treetops in the distance below. Cities had always looked friendlier to her from above than down in their dirty crevices. She figured that the illusion of cleanliness afforded by distance was a large part of the price tag up here. That, and the fact that higher ground was always the best flood insurance.

But if the Brainerd Road hill was a fiefdom, then the castle at its peak was that of a mad, syphilis-stricken despot: Allston State Hospital, one of the few insane asylums in the Bay State that hadn't yet been demolished. The chain-link fence, barbed wire, and much of the plywood boarding up the doors had, however, been demolished long ago by vandals, kids on Halloween dares, and urban explorers like Becca and Rafael. The police patrolled the area frequently enough to keep junkies and vagrants from taking up permanent residence, but there was no sign of a cruiser on the tree-lined street today as they ducked through a gap in the twisted fence.

The long, dry grass was parted and worn to a bald dirt trail by the frequent trespassers who had for years been treading on parts of the grounds the long-ago inmates would never have been granted access to.

Becca shielded her eyes with her hand and assessed the sky. The mid-day sun, diffused by a cover of stratus clouds, cast a gentle silver glow over the abandoned institution. She took her camera from the bag and switched it on.

"I checked out your web page," Rafael said.

"Yeah? What'd you think?"

"Pretty legal."

"Legal?"

"Yeah, you know: *cool.* Hey, how you get that effect? Is it Photoshop, how everything kind of glows?"

"Nope. It's in the picture when I take it."

"Really?"

She held up her Nikon. "This is modified. I removed the standard hot-mirror filter inside and replaced it with an IR filter."

"IR?"

"Infrared. People used to use special infrared film in cameras to get the same effect, but it was tricky. Infrared film is so sensitive to light that you have to process it in total darkness." She saw the glazed look in his eyes and remembered he wasn't a photo geek. He just wanted to know why the shots looked ghostly. "Infrared light is just a different set of frequencies."

"Come again?"

"Regular photography is like listening to music through earplugs. All you hear is bass. When I took that filter out of my camera, it was like taking the plugs out of my ears so I can get the higher frequencies, you follow?"

He grinned. Now she was speaking his language.

"Did you notice that not everything has that white glow?"

Poor guy. Only wanted to compliment her work after glancing at her online portfolio and now he was being quizzed on it. She wished she knew how to talk to normal people. A cool girl would undoubtedly say something mysterious about capturing the spirit of things and leave it at that. "The plants were the things that glowed the most, right?" she prodded him.

"Yeah." He looked relieved. "The weeds and shit."

She laughed. "That's because green things emit a lot of IR frequencies."

"Hey...I should take you to the arboretum sometime where *everything* is green. You'll get crazy shots!"

Becca nodded and decided not to tell him that the beauty was all in the contrast, that the weeds and vines among the dead gray concrete and plaster were the music she listened for with those earplugs out, not just a lot of cymbals crashing from every tree in the forest. She wasn't looking for a date, but it was good to have a friend, and if she was being honest, it was especially good to have a friend who wasn't afraid to go tunnel hacking and rappelling down the walls of derelict factories and mental hospitals to get to the cool parts. "Maybe," she said.

The asylum loomed over the hedge-bounded field, an imposing red-brick building topped with six gables and a domed copper cupola turned green from the weather. The windows were tall banks of small squares, and while most of those on the ground floor had been boarded up, there were some with rounded tops that were a poor fit for the straight-edged boards hastily thrown up by a demolition crew that would someday return with a wrecking ball. Through these exposed panes, rocks had been thrown and vines had grown, creeping into the dank, moldy interior of the place. On her last visit, Becca had shot a series she was quite proud of in which spirals of rampant ivy wove around the metal frames of the rotting hospital beds like leather restraints. In the photos, the vines resembled radiant silver chains.

With a glance at the second-story windows of the nearest house, Rafael swept aside a tangle of dead brush to reveal their tried-and-true entrance. Becca pulled the elastic strap of a headlamp over her hair, switched it on, and climbed through.

Inside, a long corridor stretched out around them in two directions, dappled with weak sunlight, the floor littered with clods of fallen plaster and flakes of peeled paint the size of autumn leaves. The walls seemed to be molting, and the acidic scent of bat guano hung in the cloying air. To the right, at the end of the hall, a tiled spiral stairway led to the second floor. To the left, a high doorframe opened onto the wards where Becca had shot the vine-bound beds. Rafael had covered the walls of one of the better-lit rooms on this wing with floor-to-ceiling murals: surreal mash-ups of graffiti and fine art.

Today Becca felt ready to begin exploring the second floor, and touching the scarab where it hung in her cleavage just below the neckline of her tank top, she nodded toward the stairs, her beam bouncing forward and back.

"You want to go up?" he asked.

"Yeah."

Rafael took a high-powered LED flashlight from his pocket and twisted it on. He aimed the beam at his own face from below in a clichéd parody of a ghoul, and Becca laughed at the halo of dreadlock shadows blasted onto the wall behind him.

"What's with the shit-eating grin?"

"Nothin'." He swung the light onto the floor where water-stained papers lay splayed among crushed beer cans and dirty scraps of tin foil—the only garbage the rats and feral cats hadn't eaten. "I just thought of something you'll like."

"What?"

"You'll see."

"On the second floor?"

"Yeah, you'll like it."

"Okay...." She drew out the word, infusing it with uncertain trust. Then, catching a whiff of the air, she remembered another way to explain light to him. "Wait a sec. Wanna see something cool?"

"Always."

"Turn off your flashlight."

He did, and Becca clicked a switch on her headlamp. The white LED spotlight vanished from her crown, replaced by a wide flood of purple ambiance. On the wall, neon splashes and drips appeared.

"It's urine," she said. "This is UV light. Ultraviolet, okay? Well, visible light—everything you can see with the naked eye—is sort of in the middle of the spectrum with infrared on one side, and ultraviolet on the other. Sort of like bookends."

He was smiling, his teeth glowing an unnatural shade of violet. Probably because the big piss revelation was always a hit with the boys. She continued under the assumption that he was actually listening. "Biological things emit some interesting frequencies in those two ranges. So just like how the plants glow in IR, bodily fluids do sort of the same thing in UV. But to me, the really cool thing to ponder is how all of those frequencies are part of one great big wave spectrum. Everything from the subsonic sounds that elephants send through the ground to communicate over distances, up to the ultrasonic songs of dolphins and whales, and then beyond that into where the waves stop being sound and start being light, and then into light we can't usually see, like UV, then microwaves, gamma rays.... Even matter is just energy vibrating in waves."

He uttered a nervous laugh. "Sorry, you lost me again. You're talking over my head."

"Maybe I'm just not articulating it well. You'd get it with a little time to process it."

"*Process it*. Photo joke?"

Now she laughed. "Not intentional." She took a UV marker from her camera bag and wrote on the wall: RAF & BECCA WERE HERE. The letters blazed brighter than the piss stains.

She clicked her headlamp back to white and the message disappeared.

"*Whoa*, invisible ink." Rafael's eyes and teeth were wide, but no longer violet.

"Cool, huh? Okay, up we go. Lead the way," she said with a wave of her hand, preferring him in front not just because he was strong and able to handle any squatters they might encounter, but because she knew that (gentleman or not) she could count on Rafael to stare at her ass on a staircase. She'd been told it was one of her finer features.

The twin light beams bobbed up the cavernous walls of the winding stairwell, their footsteps echoing back to them from the tiles. At the top they came to a large room, empty of all furniture except for a rotting upright piano in the corner, an abandoned wheelchair parked at the yellowing keyboard. The vast space reminded Becca of her warehouse apartment. Together, they crossed the room at a pace that felt slower than it was due to the sheer size of what could have been a ballroom but was probably a rec room for the vegetables. Passing under an arch at the far end, they found themselves in a corridor of rusted metal doors with sliding panels at eye height. Some of the doors hung open on their hinges; others were closed, possibly still locked. No light reached the hall from the open doors and peep slots, telling her that these were windowless cells. Shining her headlamp into the cells as they passed, she caught glimpses of stains and hash marks on the walls, clumps of stiff bed sheets and muddy rags.

On the cracked wall of one cell, a single line of graffiti stood out for its lack of style. Unlike the ubiquitous tags rendered in metallic spray paint, this one appeared to have been left by a patient rather than a vandal, scrawled in thick black crayon: DEAD BUT DREAMING.

Becca stared at it, chilled by the possibility that it might be the only remaining record of her grandfather's residence here. Rafael, bemused, gave her a minute to stare, then prodded her on. "C'mon, it's right up here in the next room."

Prying her gaze from the graffiti, she noticed natural light spilling into the end of the hall as a cloud shifted outside.

The last room on the right was a green-tiled chamber with some oddities that Becca didn't notice until the exhilaration of the main feature had subsided. The hospital staff wouldn't have considered it a feature, but she felt a surge of affection for Rafael for knowing that *she* would. On the far wall, where a tall window overlooked the inner courtyard, a tree had crashed through the glass, scattering shards on the dusty floor. Branches still bearing leaves reached into the room like the fingers of a giant trying to seize a sleeper from the bed on the left wall.

Noticing the bed, Becca saw that it was bracketed to the floor. The mattress had been pulped by vandals and rats, but the leather restraints on the side rails were still in good shape. She reappraised the room, finding common purpose in the buckles and straps, the row of three-foot-high electrical outlets, barren shelves which would once have housed equipment, and—among paint flakes scattered on the floor like scales sloughed off of some reptile—a rubber mouth guard with a phallic handle, and a grimy, wrinkled tube of conductive gel.

"*Whoa*. They did ECT here," she said, raising the camera to her eye and framing a shot.

Rafael put his knuckles to his temples and convulsed with a little jump, reminding her of the scarecrow in *The Wizard of Oz*. He accompanied the charade with a loud *bzzt!* Becca ignored him and moved around the bed, clicking away, capturing the juxtaposition of what might well have been a lightning-struck tree crashing into the electroshock treatment room, and knowing that in infrared the glow of the leaves would infuse all of this darkness and decay with an ethereal light.

Leaning in, kneeling, shooting, oblivious to the filth on the knees of her pants and the palms of her hands, she felt the sadness of the place getting under her skin. When at last she glanced up from the viewfinder, Rafael had left the room. She felt a flutter of fear at his absence.

Although most of the equipment had been removed from the room, there was an old-fashioned telephone handset mounted to the wall. It blazed at her in shocking red through the drab, dusty grays of the room. Had it been an emergency line? She snapped a few shots of it, becoming increasingly, irrationally certain that it would jump to life with a jarring jangle at any moment just to freak her the fuck out. And who would be on the other end if she answered? Her long-dead Grandpa who had lived out his last days in this place? Her recently deceased Gran, who had exposed her husband to certain facts about the nature of reality he had never recovered from?

Presently she realized that she was no longer photographing, but only staring at the phone in anticipation, and as her awareness shifted from sight to sound she became aware of a human voice murmuring in an unfamiliar language, what her Gran would have called a "barbarous tongue." She drew her elbows across her midriff and bit her thumbnail before thinking about where it had lately been.

"Rafael?" she said. Her voice was too thin to be heard, but now that she knew she wasn't alone, the prospect of shouting seemed reckless, a surefire way to broadcast her location. *Wait…*could the voice be him, messing with her? Had he slipped down the stairs and into the courtyard just to try and spook her?

If he knew her at all, he knew she didn't scare easy, but the boy did like a challenge. She went to the window where the chant drifted through the broken glass, muted only by the leaves clustered on the branches of the fallen tree. Taking care not to rustle those leaves or crunch the glass underfoot, she searched for a gap between the branches affording a clear downward angle. The voice gained detail and clarity, and she knew for sure that the timbre was not Rafael's.

There. A man in a black trench coat with a beaded cap on his head was kneeling in prayer or meditation, his hands flat on his thighs as he rocked back and forth to the rhythm of his mantra at the base of an algae-slicked stone basin—a defunct fountain or neglected birdbath now brimming with muck and decaying leaves.

"Whatcha lookin' at?"

Becca let out a short squeal and ducked away from the window like a cop taking cover. "Jesus, you scared the shit out of me," she whispered fiercely. Rafael crept beside her and peered through the shattered window. "What do we have here? A loony rolled back to the bin?"

Becca elbowed him in the ribs.

The song or chant had a strange, alien beauty to it. She detected a profound longing in the lilting melody. The syllables themselves were fricative and harsh wherever they broke the long wavering vowels, but they were also vaguely familiar to her, a fact that in itself endowed the chant with benign associations—the smell of her grandmother's chamomile tea, the bellowing foghorns of boats on the Miskatonic River—which emboldened her. She leaned out the window and trained her camera on the strange man, zooming the lens, which didn't have quite enough focal length, to focus on his face. His features were broad and dark, marked by a constellation of tattooed symbols arching across his left temple. Checking the display to make sure she'd gotten the shot, she disentangled herself from the tree and headed down the hall toward the decrepit emergency exit stairs that led to the courtyard.

Rafael was quick at her heels. "What are you doing? You're not gonna go talk to that guy."

"Why not?" She turned to face him in the fractured light of the stairwell, the chant permeating the building through the broken slats and crumbling mortar. "You've been down these stairs?" she asked. "They're not going to collapse on me?"

He seemed to want to delay answering just to keep her from going down, but he clearly wasn't worried about the stairs. She weighed less than he did and could see in his eyes that he'd used them. She started down, hurrying to reach the courtyard before the singer departed. "Wait," Rafael said, "Stairs won't hold us both, but...you should stay away from that guy."

"You know him?"

"Not specifically, but did you see his hat? His tattoos?"

"Yeah. Funky."

"He's a brinehead."

"A *what?*"

"He's from the Starry Wisdom Church. They're like...inbred squid worshippers."

"Little prejudiced are we?"

"Don't be stupid, Becca. There are reasons why people avoid them, believe me."

She turned the camera in her hand, reminding him of why she was on this venture. "I want to know what his story is, why he's here. He has to have a story, don't you think?"

Rafael started down the stairs. They creaked and groaned and actually swayed away from the black mold-speckled wall where the gray sky showed through. Becca hurried to the bottom and strode into the overgrown courtyard in the shadow of the asylum, with Rafael's sneakers hitting the dirt behind her and the tattooed man looking up in alarm, his mantra slipping out of rotation like a dislodged bicycle chain.

"Hey," Becca said.

The man rose and brushed the dust from his black clothes. He cast a forlorn glance at the stagnant water in the basin, and turned to go. Becca couldn't resist snapping a couple of shots of the birdbath (a concrete basin on a pedestal inlaid with a mosaic of colored glass) and the robed figure drifting out of focus in the background. At the sound of the shutter, the man spun around, the long, bony finger of his right hand outstretched in an accusatory stab, a gold ring with an onyx stone catching the light.

"Give me the memory card," he demanded.

"Like hell."

"You took my picture without permission. It belongs to me."

"Uh-uh." She shook her head, cradled the camera to her solar plexus, and stepped backward into the shelter of the building, feeling like a fool.

The old man glanced at her companion and must have seen something there to give him pause—one of those mirages of posture and facial expression that the good-natured Raf could summon in an instant if he found himself on the wrong side of the street. The man dropped his hand to his side.

"Why are you spying on me? Why do you take my picture?"

"I'm sorry, I should have asked. It's not spying. It's art."

The man scoffed.

"I'm Becca—"

"Jesus, Bec, *don't*." Rafael interjected.

"My grandfather lived here for a while," she said. "What's your name?"

His anger seemed to have abated, but he still paused before answering. "John Proctor. And your *last* name, young lady?"

"Philips."

"I don't know the name. Your grandfather was an inmate here?" he looked up at the clouds passing over the remaining windows as if he might see long-gone residents there, staring down at him.

"Peter Philips," she said.

"I had family here as well, of a kind."

"Did they die here?"

His eyes drifted down and locked on hers again. Not all of the fire was gone from them.

"That's why you pray here," she said. "I'm sorry. For intruding, I mean…and invading your privacy."

He looked at the camera and Becca deflated. "Look, I can't afford to give you the card, but I'll delete the pictures if you want. You can watch me do it." The offer pained her. She had a gut feeling they were good.

"Is it a video; with my voice, my prayers?"

"No, just pictures."

John Proctor waved his hand, shuffled his feet, and turned away. Something rattled as his hand dipped into his pocket and she saw a trail of black beads on a string vanishing into his frock, a rosary of the same stone set in his gold ring. She felt an impulse and acted on it while his back was turned, slipped a finger under the chain around her neck, and flipped the scarab from under the little bit of fabric that had concealed it. "You don't care about the pictures?" she called after him, "Just your voice?"

He shrugged. "It doesn't matter anyway. The prayers are broken."

It seemed such an odd thing to say. "How can a prayer be broken?"

He looked back, still walking away, and said, "It would mean nothing to you, but a man named Jeremy Levenda was once imprisoned here. Not my blood, but a brother nonetheless. He had the gift of tongues, a gift long ago rinsed from my race by bad breeding. One day he stood in this courtyard and summoned something glorious from the waters of this bath. And that was the last time the world has ever known such a thing. Still…I try. But as I said, the prayers are broken. And so am I."

The sun emerged and traced a wedge of light across the weedy ground. Becca leaned into it, still wondering why the chant had sounded familiar, and saw the reflection of the scarab heliographing across the man's tattooed face. It had a transforming effect: his eyes dilated, he stumbled, his finger went up again. "Where did you get that?"

She touched the cold metal, and he flinched as if she'd drawn a weapon. This wasn't the reaction she'd hoped for. She'd wanted his curiosity, not this fear written so plainly on his face. Any hope that he might tell her more about the scarab, help her understand what it meant to people, to her grandmother, was slipping away.

"Let him go," Rafael said. She'd forgotten he was there.

When she turned back from a glance at Raf, John Proctor had fled through a gap in the collapsed bricks and beams, leaving only a rustle in the teeming weeds to testify that he had been there at all.

Becca went to the birdbath and stared at the slimy leaves through the rainwater.

"What was *that* about?" Rafael broke the silence. "Your grandfather was a patient here? How come you never told me?"

Becca didn't reply. She tucked the scarab back under her shirt, and the sun tucked itself behind a cloud.

She approached one of the other doorless entrances to the hospital as if in a trance. It gave onto a common room, the bookshelves sagging and moldy, the other furnishings long since removed. Her boots, painted with Rafael's silly characters, crunched on dislodged segments of tile grout, bringing small bones to mind. She could sense Rafael behind her, wanting to say something but knowing better.

For a moment she saw the room as it had been when she was eight years old. She had forgotten visiting her grandfather here, but now, looking at the courtyard from this angle, through the empty window frame, she could almost see him, scrawny and gaunt in his gown, barely aware of his granddaughter or wife; him staring at the bright light wavering on the water in the birdbath and shielding his eyes from the glare with a hand against his brow. It had looked like a salute offered to someone she couldn't see, his hand not quite casual enough to merely be serving as a visor, his thumb pressing against the skin above and between his eyes, massaging the area where a crescent scab marked him. She remembered being afraid for him and thinking that he must have dug his thumbnail into that spot from repetition of the gesture.

It was all rushing back now, the ice cream Gran had bought her on the way home to cheer her up (black raspberry—a flavor she had unconsciously avoided since), and the vacant smile Grandpa had flashed her that made her wonder if he still knew her name. He had been semi-catatonic throughout the visit. No, that wasn't entirely true. He had said one thing to Catherine as, with her hand on Becca's shoulder, she turned to leave. The words had croaked out of him in a voice atrophied from infrequent use, through chapped lips stretched in an ironic and horrid grin.

"What I came here pretending to be…I am becoming."

Catherine had almost pushed Becca to the car after that, and Becca had been relieved to go. Whoever that man had been, he wasn't her grandfather anymore.

A scratching roused her from her reverie, and she turned to find Rafael down on one knee at the other side of the expansive room. He held a slim putty knife in one hand and was scraping dots of bright blue paint from the floor, as if it were still 2006 and he'd been hired for maintenance.

The wall behind him revealed his latest work, and her breath hitched in her chest as she took it in: a series of torrential waterfalls appeared to pour from ragged holes in the sheetrock while kaleidoscopes of blue and yellow butterflies streamed toward the ceiling from gashes in the sagging wallpaper.

"When?" she asked.

He shrugged. "While you were at the funeral. You like it?"

Chapter 3

In his dusty black frock, Reverend John Proctor climbed aboard an aboveground trolley and rode the Green Line into the city amid college students and commuters, swaying with the rock and pitch of the car, and staring out the filmy window at the darkening skyline until the train plunged underground at Kenmore, leaving his tattooed reflection staring back at him.

There were two kinds of people on the subway: those who stared *at* him, and those who stared *away* from him. His people had lived in Boston for generations. Longer than the Muslims with their burkas or the Chasidics with their braids, and yet these other religionists had been grudgingly integrated into the tapestry of Boston's rough blue-collar fabric over time. It was a white city, but its primary industry was education, making tolerance a natural byproduct that wafted like a benign emission from the towers of higher learning. And yet, for all that, the brethren of the Starry Wisdom Church were still mostly shunned, as if they'd never risen above the station of fishmongers trailing the stench of their trade.

Most of the laity in this day and age had left the docks behind and now worked in cleaner environs, in IT departments, supermarkets, and even medical centers. As a cleric, the reverend was supported by his congregation, his sole occupation the study of the mysteries. He experienced one such mystery as the train plunged belowground and sped along the subterranean tunnel beneath the brownstones and gothic hotels of the Back Bay: whenever he returned to the neighborhood he called home, a neighborhood built on marshland, something like a cold, blue current stirred in his blood.

He exited the train at Hynes Convention Center and took the stairs to street level, pushing through the doors and breaking out of the hot, stale air of the station.

The foot traffic flowed wide around him.

It had been a hot day, but with nightfall, a breeze had picked up. It flowed across the overpass, stirring his too-heavy frock coat, and bringing some relief from the oppressive air of the subway. Too many people. There were too many people in the city, crawling over every road, clogging every corridor, and there was no escape from them even in the ruins of the asylum. Perhaps the day of reckoning would come and change that. He tried to instill hope in his congregation that it would, but he harbored private doubts.

The scarab was another mystery. It troubled him. It couldn't be what it looked like (there was no possible way, and yet the girl claimed an ancestor in the place) but seeing it in that courtyard on this day of all days...what could it mean?

There were radical elements in his flock who would have urged him to view such an omen as a herald of the hour come round at last, but they were young and hasty, and one couldn't simply rouse the apocalypse like a sleeping snake, prod it with a stick at the first sign of synchronicity. He had long ago accepted that he was unlikely to see it in his lifetime. His duty was to preserve the traditions for the next generation and shelter them from persecution until their time came. That was why he hadn't smashed the camera or accosted the girl about her jewelry. The last thing the church needed was for some curiosity seeker to report him to the police and have a holy site barricaded or demolished.

Hot air rustled his vestments and bus exhaust singed his nostrils.

He didn't care for cameras in sacred places, but gazing across the Back Bay at moments like this, under falling night and rising moon, he wished there had been more of them around in the 1850's when all of this had been underwater. He could imagine it, of course, but he'd only seen one photo of the tidal marshes, and that one did little to capture the majesty of the place. He would have liked to see it beset by storms, waves thrashing and lightning lashing, but in those early days of the camera photographers had been lucky if they could capture a clear image in the bleached light of noonday.

A punk in a studded and spray-painted leather vest bumped him as he turned onto Boylston Street and he almost muttered a curse—not a swear, but an *actual* curse—then thought better of it. He would need what energy he had left for the ceremony. It was, after all, the Feast Day of Saint Jeremy. He tapped his fingers against his coat pocket, felt the crystal phial of water from the sacred fount, and made his way up the slope to the stone tower hemmed in by skyscrapers, seeing it in his mind's eye as the lighthouse it would be if ever it were the last building standing amid the roiling waters.

* * *

Darius Marlowe was being swept into a fugue state in spite of himself. He stood among the congregation of the Starry Wisdom, in their robes of purple and black, and watched the pointed shadows of hoods leaping and retracting on the carved stone walls of the temple like dark gray flames as their bodies swayed to the rhythm of the chant. It was a good bit of theater, an effective piece of hypnosis: the air heavy with the swirling strata of incense, the flickering flames, and the deep droning music of the chant rising and falling, ebbing and flowing, echoing in the vaulted peak of the chamber above and stirring the water in the stone basin on the altar below. Brine from Revere Beach, to which had been added a phial of blessed rainwater from the bath of Saint Jeremy. One ingredient remained to kindle consciousness in that water, and though Darius knew he should be slipping covertly away from the throng while their eyes were closed and their ears were immersed in the music, he couldn't resist waiting and watching for the moment when Samira would make her contribution.

It was a small thing, given willingly, but it thrilled him to witness it each time.

And there she was, stepping forward, guided by the gentle hand of the Reverend Proctor like a vassal helping a princess to step onto the running board of an opulent carriage on her way to a wedding. She stepped onto the stone dais, her simple white tunic blazing and reflecting the candlelight which the other robes absorbed, her skin flushed, black hair shining with perspiration. She held her hand above the basin, index finger extended, and though Darius couldn't see it through the throng, he could almost hear the hinges of the slender instrument case creaking open as the reverend lifted the lid on purple velvet and glowing steel. Darius had assisted at the altar often enough in the days when he'd been in the reverend's favor to know every beat in the rhythm of the rite.

Today a younger man, barely a teen, stepped up and held the virgin's wrist steady. It was a gentle grip, and mostly ceremonial. Samira Fanan, favored church daughter, keeper of keys, and tower librarian, had the resolve to keep her own hand quite steady without aid.

Proctor touched the tip of the gleaming lancet to the blue flame of a Lengian letter inked on his brow, the A that marked his pineal gland, and then reached over the basin and inserted the tip of the instrument into the pad of Samira's finger.

Darius lingered, shifting his focus from the ruby drops that swelled and dripped into the bowl of brine and holy water to the flicker of pain that rippled across her features with the transience of the tiny waves that presently stirred the waters.

Then he remembered his objective, and roused himself from the paralysis of fascination. He had already retreated to the back of the room while fading his own voice out of the chant. Now he stepped around a marble column and exited into the vestibule while all eyes were fixed on the bleeding finger.

In the women's changing room he slid the wooden box out of Samira's cubbyhole and rifled through it hastily, resisting the urge to examine her undergarments, seizing on the metallic clatter of her key ring. It was customary for the congregation to wear nothing under their robes, to allow the ethereal currents to enter their pores and stir the vortices of their subtle anatomy, their astral bodies.

Darius knew that none of that really mattered as long as the spells remained broken. The human larynx had long ago devolved into an inferior instrument for the overtones the chants required. Nothing was being stirred in that chamber but imagination. Beneath the black cotton of his robe, he had remained dressed in his street clothes, and now he touched his cell phone in his back pocket. He folded his fingers tight around the keys to keep them from jingling as he passed through the curtains of the changing room and stepped light-footed up the stone staircase to the upper library.

He unlocked the door, using his robed body to mute the sound of the tumbler. He had sprayed its hinges with WD-40 earlier that day, and it opened silently. He slipped through, leaving the door ajar, and hurried down the aisle of bookshelves, the chant fading to a low murmur behind him, the intoxicating smells of old leather and parchment stoking his lust.

The library was built around a large, square spiral staircase lined with tomes and boxed manuscripts ascending to the top of the tower. By day it was illuminated by the ambient light from the stained glass windows, but at this hour little moonlight or urban street glare penetrated those thick, dark panes depicting stellar and oceanic dreamscapes, standing stones and cyclopean mountain ranges. The tower was dark, and Darius didn't dare switch on the electric chandelier—a wrought-iron octopus with glass globes at the ends of its tentacles.

He took the smartphone from his back pocket, dexterously swiping and tapping on the glass to turn on the camera and activate the flash. He quickened the pace of his climb, the little illuminated screen swinging at his side, casting a cold glow on the stairs. At the penultimate level, with the chandelier hovering over his shoulder, the bulbous green glass eyes glaring down on his crime, he slid a worn, brown leather volume from the shelf and laid it open in the crook of his arm: *Liber Nocte Coccineae.*

The Book of Scarlet Night.

*　*　*

Across the street from the church, a homeless man reclined in a narrow alleyway, his rotting tennis shoes propped against the brick wall of an apartment building, his head resting against the graffiti-ridden plaster of a liquor store. As he tilted his head to drain the last two ounces of his 40, he considered seeking cover: the sky was flashing lightning. But before the last drop ran down his throat, he saw that the lightning wasn't in the sky.

It was in the stained glass of the stone church tower.

Chapter 4

If you're commuting out of the city tonight, you're gonna want to avoid the 93/Route 1 junction by the Tobin Bridge. A mini-twister caused a sandstorm there this afternoon at the Boston Sand and Gravel quarry. That's right, I said, "mini-twister." As if hurricane flooding wasn't bad enough, now we have sandstorms in Boston. Cue the plague of locusts. Anyway, there's sand all over the roads there. Enough to stop traffic while they sweep it off. So if you aren't already jammed in it, try to find another route out of town. Next up, I've got some Billy Moon for you. I'm Adam 12 and you're listening to Radio BDC.

The Black Pharaoh walked the winding paths of the Emerald Necklace. He followed the Muddy River north through the fens, past the war memorials and the Japanese temple bell, past the playground at Mother's Rest, through swamps turned to gardens. He walked in the dying light of a September evening, his scarlet robes burning in the last rays of the sun, and everywhere he passed, joggers and commuters, mothers and children, should have turned their heads to stare in awe at those radiant robes and the wild swamp animals that flocked at his feet, sniffing the air in his wake and leaping to lap at his long-fingered hands: rats and opossums and foxes. But no one looked in the direction of that dark man. If some rare soul had tried to focus on his face, it would have seemed indistinct and out of focus, as if glimpsed through a glass darkly. But none did. All averted their eyes as he passed like a cloud across the sun, leaving a deep chill that they would take with them to their beds when they turned in for a night of strange and restless dreams.

Walking under the Charlesgate overpass, he removed the robe and tossed it over the brownstone railing into the shallow creek where it melted and marbled the dirty water with tatters of rich blood. He emerged onto Beacon Street dressed in a gray suit, tousling his long black curls with his fingers to cover his horns, and stirring the wisps of lazy blue fire that played in his locks.

At the corner of Commonwealth and Charlesgate the Fenway Towers reared into the purpling dusk: a marvel of red brick, vine-inscribed stone, and mint-green copper, crowned with sandstone finials and iron gates along the roof.

He had absorbed enough energy on his walk through the marshes to push his form into an almost material range, enough to make it difficult not to see him, but not enough for his hands to manipulate objects like door handles. He glided through the plate-glass door into a lobby lit by wall sconces in the shape of frosted glass seashells, and stepped up to a desk of gold-flecked green marble.

The concierge was a young man in a dark blue blazer and crisp white shirt, with impeccably trimmed sideburns that stretched as his jaw worked a stick of gum. His brushed nickel nametag read "Gordon Shea," but Nereus Charobim didn't look at it; he plucked the name from the man's mind like a card from a deck.

"Gordon," Charobim said without moving his lips, "You have a vacant unit, do you not?" The ambient light from the seashells pulsed with the syllables of the pharaoh's telepathic speech, and Gordon Shea turned his head slowly to one side to watch it. Charobim knew what the man was seeing. To his human vision, it would look as if the individual photons from the incandescent lights were gliding slowly away from their source, like beads of dew running along a string, and when Charobim spoke, it was like a subwoofer in a passing car was causing those beads to buzz and blur and speed their way across the room. The sight mesmerized the clerk, and he realized that although the *visitor* knew his name, *he* no longer did: a plucked card that the magician had pocketed while he was distracted by the light show.

"Am I having a migraine?" Gordon asked.

"No," Charobim replied, somehow making the single syllable melodious.

Gordon had stopped chewing his gum, and his jaw hung slack. "Do you see those beads of light? The way they're pulsing?" He laughed at the absurdity of his own question.

Charobim studied him patiently with a not unkind smile on his face, an African face of a kind that had not been seen in this city for a very long time, save in the statues enshrined on the second floor of the MFA. He knew that Gordon Shea would now be realizing that he felt rather drunk and would feel a dim sense of alarm at the possibility that he was indeed drunk, an alarm heard distantly through a wooly dream, like pain in an anesthetized limb. Mr. Shea would be aware that his boss would not abide drunkenness on the job. Unable to recall the name of his boss, he would nonetheless retain the core fear imprinted on all primates, no matter how sheltered, before they reached puberty — that the meal ticket might be revoked.

Gordon's gaze had been drawn to the seashell sconces again, and Charobim wished he could drum his long brown fingers against the desktop to politely regain the man's attention. Instead, he sighed, and the lights flared, and the concierge looked at him, a wave of relief breaking across his brow as he remembered that *this man*, right here, the one who had asked about a vacant unit, was his boss. Of course he was. Gordon typed on his keyboard and told his boss, "Yes, sir, we do. Number seventy-two."

"Perfect. Fetch the key."

The wide drawer below the keyboard slid open on smooth rollers, and the concierge produced a key attached to a ring with a wooden diamond, the number 72 inlaid on it in what looked like mother of pearl. *My, but this place was fit for a king.* Nereus Charobim smiled at the number. It reminded him of evocations he could neither recall nor recite in this weak incarnation, of books he could no longer read. It reminded him of his old friend and rival, Solomon, who had trapped 72 demons in a box, and of the cunning-folk who had burned at the stake centuries later for merely possessing a list of their names and attributes. So much suffering for what amounted to an opening act.

"I have a job for you, Gordon."

"Anything," he said, still holding out the key, waiting for the boss to take it.

"Put that key in your pocket and take it halfway to hell. Do you know where that is?"

The young man laughed. "Sure," he said. "I mean, yessir."

Charobim turned and silently tapped the desktop with the palm of his hand. "And don't lose the gum," he said, "You're going to need it."

Charobim showed Gordon exactly what to do; an image flashed in the man's mind.

Gordon Shea's final act before abandoning his post and strolling out into the night with his Velcro ankle weights and bicycle security chain in his hands was to press the elevator button for the boss.

* * *

On the fourth floor the pharaoh walked through the solid mahogany door of unit 72. His feet were clad in sheepskin loafers, but no footsteps echoed in the sparsely furnished suite as he strolled across the gleaming hardwood floor; nothing changed when he stepped onto the plush white carpet and passed the fireplace on his way to the big window overlooking Kenmore Square and the antique vanity on the south wall. Recessed lights cast their full-spectrum illumination over a white leather couch, white armchairs, and white curtains. It was museum-quality light, and it seemed wasted on blank walls. Charobim doubted that Darius Marlowe would hang art when he moved in. The young scientist was fiercely loyal, but to say that he lacked culture would be putting it mildly. Charobim looked down at the foot traffic and streaming headlights on the street below. The red neon pyramid of the Citgo sign loomed over the square, reminding him of home in the crassest possible way; and despairing at the cheapness of the symbol, he shifted the focus of his eyes to his own reflection. His hair had settled around the ridged black horns. He smiled, a white crescent hanging in the sky.

Nereus Charobim, the Black Pharaoh, avatar of Nyarlathotep, thought of old acquaintances. King Solomon, Pontius Pilate, Franz Mesmer, Harry Houdini.

Houdini had been a fake, but he'd at least never made serious claims to the royal arte. Macgregor Mathers and Helena Blavatsky on the other hand…well, let's just say Mathers was no Hermes Trismegistus.

The last time Charobim had visited this city, a city known as "The Hub," even though those who used the moniker had no idea how true it was, he had been just one of many souls gathered on a Beltane morning to watch Harry Houdini, bound in manacles, jump from the Harvard Bridge into the frigid waters of the Charles River, where he managed to shed his chains while holding his breath. May 1, 1908 that had been. *Escape Artist* they had called Houdini. That, more than *magician*, had become his identity by the time he performed the death-defying stunt to draw rubes to his two-week run at Keith's Theatre.

As Charobim approached the antique vanity, he ruminated on the fact that he too had begun his career as a magician and was now a kind of escape artist. Only *his* aeon-long feat had more to do with helping others escape their manacles. In any event, it was fitting that one cog turning in that cosmic lock was now riding a bicycle across the Harvard Bridge, perhaps coasting to a stop with a pump of the handbrake at this very moment, and preparing to pay homage to Houdini's daring dive.

The concierge would be slicing into the dark water like a dropped knife, the Velcro ankle weights he wore on his morning bicycle commute dragging his body down into the weedy blackness of the river. Picturing the body piercing the glassy water, Charobim exhaled and glided into the beveled, ironbound mirror, and made himself at home.

Chapter 5

Darius Marlowe was used to dreaming in the language of numbers: square roots, prime integers, angstroms, and Ohms. But on the morning of September 17th he awoke from a dream of smoots.

In October 1958, members of the MIT fraternity Lambda Chi Alpha carried a young pledge dressed in black clothes and black gloves across the Harvard Bridge from MIT to Boston, laying him down at five foot, seven inch intervals (his height) and marking his progress with chalk followed by paint so that he, one Oliver R. Smoot, could be used as a unit of measurement. To this day the bridge bears painted markers every ten smoots, beginning with an arrow pointing toward MIT on the Boston side of the bridge and the indicator: 364.4 SMOOTS + 1 EAR.

Whether the 1958 fraternity brothers selected the subject of the prank with preternatural insight into his destiny, or the ninety-minute prank itself fixed the course of his life, it should be noted that Mr. Smoot went on to become the chairman of the American National Standards Institute and the president of the International Organization for Standardization, and Google now offers the smoot as a unit of measurement in their calculator, maps, and Google Earth tools.

The marks are repainted each semester, and when the bridge was renovated in the 1980s, the Cambridge Police department requested that the marks be maintained, as they had come to rely on them for identifying the locations of accidents on the bridge.

Darius Marlowe was as familiar with the marks and their legend as any MIT student. He had walked over them countless times in waking life, and recognized them in the nascent hours of the 17th as he tossed and turned, winding himself in his dirty bed sheets in a double dorm room on the fourth floor of Fairborz Maseeh Hall while his roommate snored.

Darius was dreaming of the pharaoh again, the black man, the faceless messenger who had introduced himself in other dreams as Nereus Charobim. In the dream Darius stood among the muddy reeds on the riverbank and watched the rain-lashed waters rushing and churning like the Mississippi in flood, carrying flotsam out to sea: a clapboard shed, a metallic blue car (desperate, prying fingers behind a slice of submerged window), a drowning Doberman, and a bicycle.

Darius tracked the quick progress of these objects past the Community Boathouse where a fleet of Mercury keelboats rocked and strained against their tethers on the overwhelmed bank, toward a tattered mass of whirling black cloud downriver, from which sinuous, ashen tentacles and sheets of black water whipped around in rising spirals.

The scene was washed in a cacophony of noise—wind and screams—but the pharaoh's voice was loud and clear above the din, speaking, not shouting, Darius's name, commanding that he turn his attention to the object in the palm of his hand. A key on a ring; the ornament on that ring a silver oval reflecting the storm-diffused September sun up at Darius's face, washing his dark, heavy brow with its flickering light. Was it a signal mirror that he was supposed to use to send an S-O-S, he wondered, in the logic of the dream?

No. The unmistakable face of Nereus Charobim now stared at him from the little mirror, features distorted as if sketched by a shaking hand or seen through a ragged glaze of Vaseline.

"I have prepared a room for you in the Gryphon Tower," Charobim said. "Cross the bridge and join me. I have work for you."

The face faded from the oval, the silver faded to onyx, and a green digital number glowed from the little window in Darius's hand: 182.2 S.

A measurement in smoots.

Darius woke up tangled in sweaty sheets. He gazed around the room, expecting to see the pharaoh standing among the stacks of books and piles of dirty laundry. The only other body was his detested roommate, Mitchel, an acne-scarred robotics geek from Pennsylvania who either thought Darius couldn't hear him when he jerked off or didn't care if he could. Bottles of Mountain Dew lay in and around the too small trash basket beside Mitchel's desk, evidence of a late-night study binge.

Darius sat up and put his feet on the cold floor. He let the reality of his surroundings sink in and felt disappointment swirling around the drain of another morning. He needed to piss, needed to step into his slippers and head to the dirty bathroom, but he held it in and focused on the gossamer-thin threads of the dream, combing through them gently, so as not to break them with the crude tool of his intellect. What had the number been? A weight on a digital scale? A time on a clock? No. It had been a mile marker on a road. No... a marker in smoots!

The elation of remembrance was shattered by the absurdity of the notion that the messenger of the gods would communicate to him in such nonsense. The idea was surely a product of his tired imagination. And yet, what would it hurt him to check? 182.2 S. He saw the number in his mind's eye, as if it were emblazoned on his forehead, and its specificity soothed him. He didn't even need to write it down to remember it, and he smiled as the little joke began to dawn on him. Maybe the black pharaoh had a sense of humor after all.

As the shackles of sleep fell away, he moved to the bathroom, emptied his bladder, and brushed his teeth without losing sight of the number. He took a handful of water from the tap in his cupped hand, rinsed his mouth, and met his own eyes in the dusty mirror. He smiled at his reflection. There had been a mirror in the dream, and a promise.

Less than ten minutes later, dressed in jeans, a brown suede jacket, and a scarf, he walked out of the front doors of Fariborz Maseeh Hall and trotted down the steps. The cold morning air invigorated him as it stung his cheeks. He dug his hands into his pockets, turned right past the chapel, and stepped onto Mass Ave.

The street bustled with the usual book-laden students and neon-clad joggers amid the buses, bikes, and cars. A quarter of a mile on, he realized that the bank of the Charles River across the street was congested with a crowd of onlookers, blue lights flashing in the gaps between them as they milled around near the new tide line. The Mass Ave Bridge wasn't as high above the river as it had once been. What had never been a bridge worthy of a suicide attempt was now too low to allow more than the passage of kayaks underneath. And yet, as he drew nearer, it became apparent that someone had been drowned. Maybe the victim had capsized a small boat, an inexperienced operator in a rental.

The flashers turned out to be an EMT truck, beyond which a police boat was bobbing on the gray water, twenty yards out. The bridge wasn't closed; and, while there were a couple of officers in police windbreakers out on the footpath with walkie-talkies, traffic was moving to the Back Bay side, albeit sluggishly, as drivers strained to catch a glimpse of the tragedy. Darius succumbed to the same curiosity. He watched for a break in traffic and jogged across the street to the back of the crowd, where bystanders were searching their phones and making speculative chit-chat with strangers. One man had a young girl seated upon his shoulders, her cheeks rosy beneath a yellow knit hat. Darius sidled through the crowd until he had a better view of the boat.

It wasn't just morbid fascination drawing him closer. He felt a compelling sense that whatever had happened here was linked to his dream, that there was personal significance in the tragedy, and that, if he were observant enough, providence would put him in the right place at the right time to interpret it. This sense had been growing in his waking life over the past month, a feeling that not only were his dreams a conduit for messages from the master, but that even everyday reality had taken on a dreamlike quality rife with coded symbolism and cabalistic significance. Perhaps the patterns had always been there, but he'd been too distracted and unfocused to see them. Perhaps the initiation he was undergoing each night had removed a filter and attuned his consciousness to the rich, synchronistic alphanumeric soup that all modern people waded through without the ability to read it. Or maybe he had been set on a path that consistently put him in the right place at the right time to see it.

Here was another confirmation: the police boat drifted sideways in the water at his approach, granting him a clear view of a large white 23 at the back of the hull. He thrilled at the sight. That number was a key to a door that he would arrive at one day. It had been appearing to him daily, hinting at some titanic truth, teasing like a harlot, flashing like a beacon, leading him on toward revelation.

Darius took a pocket-sized marble notebook from his jacket and flipped it open to a clean page. With a pen plucked from his jeans he scribbled the latest entry: "9/17 Police boat trolling for body near Mass Ave Bridge—23."

A pair of scuba divers broke the surface with an unmasked face between them; a doughy white visage with weedy black curls clinging to the forehead. The crowd gasped almost in unison at the sight, and those at the back pressed forward. The man with the little girl finally seemed to awaken to the fact of what he was doing. Darius saw him reach up to cover her eyes with his cupped hand as he turned and headed back toward the street.

Darius moved in closer, stepping into the gaps left by those with weak stomachs and minds. He didn't think he recognized the drowned man, but it was hard to be certain from this distance. The divers were passing the body to a burly officer perched on a diving platform at the stern of the vessel, and now Darius could see that the corpse was wearing an unusual accessory: a bicycle security chain coated in translucent red vinyl wrapped and locked around his knees.

He lingered until his intuition told him there would be no more revelations here. It was time to get ahead of the dispersing crowd if he wanted to cross the bridge mostly unaccompanied.

Turning his back on the scene, he felt a thrill of empowerment, an inarticulate *knowing* that this was somehow for him, a performance for an audience of one. The feeling grew with each step, each meter, as he passed the broad-brushed markings on the sidewalk. 50 SMOOTS. The wind picked up on the open water, and his scarf trilled against his ear. 100 SMOOTS. A cloud of starlings burst from a tree on the far bank of the river and wheeled through the sky, a secret alphabet written against the clouds in the geometry of their ink-black choreography. This too, was meant to speak to him in a language he teetered on the brink of deciphering.

The hairs on his arms pricked up beneath his jacket sleeves. The sense of power and portent swelled with each step he took. In the middle of the bridge, he found confirmation. At the 182.2 mark he came to the place where the original pranksters (and every freshman who had come after and preserved their markings) had set down not a number, but a slogan, "HALFWAY TO HELL" with an arrow pointing back toward MIT.

He stood on the letters and looked away from the college, away from the police vehicles and the dispersing crowd. He gazed across the choppy water toward Back Bay and Kenmore Square, toward the neon Citgo pyramid near Fenway Park, and ran his fingers along the underside of the pale green metal railing until they found something stuck there: a metal object in a wad of gum. He peeled the object free and folded it into his palm. He had lingered only for a moment, and now, walking on toward the other bank, he looked down at the treasure in his palm. It was a key on a ring with a diamond shaped tag inlaid with the name and unit number of his destination:

FENWAY
TOWERS
72

Darius Marlowe reached the Back Bay side of Mass Ave with a spring in his step.

Chapter 6

Becca had last seen the dog she'd begun thinking of as "Django" in a tunnel beneath an abandoned textile factory in Cambridge. Today she was going back for him. The factory was a favorite site for her little band of urbex friends, and she had already milked it for most of the decent shots she was likely to get, but she brought her camera anyway, because she thought, *you never know*. What she didn't bring was a partner. In fact, she didn't even tell Rafael she was going back to the mill. Reckless? Sure, but he was stubborn about safety protocols and wouldn't take no for an answer. She figured there was no point in telling him if she didn't want an argument and an uninvited escort.

The dog had come within arm's reach on her last visit, but he was skittish. She didn't know how she knew it, but she felt sure that if he scented or heard anyone other than her, he wouldn't allow himself to be seen at all...*if* he was still haunting the place. So she went alone.

The mill was a huddle of loosely connected ruins in red brick beside the river. Twin stacks that hadn't belched smoke in decades loomed over a rusting water tank atop the main structure, above grids of shattered windows. Most of the graffiti was old and faded, except for the metallic paint, which caught enough light even on an overcast day like today to render well in photos. The weeds were prolific, and Becca had used them to great effect in infrared sets; but today they presented nothing she hadn't captured already. She kept her camera in her bag as she ducked under the barbed wire and made her way along the well-trodden paths to her favored entrance: a brick archway before which lay a rotting wooden door.

Here were long rooms that still housed moldering spools of green and blue thread piled high like mounds of plague-ravaged corpses, and rows of rusting machines, their rollers clogged with crumbling asbestos tiles. The long halls were illuminated from collapsed ceilings. Passing through them on her way to the deeper, darker chambers, Becca tuned her ears to the flutter and chirp of birds nesting atop unmoored pillars and in the corners of roofless brick walls.

Last time, she'd seen the dog on one of the sublevels, in a utility tunnel that connected the main factory to an outbuilding. Eventually she would make her way down there by the light of her headlamp. For now, she paused only to put on her trusty leather work gloves. Every surface in a place like this was rife with tetanus.

She walked over tangled branches and under slopes of collapsing corrugated metal, her Doc Martens crunching on broken glass and chalky tile shards. Her breathing deepened and slowed with each step. There had always been something soothing to her about decaying places, something peaceful in their absolute abandonment. These failed structures existed in a realm beyond effort and ambition, beyond maintenance and manicure. In contrast, the self-conscious facades of high-rent shops on Newbury Street where she worked in the gallery often threatened to suffocate her with their pretense that life could be beautified and preserved indefinitely, that order and tidiness were some kind of natural state, and that the chaotic and rustic, the rough edges of art, were only beautiful by contrast to the austere and immaculate and could only be acknowledged when safely contained within the protective foursquare boundary of a frame.

She sought out the ruins of her city because they seemed to speak a plain truth: that all things aged and transformed and withered and died, and that all effort and industry, however dazzling, would have its day in the sun and then fade. In this she found peace because it aligned with her own sense that in the long run the only precious things might be captured frozen moments in a chain of continual change.

Nina, her therapist, had asked her recently if she thought it was odd for a person who suffered from Seasonal Affective Disorder to make a hobby of delving into the dark bowels of the city, places where not even electric light continued to flow. And Becca supposed there was some irony there. But she'd never been comfortable with painting over rot. Better to face it. Better to accept it, maybe even to revel in it and embrace what was hardest for her. Embrace the darkness and decay, and find beauty in them.

She had tried denial for a while in her teens, but it hadn't worked out long term. Taking the headlamp from her bag and slipping it over her crown, she remembered the November day in her junior year when a UPS truck had dropped a package addressed to her on the front steps of the house on Crane Street. Catherine had been excited to watch her open it, had told her as she ran a pair of scissors across the packing tape that it would hopefully take some of the misery out of her mornings in the darker half of the year, and make it easier for her to stop missing the bus.

"What is it, a clock?" Becca had asked, knowing already that it wasn't as she lifted the heavy object from the box. Styrofoam peanuts rained down from what looked like an opaque plastic half-moon mounted on a black base trailing a power cord.

"It's a dawn simulator," Catherine explained. "Not that different from an alarm clock, but it comes on gradually and fills the room with full-spectrum light. It's supposed to prime your pineal gland before your other alarm goes off."

Becca turned the heavy object over in her hands, skeptically. A plastic sunrise—weird. But later, standing in her room beside her Gran with the curtains drawn and watching the light slowly growing in the frosted dome, she felt a little thrill of hope; not because she believed the gadget would make much difference in her daily life, but because Catherine had thought of it, had pulled her head out of dusty tomes long enough to get on the internet and find something that *might* help, and had cared enough about her struggle to buy it for her.

"*Yehi Aur!*" Catherine proclaimed, her fingers splayed toward the corners of the room where the shadows were shrinking.

"Huh?"

The old woman looked askance at her, an eyebrow raised and a sly grin wrinkling the corners of her mouth. *"Let there be light,* dear. It's Hebrew."

The dawn simulator had helped a little in finishing high school, but in college she'd never taken it out of its box and reverted to oversleeping. That was when she'd started experimenting with reveling in her condition—seeking out dark places in her city and in her art, her only remaining crutches the vitamin D supplements and SSRI prescriptions, because without those she'd likely cut her wrists in the bathtub sometime in January.

She had also discovered along the way that it was easier to get out of bed when she had a goal. And today the goal was finding Django. She had already named him. Hadn't earned his trust yet, and certainly hadn't succeeded in rescuing him, but had named him, after one of her favorite guitarists, Django Reinhardt.

On the previous occasions, when she'd caught sight of the dog, she had been wary of spooking him with the camera. Shooting him with a flash was out of the question, but she had managed to get one decent photo. He appeared to have some German shepherd traits, probably mixed with smaller breeds.

She took a piece of dog biscuit from the front pocket of her cargo pants and ducked under a fallen steel girder, treading softly. The only urine stains on the walls were at human height and appeared dry. She'd seen no dog shit and couldn't imagine what he ate to survive. He was a skinny thing, a real bag of bones, judging by the few glimpses and one photo she had to go on.

She had entered a long, narrow room with the ceiling mostly intact. Decrepit mechanical looms hulked in the shadows, making an obstacle course of the place. When she'd first entered the room, a few stray shafts of sunlight had cut the air and glanced off of the machinery, highlighting random bits of crusty white corrosion. But now clouds had overtaken the sun again, and the light had faded, casting the entire space into murky, indistinct gloom.

She heard a rustling from one of the corners, and turned her head to pinpoint the origin. Knowing that it could very well be a rat or a raccoon, or even a savage fisher cat, she crept closer, the dog biscuit trembling slightly between her gloved fingers.

She smelled the animal before she saw it—a pungent concoction of swamp water and breath that could only come from rotting teeth and a stomach eating itself from hunger. Knowing that no small wild animal she'd ever encountered had smelled so desperately canine, she was emboldened, and, stepping around a wide pillar, she caught sight of him, nose to a pile of rubble, mangy black and tan fur poking at odd angles between bald spots where he'd probably licked himself raw from flea infestations. One ear was split at the tip (probably from a fight), and she shuddered to think of how thin he'd look if not for the long fur.

She wished for clean water to offer him and regretted not bringing wet dog food. Even the cookie might be too much for him to digest in his emaciated state, and she had to stifle a hitching sob, had to catch and suppress it in her breast at the sight of the poor thing. He scratched and pawed at the rubble until he succeeded in unearthing a crumbled shred of dirty tin foil left behind by some vagabond or junkie. Whatever juices the treasure had once contained, their residue was surely rank by now, and she had to resist the urge to shout a command at him to drop it, as if he were already her own and would listen rather than flee.

Becca crushed the biscuit in her hand and watched the dog tear the foil with a shake of his muzzle. He lapped at the scrap, and she hoped it wasn't coated with narcotics that had been boiled over a garbage fire.

Dropping the foil, the dog snuffled along the dirty concrete floor for a few inches, then catching either Becca's scent or that of her offering, he looked up and locked eyes with her. His fur rose in a ridge along his spine and his tail stiffened, but his ears remained cocked forward.

She held her palm out, displaying the crushed cookie, and blew a breath down her arm to carry the taste of it to him.

He took a tentative step forward, lowering his head between his shoulder blades, but stopped a good yard away from her, uncertain.

"Hey, little guy. You're a boy, right? You want a cookie?"

Ravenous as he was, he bided his time, waited for her next move.

Sensing that a dance had begun between them, Becca tossed a piece of the biscuit. It rolled through the dust and landed a foot from the dog's nose.

Now it was she who waited.

The dog seized the morsel and retreated to his original position where he chewed it with a jerky crunching and swallowed it down.

"Django," she cooed, trying the name out for the both of them. She liked the way it sounded. He took a tentative step toward her. She held her hand out. But he wasn't quite ready to eat from it yet.

A new smell reached her nose now, overpowering the funk of the dog, an aroma of earth and fire. It took her a moment to identify it, but then it came to her: burning sage, and with it a voice, a muted baritone echoing through the labyrinth of brick and metal and broken glass. They weren't alone, and *damn it,* whoever he was, he was going to scare the dog off before she could finish earning his trust.

The voice grew louder—it sounded like a chant, a droning litany, and she started to think it might be more than one person. Her mind's eye conjured a fleeting vision of robed ritualists walking in a procession through the derelict mill, carrying candles and swinging censers on chains. But then, despite the dirge-like rendition, she recognized the melody and her tense muscles relaxed. It was a song, "Dirty Water," by the Standells.

Becca stood frozen, peering through a narrow doorway into the next room, where a jungle of hanging swathes of moth-eaten cloth obstructed her view of the singer. When she turned her gaze back on the cracked floor at her feet, the dog was gone.

"Fuck." She retraced her steps, checking between every pillar and piece of machinery but finding no trace of the poor mutt. The singing increased in volume behind her, and now, as it moved into the room she was in, she could tell that it was a solitary voice, gravelly and tuneless. She wheeled around, prepared to give the intruder a piece of her mind, but as she drew the breath to launch a tirade, his sheer outlandish bulk silenced her.

Becca was face to face with a black-bearded giant in a green army trench coat. Several layers of frayed sweaters hung around his wrists and neck so that it was impossible to guess his true girth. He appeared to be the sort of homeless person who wears his entire wardrobe at all times. What little she could see of his skin looked African American, and the texture of his dense beard would have supported that assessment; but as with the clothes, it was impossible to tell how many layers of dirt and ashy grime the man was wearing. He might have even been white underneath. But at a glance, Becca found it difficult to focus on any one detail beyond his distracting headgear. His hair was mostly hidden beneath a golden cardboard Burger King Crown, his eyes behind a cheap pair of red-and-blue 3D glasses. In his left hand he held a smoldering bundle of burning sage tied with a red string, and in his right, a small laser pointer.

He bustled past her without acknowledgement, wreathed in smoke, still singing and waving the pungent bundle. Becca recoiled in the wake of the fumes and coughed out a lungful of the stuff before burying her nose in the crook of her arm. The man seemed to give her a shallow nod as he passed, but with his colored plastic lenses, she couldn't tell if they'd made eye contact. She had begun to wonder if he was blind when he turned to her and said, "What up?"

Apparently a rhetorical question because he didn't pause in his genuflections for her reply but spun on his heels in a kind of dance, the trench coat flaring out and swirling around his surprisingly graceful axis, the orange terminator line of the burning ember on the blackening leaves tracing a fiery circle in the air above his head.

He completed the revolution by landing, left leg in front, bent at the knee. From this position he pointed his right hand at the brick wall and traced a perfect pentagram with the ruby bead of the pointer. The chrome barrel poking out of his folded fingers looked like the type she'd seen at the checkout counter at pet stores for teasing cats, usually for less than three dollars.

Pointing the dot at the center of the now invisible pentagram, he broke from the Standells' song and bellowed, *"Apos pantos kakadaiminos!"*

Becca backed away from the madman into the corridor of machinery and shadow where she'd last seen the dog.

The man came up from the weird martial arts stance, surprising her with his agility (she had guessed that he might get stuck there), and proceeded along the wall to the far end of the room, where he repeated the same spin, drop, and pentagram tracing, this time ending with the cry, *"Hekas, hekas este bebeloi!"* When he rose, he stared at the wall, head cocked as if trying to discern some hidden code in the cracks and graffiti. He whispered a word that might have been *skidoo*, and dropped the laser pointer into his pocket. He stubbed the sage bundle out in a cement seam on the brick wall, and, touching his cardboard crown to keep it from tumbling off his head, turned with a bow and flourish of his trench coat and addressed her: "Milady."

Becca couldn't help herself; she laughed into the back of her hand to release the nervous tension before remembering how pissed she was about losing Django. When she did, she set her hand on her hip and said, "You scared my dog away, asshat."

"Your dog? You mean that shepherd with the split ear?"

"Uh-huh."

"Shiiit. I din't know he belonged to nobody. Been sleeping rough like me. He belong to you? For real?"

She sighed and picked up her camera bag, hoisted the heavy thing over her shoulder, and girded herself to push past him on the way out if she had to.

"Never mind."

"He's not yours *yet*, is he?"

Becca shook her head. "But he needs someone to start feeding him or he won't last long."

"Mmmm. True dat."

"Well, nice meeting you," she said with a tight, sarcastic smile. "Gotta go."

"But we *haven't* met. Not yet. Name's Moe Ramirez," he said, approaching her with some of the same caution she'd shown the dog just moments ago. The similarity was so striking that she couldn't help laughing again—it was hard to stay mad at this freak when he was stalking toward you on tiptoes. She decided to let it go. Punishing him for existing wouldn't bring the dog back.

"Becca," she said, not quite ready to give up her last name, although he didn't look equipped to Google it. Then again, he did have a laser, so who could say? "What're you doing, anyway?" she asked.

"Banishing. Cleansing."

"Kinda figured something like that. Banishing *what*, exactly?"

"Little nasties, psychic chum in the waters of the C.U."

"C.U.?"

"Collective Unconscious." He squinted at her through the colored lenses. "I *see you*." He chuckled. "And you ain't one a them. That's why I din't chase yo ass outta here, you dig?"

"Not really.... One of who?"

"The cultists, that's who. The brethren of the Starry Wisdom Church. *Wisdom* my *ass*. I got more wisdom in my teeth than those motherfuckers got in they heads all combined." Moe cackled and

Becca jumped. "S'all right, s'all right, I'm just sayin'...." He was wagging his head from side to side now, and it gave him the look of a giant insect with cardboard antennae and red and blue eyes.

"I met one of them," Becca said. "Didn't seem so bad."

He leaned in close, as if smelling her. "Met 'em? Did you, now? Did you meet him in the flesh or in the astral? Huh? That's what I thought. Not all of 'em can access the ethers, and for now those what can, can only do it when they dreaming. But that's all gonna change if the wards ain't kept in place."

"I have no idea what you're talking about."

"Well, see here now, my fair lady. They call Boston *The Hub*, right?"

"Sure."

"How true it is. And when you at the hub, you bound to see some of the cracks. That's what I'm talkin' about. And Maurice, that's me but you can call me Moe 'cause we friends...Maurice is charged with sealing those cracks best he can. There's one among them been buildin' a infernal machine gonna change everythang. You watch for it. I hope the day don't come when it works its dark magic, but if it does, you keep your music on, you hear?"

"Yeah, okay...I need to try to find that dog, Moe, if you don't mind. The one you scared off."

"Right. I know you think I'm fulla shit, but heed my words, Lady. There ain't no such thing as coincidence. And that means that we are well met. We may not know the reason yet, but you keep that in mind."

"Okay, I'll do that."

"The one I spoke of been haunting the riverbank, doin' experiments in desolate places like this here mill, seein' if he can get a rise outta the dirty water. So you be on the lookout. I seen that there urbex patch on your camera bag, and I knew you was all right, but you shouldn't be in a place like this alone."

"I'm not alone." Becca grinned, and realized that she'd already developed an inexplicable affection for the crazy old bum. He had a way about him.

He smiled back at her, revealing a gold tooth. "See, I knew you was all right. Told you we was well met. You got headphones?"

"Uh...no, not on me, no." In fact she might have had ear buds in her camera bag with her iPod, but affection or not, the thought of letting him borrow them skeeved her out.

"Get some. Noise cancellation is best if you got the Benjamins."

"Thanks for the tip," she said, mustering as much sincerity as she could for the simple reason that he seemed genuinely interested in protecting her.

He dug in his ear with a thick finger and removed something gray. "You do what you can," he said, "within the budget you got. Me? I use chewing gum."

Becca suppressed the urge to retch as she stepped back and to the side. "Okay. You take care."

He called after her as she walked through sun-dappled litter and leaves back to the fallen door. "Look out for the cracks!" he said, and she waved without turning to look back at him. When she reached the empty doorframe, she noticed a piece of graffiti she hadn't seen on the way in. The runny blue spray paint looked fresh, maybe even still wet. Something about the shape looked familiar. Had she seen it at the asylum? She drew her camera from the bag at her hip and snapped a shot of it, thinking that it resembled a tree branch: a straight line with five short lines branching off of it.

When she stepped out into the light, she scanned the overgrown lot, but Django was either hiding well or had gone prowling the flooded riverbank in search of sustenance.

Chapter 7

Darius Marlowe had spent most of his time in the city with eyes
downcast, looking at the stones in the pavement; the flattened gray
circles of gum permanently melded to the sidewalks; the plodding
shoes, rustling skirts, and swirling overcoats of his fellow
pedestrians. If he did look up, it was to read signs and scan
storefronts. At night he might use the lights at the top of the
Prudential building—Boston's North Star—as a landmark to orient
himself, but on most nights, against a ceiling of cloud, the pulsing red
radio aerials and low-flying aircraft were the only lights in the sky,
and you couldn't predict the coming of the Great Old Ones by their
alignment.

He saved his sky-gazing for trips out of the city on clear
moonless nights in the Blue Hills to the south, where he could escape
the light pollution, lie on his back, and let his mind fall into the black
expanse of night, or alight like a swinging spider from point to point
of the Dipper hanging by its handle from Polaris. Tonight however,
he cast his gaze at the skyline as he approached his new home and
basked in the majesty of the gargoyle-topped columns and green
copper gables of Fenway Towers.

He had been living there a week, but it still gave him a sense of
empowerment to climb the steps and pass between the twin griffins,
to walk under the oak-leaf-adorned stone arch and enter the place

knowing that his rooms there—sprawling, white, and luxurious—were a gift from his benefactor, guru, and guide.

He nodded at the concierge and pressed the elevator button, turning his back to the desk while he waited, and cradling the white cardboard animal carrier against his jacket to muffle any sounds that might escape through the air holes. He had no idea what the pet policy was and couldn't take no for an answer. He had read in the *Globe* that the previous man on the desk was the drowning victim recovered from the river on the day he'd found the key. He couldn't claim to understand all of the pharaoh's designs, but he guessed that the dead clerk had stuck the key to the bridge handrail as an errand for Charobim before checking out permanently, leaving the lobby job open to a new face, one that would not find Darius's out of place when he took up residence in an unsold unit.

On the fourth floor he turned his key in the lock of unit #72. The door glided open on well-oiled hinges, and he entered his private domain. He stepped out of his shoes in the foyer and tugged his socks off, draping them, with his jacket and scarf, over an art-deco metal chair. He savored the feel of the polished wood floors beneath his feet as he moved to the west wall, where a bank of tall windows offered a panoramic view of Kenmore Square. The streets below were dark, but the ruddy glow of the vanished sun still clung to the underbelly of a thunderhead over Brookline. He closed the sheer curtains and turned to face the room.

Darius had few possessions and had left most of them in his abandoned dorm room at MIT. It would have felt somehow sacrilegious to clutter this austere white space with the cheap artifacts of his old life. He still took most of his meals on campus where they were already paid for, but he slept here and would soon work here as well. For now, the beautiful empty space was neither lab nor home. It was more of a shrine and monk's cell. There was no TV and little furniture. He slept on the floor in a sleeping bag he'd picked up at an Army Navy store, and he liked this, too. It felt good on his back after the lumpy dorm mattress, and if he felt any aches, he reveled in them as daily reminders of the Spartan luxury his guru had established for him.

What little he needed for living he kept in the bedroom, reserving the larger space for use as a private temple. The ceilings were high, the floor taped with arcane geometry, the sole piece of furniture an antique vanity with a swivel mirror in an iron vine mounting. Darius didn't know if the vanity had been provided by the landlord, or if Nereus Charobim himself had arranged to have it delivered. In any case, it was perfectly suited to his purpose. He had recognized this at first sight and adopted it as an altar immediately.

At the flip of a switch, the propane fireplace roared to life in the black iron grate. He opened a box on the mantle, rustled through red tissue paper, and removed two sticks of incense, a special blend formulated by a cultist with a backroom shop that was taboo enough to remain clandestine even in Salem, where you could find a pagan emporium on every cobblestoned corner.

He touched the sticks to the flame and inhaled a taste of their acrid fumes before placing them in the twin burners on the hearth. Then, with ribbons of smoke rising behind his shoulders like angel wings, he approached the vanity. He took a ceramic bowl from the floor and ceremoniously placed it in front of the mirror. He opened the drawer where a woman would have kept her brushes and rouge and removed a long dagger. This too was from the shop in Salem, modeled on a Tibetan *phurba*, a three-sided blade descending from a handle carved in the shape of a bulbous head with tentacles wrapped around the base of the blade. The knife was black from pommel to point and flecked with sparkling minerals. He set it on the table, uncorked a phial of virgin olive oil, and poured half of it into the bowl.

The white cardboard box jostled.

He stripped off his clothes, tossing them piece-by-piece into a corner, and beheld his sinewy form in the dark mirror. With a match from the drawer he lit a pair of thick black candles that flanked the bowl of oil and tilted the mirror downward to reflect the golden liquid. He dipped his thumb in the oil and rubbed a drop across his forefinger, softening and glazing his hand before taking up his cock and stroking it to erection.

He thought of Samira. The look on her face when the lancet pierced her finger, and the image brought him to fullness.

Awkwardly, he bent and opened the white box with the garish pet store logo. He reached in and cupped his hands around the bird—a diamond dove—and lifted it out. The dove trilled and tried to stretch its wings against his fingers.

He set it down on the vanity beside the bowl and held it there gently with the webbing between his left thumb and forefinger, while with the same part of his right hand, he took up his cock again and stroked himself to the brink of orgasm.

He stopped there and conjured the sigil of the messenger in his mind's eye, blazing in blue flame. He drew a deep breath tinged with charred nettle, and on the exhalation, as the wave of ecstasy broke over him, he lifted the dove by the neck and squeezed the life from it while his semen jetted into the golden oil. Before the final convulsions of dove and cock relented, he seized the dagger and plunged it into the dying bird's chest, spraying dark blood across the bowl and the linen cloth on which it rested.

A twitching talon cut the heel of his hand, and he tossed the bloody white body to the floor, all the while keeping his eyes focused on the silvered glass and the wavering golden light of candle flame and oil.

Now he stirred the contents of the bowl with the dagger, making a marbled swirl of blood, semen, and oil, removing the black blade only when the widdershins motion of the liquid had taken on sufficient momentum to keep swirling without assistance. He watched the vortex in the mirror taking on depth and dimension, continuing to rotate long after inertia should have stopped it.

With the tip of the dagger he traced the sigil of Nyarlathotep on the glass, consecrating the mirror, making a portal of it for daily use, opening the way for a conversation and communion that had until now been relegated to the domain of dreams.

A face appeared in the marbled vortex, austere and African, eyes twin points of icy light, features shifting like a heat haze mirage, in a scarlet hood from which a writhing appendage fell—a tentacle that breached the glass boundary of the mirror and dipped into the liquid, then retracted with a drop of the offering quivering on its tip, which then darted into the mouth of the master, bringing him a taste and sealing the covenant.

"I knew you would come," Darius said in a flood of relief at the sight of the face; all of his fears of rejection and delusion allayed at last.

"And I you," the pharaoh said, his voice like a purring engine crackling with sparks and thrumming through every atom of the air, the floor, the walls.

"I knew you were more than a dream."

In reply the face retreated into the red hood, and the fractal swirl in the mirror transmuted into a series of images that had haunted his dreams: flooded subway tunnels, a night sky marked by a unique conjunction of planets and constellations that had not been seen since the time of the Mayans, a mathematical theorem written in blood and light, and a spell written in Sanskrit. Each had visited him in his sleep, but now their order and juxtaposition took on new sense.

The face of the pharaoh appeared again, and its lips, like ripe black worms, spoke to him. "You are my hands, Darius. Your works grant me substance, but until the stars are right, I act through your agency."

"Yes, Lord."

"We must be prepared for that time. We must open the way."

"*Yes.*" He breathed the word in a fugue of ecstasy.

"You have obtained the verses I requested? The calls and keys?"

"I have. I'm ready to leave everything behind…school, church. From this day I serve you, only you."

"Leave nothing behind, for all things serve me through you, just as they serve the Great Old Ones through me."

"What would you have me do?"

"I have secured a laboratory for you at the institute."

"A lab of my own?"

"Not of your own. You will be a guest at odd hours of Dr. Leonard Martin."

"Martin? He's an arrogant megalomaniac. He'll never let me near his precious equipment."

"He will. I have seeded his dreams. You need only present him with this glyph, and he will stand aside."

The mirror went opaque as a fogged window, and the black tentacle traced a geometric form in the condensation. Darius, naked, scanned the altar and realized with dawning alarm that he had no pen and paper. He dashed to the corner of the room where he'd thrown his clothes, slipped on the blood of the bird and slammed his hip against the hardwood floor. He crawled to the bundle of clothes and dug his smartphone from the pocket of his jeans, staggered to his feet, and returned to the vanity.

He took a picture of the symbol on the mirror, then checked the file, almost certain that the image wouldn't transfer properly, that all he would have captured in pixels would be a reflection of his hand holding the phone. But it was there, a matrix of angles and crescents inscribed in gray condensation. He set the phone down beside the dagger, and the mirror went fractal again, sliding through kaleidoscopic transitions and imprinting his retina with a series of calculations and diagrams that he didn't need to document because they made perfect sense to him as they opened new vistas in his mind. All of the obstacles in his work fell away in a flash. At last, Charobim appeared again to deliver a parting injunction. "Build it, and they will come."

Chapter 8

Becca made a cup of tea in the microwave and settled cross-legged in her rickety gray office chair, waiting for the SD cards from her modified Nikon to load into the iMac. Images flashed before her eyes like a shuffled deck of tarot cards: too fast to focus on but chilling her nonetheless. She leaned forward squinting, as if that would reconcile the mystery.

"*No....*"

On the screen were elements she recognized from vague oppressive nightmares she'd had before Nina prescribed something for dreamless sleep. Drawn into the procession of aberrant thumbnails, it took a moment for her to realize that a distant sound from the bedroom was her ringtone. She stepped away from the computer desk and, when she saw it was Rafael, answered the call.

"Hey, Raf, what's up?" she said, moving to one of the wall-length windows, her gaze roving idly over the rain-drenched rooftops spread out below, most of the houses abandoned in the flood zone, some lit against the dark afternoon and the thunderheads that had settled stubbornly on the city.

"Just checking to see how you're doing... after, you know, losing your grandmother and all. How's it going?"

"I'm all right."

"Well, I know this time of year isn't exactly easy on you anyway. Then that happened."

"Yeah." She sighed. "I probably should have moved to California by now."

"You sound distracted. Is this a bad time?"

"No. Sorry. Is that rain I hear? Are you outside?"

"Actually, I'm outside your building. I brought you some soup."

"And you're making small talk?" She laughed. "What is wrong with your brain, boy? I'll be right down."

His dreads were dripping like a rope mop when she opened the door for him. "Get in here. You look as bad as the dog I've been trying to rescue."

"What dog?"

"Doesn't matter. He got away."

"Sounds more like attempted abduction than rescue."

"If you weren't bearing a gift of soup...."

"Yeah, well, somebody's gotta feed you. I stopped by the gallery but they said you were out sick."

Becca sighed. "I'm okay. I'm just not up for dealing with people."

He stopped climbing the stairs midflight, nodded, and said, "Okay, that's cool."

She grabbed him by the bicep and tugged. The muscle gave more resistance than she expected. He always looked so lanky and mellow; she forgot how athletic he was. "I don't mean *you*. You don't qualify as people."

"Gee, *Thanks.*" He smiled and followed her up the stairs, closer to the sound of the rain on the roof and the muted rumble of thunder.

The soup was vegetarian curry from a café near Rafael's apartment. He'd known it was a favorite of hers from lunches they'd had there at the outdoor tables on Boylston Street. On their first visit, Becca had asked the waitress about the broth to make sure it wasn't chicken stock, and Rafael had apparently filed away the information for future reference. Becca relished the warmth from the cardboard canister as she carried it to the kitchenette and ladled the soup into bowls. The rich smell awakened her hunger.

She brought a bowl and spoon to Rafael, who sat on the futon by the windows, and had almost settled into a stuffed chair with her own bowl when he jogged her memory by asking, "So tell me about this dog."

She straightened up, sloshing a dollop of broth over the brim of her bowl. She licked it from the heel of her hand and said, "That's right—I was downloading pictures when you called. You mind eating at my desk? You don't have to, but I want to look at them. They're fuckin' weird. And I might have one of the dog."

"Weird how?"

"C'mon."

*   *   *

"Okay, that *is* weird." Rafael had forgotten his cooling soup. He sat in Becca's swivel chair, squinting at the widescreen on her desk. "What is it?"

"I don't know...." Too hungry to forget her own food, she stood behind him, slurping the dregs from the bowl. They had watched the entire set from the mill as a slideshow, and now he was zooming in on one of the better examples.

"It looks like that kelp you find at the beach," Rafael said. "The brown stuff with bubbles. You ever pop those like bubble wrap when you were a kid?"

"Sure. Yeah, it kinda does, but it's...."

"Much bigger. This is to scale with the bricks? It's not a double exposure?"

She shrugged. "I didn't see anything like this on the bricks at the time, but I don't even know how to get a double exposure with a digital camera. Not on the card. And even if I did, I haven't shot any close ups of seaweed, and it only *sort* of looks like that."

"Yeah...I just meant how that batwing stuff connects them. The actual bubbles are more round and...oily."

"I know what you mean. Like giant soap bubbles right? You can't see the colors in black-and-white infrared, but I know what you mean. Those swirly shades of gray look like they'd be iridescent."

Becca leaned over Rafael's shoulder (he smelled good, like coconut oil) and clicked on a thumbnail in the viewer. Another image of a brick wall expanded to fill the screen. The bricks were flaking with weather-cracked paint and lichen, but overlaying these textures was a ghostly pattern of gray whorls spiraling from pinpricks of blackness. The pattern ran rampant over the entire wall with the exception of a clear area at the focal point of the photo, surrounding the graffiti of a five-branched rune, as if the symbol were repellent to whatever psychedelic infestation had overrun the derelict mill.

"They look like spirals made of spirals," Rafael said.

"Or fractals. Fractals made of tentacles."

He looked away from the screen and scrutinized her face. "When did you take these, anyway?"

Becca didn't meet his eyes when she replied. "Yesterday."

"You went to the mill without me? The *fuck*, Becca. Have you gone on any other expeditions alone?"

"A few. Look, I know what you think, but this dog is really skittish. I'd have no chance if I wasn't alone."

He shook his head. "Becca, what if you fell through a floor? Or if something collapsed on you? These places aren't safe, and without—"

"Without a partner, I know. I *know*. Okay? I promise I'll at least tell you where I'm going next time."

"No, you'll bring me next time."

Now she did meet his eyes with a hardness in her own. "You're not my father. And I *wasn't* alone. There was some crazy guy there. Like a tinfoil hat dude."

"Oh, you're really making your case now. Good thing he didn't rape you."

"Too paranoid to be rapey."

"Or murder you in a paranoid rage."

"His only weapon was a laser pointer. One of those cheap ones you use to fuck with a cat."

Rafael sighed. "What, did he give you a PowerPoint presentation on Ancient Aliens?"

Becca laughed. "Almost. I wonder if he painted that symbol. You ever see it before?"

"Can't say I have."

"It looks familiar, but I don't know from where."

"He didn't point it out to you with his laser?"

"No. He was using that to draw red pentagrams on the walls. Wish I'd got a shot of it. He was so freaky cool with like this cardboard crown and 3D glasses."

"Sounds certifiable. But you *did* get a pentagram picture. There, right?" Rafael pointed at one of the thumbnails he'd clicked past quickly a moment ago. Becca enlarged it. It was a shot of a different wall with the same sort of infrared fractal pattern, except here the pattern vanished around a five-pointed star delineated by the absence of the fractal, the same way the five-branched symbol had kept it at bay in the other photo.

"Wait a minute," Becca said, "That shot isn't from the mill, it's from the asylum."

"Are you sure?"

"Positive. And Moe, the freaky guy with the laser, he wasn't there that day when you and I went."

"Maybe he was there before us. Can a laser leave some kind of uh... radiation traces that would show up on an infrared photo?"

"I doubt it, but now I kinda want to buy one and experiment." She went to her shoulder bag where it hung from a chair, dug out the camera, then snapped a few quick shots of the nearest brick wall and of Rafael seated at her desk, the screen glowing behind him. She ejected the card and inserted it into the computer.

"What are you doing?"

She clicked on all three photos in quick succession. They opened, filling her screen. "Just testing the camera to see if we get the same effect here. In case there's something wrong with the sensor or the lens, but...no.... No spheres or fractals."

"So it's not the camera."

"No."

Rafael took a spoonful of soup and watched her as she tucked the camera back into the bag, slipped into her jacket, and slung the bag over her shoulder, pulling her ponytail from under the strap.

"Where are we going?" he asked, and sipped from the bowl as she had, eyeing her over the brim, intent on finishing before she left without him.

"Back to the mill."

* * *

Becca convinced Rafael to wait outside while she went in to take another set of photos, this time documenting the walls extensively to see if the phenomenon recurred. She was also hoping she might see Django or Moe again and didn't want her companion scaring either of them off. There was a semi-collapsed outbuilding where Rafael could have taken shelter while he waited for her, but the rain had let up while they were on the T, so he wandered the weedy lot and smoked a joint. A few rooms in, Becca caught sight of him through a broken window. He produced a tube of oil paint from the pocket of his hoodie, squeezed some purple onto a small brush, and set about dashing off one of his trademark characters on the damp brick façade, his nimble brown fingers amazing her with their innate fluency.

She smelled no sage in the air this time, and as she progressed deeper and deeper along the ground floor through the labyrinth of abandoned machines and rotting textiles, she became increasingly sure that she was alone in the place. In one empty room she found paw prints in the dust and followed them, but they vanished in a roofless hall where the rain had recently assaulted the dirty tiles, pooling in the cracks and empty grout channels. Her footfalls echoed amid the *drip-drop-plop* falling from the heights where tangles of rebar clawed at the pewter sky.

She came to a descending steel staircase and took it one tentative step at a time, the metal groaning under her weight. At the bottom she found a utility closet the size of a bathroom. It was almost empty of evidence of its original function, as all of the circuit breaker boxes and conduit pipes had been stripped of copper, probably by looters. At the far end where the ceiling sloped into shadow, she saw a bed of cardboard scraps and musty blankets. Was this where Moe Ramirez slept? She waited for her eyes to adjust to the dark.

As the room took on detail, she saw that the walls were marked with colored chalk in a profusion of geometric forms, Hebrew letters, and numbers, along with what appeared to be other letters as well, but in no alphabet she recognized. The branch symbol was there again, and what looked like the connect-the-dots mapping of constellations unknown to her on the slanting ceiling. The centerpiece of that ceiling gave her a shock: a perfect rendering of the winged scarab she'd inherited from her grandmother, carrying a blazing red star in its pincers.

There was a light bulb with a chain, but she could tell from the dark sediment settled in the bottom of it that it wouldn't have promised light even if the breaker boxes hadn't been gutted. She didn't even bother trying the chain.

She took a step toward the bed, realizing now that what she had at first sight taken for cans of food were actually squat candles. A few books of matches lay beside them, most stripped to fringed booklets, but she found a pack with three intact atop a dog-eared spiral notebook, and struck one to light a candle.

The little cell seemed to careen like the cabin of a boat at sea for a moment, throwing shadows at vertiginous angles as the flame was tossed by the wind of her hand shaking out the match. In the gold light she saw that the floor and bed were cleaner than she'd supposed, and she noticed a whiskbroom leaning beside the entrance, its straws worn down almost to the stitching. She saw no sign of the cardboard crown or glasses, but this place had to be Moe's room, judging by the occult graffiti. She eyed the notebook with a guilty weight in her stomach, knowing that there was no way she wasn't going to peek at its contents.

It might explain why her grandmother's beetle was etched on the ceiling where he would see it every night as he fell asleep and every morning when he woke.

The door creaked shut behind her, causing the hairs on the nape of her neck to prickle. She went to it, wrapped her hand around the knob, but hesitated, afraid to turn it. She didn't give herself enough time to let that fear blossom into paralysis; she cranked the knob and pushed the door harder than necessary, intending to shove anyone who might be lurking on the other side, who might have shut her in. There wasn't time to wonder if she might be knocking Moe or Rafael to the floor.

The door met no resistance, and she found no one there. She looked around for a piece of broken brick or something to prop it open with, and finding nothing suitable, took her chances that it would close again while she hurriedly retrieved the spiral notebook from the floor.

In the hallway, by the light from the stairwell, she flipped through a few pages, nervous that Moe would find her plundering his private journal, a feeling intensified by her recently rattled nerves.

The same crazed metaphysical calculations that lined the walls also filled the pages, as if having run out of paper, the author had put down his pencil and taken up chalk to continue his train of thought. She turned to the back of the book to check, but there were still some blank pages. Starting at the beginning again and doing a quick, methodical scan, she found no other diagrams of the beetle.

Interspersed between the cabalistic calculations she came across the occasional list or journal entry in plain English. Such as:

7/19/17 Acquired the power objects to complete my vestments today. A golden solar crown, ruby scepter, and spectacles for activating the R/L hemispheres. I stand at the axis mundi *now, between the pillars of Mercy and Severity, and assume the mantle of Guardian of the Wheel.*

He sure didn't write like he talked. Becca heard something shift and crash on the ground floor above, and almost set the book down to run to see if it was Django, but she knew if she left it here she wouldn't come back, and now she wanted to know more, needed to know more. Did Moe's 3D glasses somehow enable him to see the invisible patterns on the walls, the alien shapes that her camera could only catch in the infrared part of the spectrum? That seemed impossible, but she had often wondered if schizophrenics were simply people whose consciousness was attuned to a slightly different level of perception than the rest of society. The books she'd read about shamanism in her grandmother's library seemed to suggest that possibility.

She wished she'd found Maurice at home and could just ask him about the photos and the beetle, maybe buy him a hot cup of coffee and a sandwich, but she also knew that the notebook in her hands might reveal more truth than any oblique explanations he might give her face to face.

Another entry:

The young man was back today in the flooded buildings on the riverbank, testing different labia for the Voice Box of the Gods. Like reeds for a flute. He's getting closer to the right harmonics. The membrane tween worlds is wearing thin. Took me all night to seal the cracks.

What the hell did that mean, if anything? Maybe *she* was the crazy one for thinking she could decode the ramblings of a burnt-out mystic. Still, she flipped the pages, searching. There were some drawings of what looked like alien landscapes and inhuman sexual anatomy, but nothing that quite resembled the fractal patterns she'd seen in the photos, and no scarabs.

Another small crash echoed down the stairs, followed by a scampering rush, and this time she shut the book, tossed it atop the pile of ratty blankets, and blew out the candle.

She climbed the stairs quickly and quietly. As her head cleared the floor, she glanced around the room and caught sight of the shaggy black-and-tan tail swishing out of sight around a corner where black mold clung to water-stained cinderblocks.

Abandoning stealth, Becca took the remaining steps at a dash and gave chase. She hurtled around the corner and splashed through a stretch of stagnant puddles, cloud-filtered sunlight strobing against her face from holes in the roof, dazzling her eyes with its brightness after their acclimation to the darkness of the basement utility closet.

She stopped short at an intersection of corridors, her green canvas bag swinging at her hip with the weight of the camera. Between her boots, she saw the gray impressions of paw prints in the dust, and followed them down the center corridor, wishing for a flashlight. She'd come less prepared than usual today. Her typical urbex kit included the headlamp, a Swiss army knife, and enough nylon cords, cleats, and hooks to satisfy a rock climber. Rafael called her a "girl scout," but today in her haste to take more photos and interview Moe, she hadn't expected to explore the bowels of the building.

The paw prints led through an interior hall built of sheet rock and wood that had suffered more water damage than the brick walls of the outer rooms. In places she could see through gaping holes in the walls where she supposed vandal kids had thrown karate kicks and chunks of bricks for the sheer pleasure of destruction. None of these offered her another glimpse of the dog, though, and eventually she walked out of the far end of a long puddle, her boots glazed with gray water, and no tracks on the dusty concrete to follow. It took her a moment to register the absence of the paw prints because there were other markings on the floor; dark and geometric and hard to read in the darkness.

She now wished she'd taken the book of matches with her, maybe even the candle. She could have stuffed them in her bag and returned them to Moe's lair before leaving the mill. But now it was as futile to wish for matches as for the headlamp she'd left at home, so she took out her camera, turned on the LCD, and shone the little screen at the floor, straining to see the marks by its weak light.

Becca didn't like what she saw in the half-second before the light automatically dimmed. It looked like blood.

She switched the flash on and took a shot of the floor at her feet, looking directly at it rather than through the viewfinder. The burst of light turned the odd shapes on the floor deep red for a blazing instant, and then she was doused in darkness again, looking at the photo on the screen: three exploded drops of blood on the concrete (drops that had fallen from a greater height than that of a dog judging by their spiky coronae) and a set of bloody, blocky sneaker treads smearing toward the wall. But the dark red skid marks ended there, as if the wall had been built across their path, or as if the body had been pulled through the wall, which was itself devoid of bloodstains. In the dark she could almost imagine she was standing beside a barrier of thick fog, but when she touched it, the eggshell paint was cold, damp, and solid beneath her fingertips.

She backed away from the wall until her shoulders touched its opposite, raised the camera, and shot six photos—three with flash and three without.

Her heart quickened as she thumbed the buttons, standing in the dark, waiting for the last photo to load and light her face. When it did, her breath caught in her throat. The pattern of fractal tentacles was here, just as it had been in the pictures of the brick walls from the previous day. But in the dark, the infrared textures were stronger, as if they'd been weakened by ambient sunlight in the other room, or had grown more tangible, more present in the mill since last she'd been here. And that felt right. The pattern reminded her of the restoration of some fresco from antiquity, the details of the paint emerging from under a layer of grime and soot. Only here it appeared that a layer of some reality or dimension adjacent to our own was revealed.

Becca wiped her clammy hand down her thigh, then turned the thumbwheel and checked the previous shot. In this one, she had aimed at the base of the wall where it met the floor to capture the bloody sneaker treads. A cold dread woke in her, a sense that some grave threat was closing in on her in the dark. Her animal instincts urged her to look away from the camera screen and search the shadows for whatever had spilled blood here, but she couldn't look away because the terrible and impossible fact confronting her from the brittle light of the LCD was that the monsters were inside the walls, all around her, and in the floor beneath her feet as well. Or that matter itself, the three dimensional space she mistook for floor and wall and God help her maybe even the sky itself, was made of monsters.

Her breath had grown shallow and her limbs felt numb, the onset of terror threatening to immobilize her, and with her eyes still locked on the image, she forced herself to step away from the blood, to back down the corridor in the direction from which she had come...because in the photo the blood smears didn't end at the wall; they continued through it, and there on the other side was an object she feared she recognized, sitting in a puddle of blood. It was impossible, and she told herself so. It quickly became a mantra, "Not possible, not possible...."

Not possible for a digital camera to function like an x-ray scope, to turn a wall into a window. Not possible for a cardboard crown to be overturned in a pool of blood in another dimension at her feet, inside a solid wall.

* * *

When Becca emerged from the mill, staggering over the fallen door and through the brambles, clutching her camera to her chest, sweat beading on her forehead and chilling in the cold air, she didn't see Rafael. Her panic increased at the idea that he might have gone into the building looking for her, that she might have to go back in there instead of just getting the hell out of here, and the inarticulate fear underlying these other concerns but rapidly rising to the surface of her consciousness—that he could be trapped in the walls, like a fly in amber, among the oily spheres and fractals.

But then she heard a gentle, lilting voice on the breeze, *Rafael's* voice, and coming around a corner she found him squatting in a bald patch of the weedy lot where the rusty rings of beer can lids poked from the charred ground and shards of dirty glass glinted silver in the diffused sunlight of the dim day.

Sensing her approach, he turned to smile at her, a smile that faded when he saw her. He was holding something in his fingers, something she would never have thought to pack in her own bag. He was feeding a piece of beef jerky to Django.

Chapter 9

Darius Marlowe was a man with many keys. He had an ID that served as a key to the building that housed the lab; he had a magnetic card that served as a key to the lab itself; and he had a photo of a sigil drawn in condensation on the surface of a foggy mirror—a mirror misted with the water of another world—on his phone, which served as a key to the mind of Dr. Leonard Martin, who was himself a kind of key to the best 3D printer at MIT.

He flashed the sigil at Dr. Martin as he entered the lab. It probably wasn't necessary to show it to him every time, but Darius wasn't sure of the rules for keeping the suggestion effective, so he didn't take any chances. His recent communications with Charobim had focused on only his most vital technical questions. The face-to-face summoning was an exhausting process, one he resorted to only when the instructions from his dreams required clarification.

The dreams had grown more vivid now that he slept at the Fenway Towers, close to the mirror. Maybe it had nothing to do with the mirror. Maybe he was developing some part of his brain, some facet of his active imagination through regular exercise. He thought of it as a kind of muscle deep in his brain, something serpentine coiled around his amygdala.

Martin had glanced up at Darius's entry with perfectly lucid curiosity on his face, but at the sign of the pharaoh his features slackened immediately, and, resembling a lobotomy recipient, the distinguished scientist shambled to a corner of the lab to busy himself with whatever amusements he could find there (probably the non-Euclidian sculpture he'd been building out of coffee stirrers whenever Darius visited) and clearing the way for the protégé to use the lab.

Darius opened the glass specimen case at the end of the bay and checked on his latest prototype. It was a thing of beauty: a bionic larynx built in the Plexiglas box of the 3D printer from bovine cells, silicone, and silver Nano-particles in a mere five hours and then left to cultivate in a Petrie dish for two weeks, a process accelerated by a formula that Charobim had inscribed on the mirror one midnight. Dr. Martin would have been duly impressed if he were in his right mind in Darius's presence. But then, if the professor were in his right mind, the student would have been ejected from the lab by campus security long before he'd had a chance to exhibit his genius for biotech innovation.

The project followed a trail blazed by McAlpine and Mannoor at Princeton, where they had developed a bionic ear that could transmit and receive electromagnetic frequencies beyond the natural human range. But their models took four weeks to cultivate and couldn't detect acoustic sound waves. The work of Charobim and Marlowe would never see the pages of a peer-reviewed journal, but it broke new ground in that it produced actual acoustic speech via a voice box made of similar biosynthetic materials for the vocal folds, cartilage, and epiglottis. Of course, the production of language depended on the entire vocal system from lungs to tongue and teeth, but Darius wasn't interested in making it speak English or any other known language.

He had built the Voice Box of the Gods to reproduce a lost language, the *first* language, which man had once sung in wordless adoration of the dark gods who had birthed him from the amniotic tide pools of his marine incarnation.

It was a language of vowels and overtones preserved by the priest class of ancient Sumer long after the evolution (or devolution) of the human organism had left such utterances behind. Some volumes of occult history claimed that the priests had cut out their own tongues or mutilated their mouths in excruciating initiation rituals to reclaim the gift of black song. Charobim would neither confirm nor deny these accounts when Darius probed him in the deepest hours of the night, when drunken B.U. students would catch glimpses of unearthly lights and colors from a fourth-floor window of the gargoyle-haunted Fenway Towers. The methods of the past were abrogate, Charobim declared in his true form as Nyarlathotep. New science had granted the ability to produce essential harmonics in purer form, and the phonetic codes that Darius had transcribed from the old tomes in the tower library of the Starry Wisdom Church were the keys.

The first prototypes had failed to reproduce the sounds properly and had only succeeded in thinning the membrane between the dimensions in the abandoned buildings where Darius had tested them. He had gone back to the design, had spent hours with his laptop on the vanity beside the swivel mirror, the two glowing windows exchanging information, his blood-shot eyes and blood-stained fingers serving as the interface. And now he sensed that success was nigh. He could almost taste it.

He pulled on a blue latex glove and gingerly lifted the larynx from the Petrie dish. A pair of spiral wires trailed from it, their gold contacts brushing against his wrist as he turned the organ this way and that, admiring the translucent pink sheen of its semi-sexual aesthetic.

He opened the cabinet at his feet and removed an object that had once been, and still resembled, a battery-powered Aiwa boom box. He had gutted most of the electronics and replaced them with a small fan and silicone ductwork which functioned as an esophagus for driving breath through the vocal folds, and a digital chip programmed with the incantations: the Sanskrit, Enochian, and Lengian vowel sequences distilled to ones and zeroes.

He had encoded the mantras into data strings at the Stata Center for Computer, Information, and Intelligence Sciences, a complex he loved for its non-rectilinear Deconstructivist architecture—the walls teetering at sickening, random angles around him while he worked. Some sensitive students found the place nauseating, but it delighted Darius, and he reveled in the critique of mathematician and architectural theorist Nikos Salingaros, who said, "Housing a scientific department at a university inside the symbol of its nemesis must be the ultimate irony."

Darius took a screwdriver from the bench and removed the left speaker grill to reveal the custom port he had installed in the boom box. He plugged the contact wires into their jacks and secured the bionic voice box in its latex brace, making sure to position the labia over the air channel. The juxtaposition of bionic bovine tissue and ghetto tech gave him the same thrill it always did, and he took a moment to admire his handiwork before realigning the metal grill and replacing the screws.

He picked up the finished device and made for the door. "Later, Professor," he said with a two-finger salute, then paused with his hand on the door handle. It occurred to him that if his newest prototype did the job, this might be the last time he would see Dr. Martin, and he realized he had developed an unexpected affection for the man.

The hypnosis usually wore off within a couple of hours, and Darius had gotten used to flashing the old coot's retinas at least once per session to gain an extension of lab time, but now he set the boom box on the floor and dug his smartphone out of his pocket. With a tap he inverted the sigil, then showed it to Martin, who was looking up from his stick sculpture like a dim-witted child, an expression of good-natured curiosity puffing his salt-and-pepper whiskers into a smile that would have shocked his students. But the smile faded as the sigil sunk in, and his brow furrowed into its natural state. "Who are you?" he asked.

"An admirer of your work. Listen: you should leave the city for the weekend, okay? Just a word to the wise. There's a new kind of storm coming, and you'll want to seek out higher ground."

And with that, Darius Marlowe slipped out the door, jogged down a square spiral of stairs that echoed with his footfalls, and stepped onto Mass Ave leaving MIT behind.

Chapter 10

Caring for Django turned out to be a welcome distraction from the mounting fear Becca had felt in the dark corridors of the mill. She knew her camera held clues to a mystery that she would need to confront, but in the hard, gray daylight of the outside, those mysteries took on the bleached-out hue of a fading nightmare, and the dog's needs took precedence, enabling her to shift her focus from cosmic dread to personal responsibility. Part of her mind was already ticking off things she could do about the photos, like making backups and showing a couple of the best examples to either Clay Dalton—her mentor at the Museum School—or Uncle Neil, who now ran a camera shop after retiring from forensic photography.

The fact was, she didn't want to think about what she might have captured in the corridor, so she tamped it down by telling herself that when she did look at the shots on the big screen, the images would somehow make sense in a way that had eluded her while she was freaked out in the dark, with only the LCD for reference. It would make sense, or one of her mentors would make sense of it for her. For now, she focused on the dog. She might not be able to help Moe Ramirez, but she was pretty sure she could help Django.

When they arrived at her warehouse apartment, she offered Rafael a beer and asked him if he wanted to watch TV while she groomed the dog, already feeling self-conscious about just how prepared she was to take care of an animal she'd been unlikely to ever see again. He accepted the beer but not the remote, and ended up following her around while she fussed with the dog, trimming clumps of matted hair with a pair of shears. To his credit, he did hold Django to keep him from jumping out of the claw-foot tub while she worked what was left of his fur into a medicinal lather. By then Rafael had finished his beer and was shaking his head with a smirk she found infuriating.

"What? What's funny about this?"

"You."

"What about me?"

"Flea shampoo?"

"Well, duh. I don't want fleas in my apartment."

"So you just keep the stuff on hand?"

"No, I bought it when I decided to rescue him."

"I just think it's cute you've been planning this for a while."

"He needed someone."

"What if he belongs to someone?"

"He doesn't. He's a hurricane dog."

"So you're gonna have the vet scan him for a microchip?"

She hadn't thought of that, and knew he could see the trepidation on her face as she considered it. He laughed. "Fuckin' dognapper."

Becca aimed the shower wand at him. He flinched at the spray and let go of Django, who immediately shook off and soaked the both of them.

From there it escalated into a water fight, with Django happily yapping between the pair. Later, when Rafael had gone home and Becca was curled up on the futon with a glass of red and the dog on a blanket at her feet trying to burn his nose on the little electric space heater she'd set up for him, she thought of how good it had been to laugh. She'd almost forgotten what it felt like after putting her grandmother in the ground and then succumbing to the encroaching paranoia that had come with the odd encounters she'd had these past few weeks—first with the tattooed reverend at the asylum and then with Maurice and his talk about cracks in some cosmic wheel. She supposed her attraction to the margins of society was responsible for those encounters. She'd never wanted to photograph shiny, happy people, and if you were going to go poking around in abandoned asylums on forsaken hilltops and collapsing mills beside rat-infested wharves, you had to expect to meet your fair share of people who had *fallen* through the cracks (ha-ha). *Lovers, buggers, and thieves.* Wasn't that what Maurice had been singing when she met him? *Down by the river Charles.* The thought stirred a worm in her stomach, and she wondered if she'd ever be able to hear that song again without a chill running down her spine.

Well, you were bound to find some crazies when you went looking for them, poking around in the rusty wreckage. But it didn't help when the paranoid schizoid who wanted to warn you about a cosmic invasion ended up getting pulled through a solid wall into some sidelong dimension by fractal tentacles and iridescent spheres or some such fucking thing, did it?

She rubbed her stocking foot against Django's head, scratching between his ears with her toes, and her eyes wandered reluctantly to her workstation across the vast room. Would she be able to sleep tonight if she looked at those pictures? It had been bad enough to look at them in the little LCD window on the camera. She took another sip of her wine and almost regretted letting Raf go home. Examining the photos with a friend might have been easier.

Or sleeping with a friend might have been easier.

But fear of sleeping alone in the big loft with those uncanny images slumbering on her hard drive was no reason to cross a boundary in her most precious friendship. One that couldn't be uncrossed. The fact that she sensed a depth of feeling from Raf that she couldn't reciprocate made her sad. It had been good to laugh in the spray of the shower wand, but if she wanted to be able to keep laughing with Rafael, she would have to be careful not to hurt him. The medication was getting her through for now, but she knew what was coming with the longer nights, and the ice and snow. Days when she would barely be able to function, when she would fluctuate between catatonia and flashes of misplaced rage. Raf didn't need that, didn't deserve it.

"And I'm *not* alone, anyway," she said to Django, bending down to pet him.

He thumped his tail twice on the wood floor. Soon she realized she had absentmindedly moved from scratching the dog's fur to scratching her own forearm, picking at an itching scab that she couldn't recall the origin of. She was always getting banged up on urbex outings, but the scab picking was a nervous habit that Nina had pointed out to her, and she forced herself to stop.

That crown was in a pool of blood and you know it, and seeing it on a big screen will only be worse. Far worse.

She should have told Rafael to stay. She was more rattled than she'd realized because the dog had kept her mind off it until now. And yet she wasn't finished tending to his needs. She'd been happy to watch her new companion clean his food dish, but now he was due to go out before she could sleep. God only knew what would come out of him, with all of the standing water he'd been drinking. In hindsight, the beef jerky didn't seem like such a great thing to have given him on an out-of-practice digestive system, but she knew they never would have won him over without it. Not today, anyway. She had done better by him for his first meal at home: kibble soaked in warm water to keep him from bloating. She stretched and cracked her back, trying to let go of the tension, then grabbed a couple of plastic grocery store bags from a cabinet and stuffed them into her coat pocket.

Django didn't need to see the leash to get up and follow her. He gave up the blanket beside the heater as soon as she started moving. Apparently they had already formed some kind of bond on the basis of one meal and a roof that didn't leak. He looked both sad and comical with his botched haircut. She'd need a proper electric trimmer to do it right and she wasn't sure she could spare the expense. There were going to be some significant vet bills in the next few days, with vaccines and maybe even an antibiotic for that ear. She'd asked around and found that even the flat rate for an office visit was steep, but she did have a bit of money now from her grandmother, and groceries were overrated anyway. She wasn't going to splurge on a groomer, but for now, at least he wasn't flea ridden and chewing the hell out of himself.

She slipped the collar over his head—black nylon with a red Celtic knot that matched the leash. Then, pausing to grab the headlamp and pull her jacket on, she led him out the door, down the stairs, and into the night.

She could see her breath against the black sky as soon as they stepped out onto the sidewalk, and it reminded her of the nights when she used to step out into the cold to smoke. Django peed on the side of the building before she could even get him near anything resembling a tree. She started to reprimand him but instead said, "You know what? That's perfectly cool, dude. It's your territory now, you go ahead and mark it. Rite of passage."

He looked up at the sound of her voice and seemed to grin while the last few bursts splashed a dark spray across the bricks. It almost frosted on contact.

Looking at the urine-stained side of the warehouse brought to mind the fractal patterns she'd found lurking in seemingly plain surfaces, and she wondered if the same shapes were concealed here. There had been no sign of them in the indoor photos she'd taken earlier, but down here on the shadowy street it wasn't hard to imagine that there might be traces of whatever had infested the mill, like an encroaching fungus striving steadily toward the second floor. She dismissed the notion with a shiver, gave the leash a little tug, and prompted Django to walk with her around the building. He trotted along willingly, and she took courage from his company when they stepped out of the orange glow of the sodium lights and into the weed-choked horseshoe courtyard.

Django sniffed around, eager to scout new territory even in the bitter cold, and in no apparent hurry to drop a load. Becca followed him, bouncing on her feet to keep warm through each pause.

From the courtyard she could see across Fort Point Channel to Southie. The sight of phone wires swaying in the biting wind made her grateful for the shelter of the building. Django tugged, and, not daring to risk letting go of the leash, she let him pull her around the lot for a while, on the trail of some scent. She gazed at the sky and saw a couple of stars like ice chips through tatters in the gray cloud cover. She cupped her hands around her nose and breathed warm air into them. The heat felt good. It brought feeling back to the tip of her nose, which started to run. She had no tissue and tasted the saline on her upper lip with her tongue. "Okay, buddy," she said to the dog, "Time's up. We're going in. You shit on the floor, so be it."

But Django's body had stiffened, and not from the cold. His snout low and ears cocked forward to tune in on some sound, he had dropped into a ready stance, as if preparing to spring. Becca saw that his tail was curled down, the fur raised near the base, and as she bent to stroke it smooth and utter reassurances, she heard a low growling. Within a few seconds it became clear that the rumble wasn't coming from the dog but from something much larger approaching, and before she could figure out what it was, Django had yanked the leash from her hand and was charging toward the street, barking furiously.

She chased him, stomped on the leash, and put all of her weight on her front foot. It wasn't much, but it was enough to halt a malnourished mutt. Django strained in his collar and directed a barrage of territorial barks toward the street where the rumble of an engine was growing louder. Becca didn't take her boot off the leash until she had a firm grip on it, and by then Django was reconsidering his bluster.

The rumble had quickly grown to resemble the din of a small army of dragons—not just one engine cutting the quiet night, but a cavalcade of them buzzing the tarmac. Tail tucked between his hind legs, Django backed against Becca just as the first vehicle came into view. It was an armored tactical truck, like a Humvee but not quite. Becca was no expert on military machines, but she'd seen Humvees on the news and parked around town as gas-guzzling status symbols. This truck was bigger. It sported what looked like a bulletproofed grill emblazoned with a cougar's head and the word LENCO in white beneath a black hood cut to the angles of a stealth bomber. As the thing rumbled by, she saw some kind of binocular scope mounted on the roof beside a domed hatch. She had glimpsed the shape of a helmeted driver through the windshield, but the only windows on the back and sides were small rectangles of smoked glass.

It was the first of several, and when she looked at the iron bridges that spanned the channel, she saw a black SWAT van led by two police motorcycles with their flashers on racing to catch up with whatever this procession was that had army trucks for a forward guard.

Her hair blew around her face as the cavalcade passed, and she watched them trundle northwest toward the Back Bay. When the rumble had mostly faded she led Django back inside and rode the freight elevator with him up to the loft. The stresses of the day were catching up with her, and now she only wanted to sleep. Hopefully the dog would let her. The idea of making him a fluffy bed of old blankets and towels kindled an unfamiliar maternal feeling in her, and she decided she would set it up beside her own bed.

Entering the building, she'd had it in mind to get on the computer for a brief scan of the local news sites and maybe Twitter, to find out what that police ruckus was all about, but back in the relative warmth of the loft, her head grew heavy, and by the time she'd made the dog a bed, her curiosity had faded into fatigue. Except, that wasn't entirely true. What she'd lost was not her curiosity but the resolve to approach the machine where those impossible photos slumbered behind an eighth of an inch of hi-def liquid crystal. Those could wait for the light of day, and so could news of the world beyond her door.

Chapter 11

Jason Brooks had given up on the hope that a dog might change his life back in 2010 when the Wonderland greyhound track was shut down by popular vote. After that he had moved on to horses, but he still missed the dogs. Horses made it look too easy, until one of them wiped out and threw a jockey and reminded you just how much mass and muscle was flying over the dirt; but dogs…dogs looked like they had a personal stake in the game. And a greyhound running like a mad motherfucker was a sight to behold. The track closure didn't surprise him. Attitudes toward animals were changing in the twenty-first century, and of course the blue bleeding hearts of Massachusetts led the trend. The horses would probably be the next to go, but by then the state would at least have more casinos. For now, he divided his weekends between the First Light Casino on the Wampanoag reservation thirty minutes south of Boston, and the Suffolk Downs track just north of the city.

On the Saturday in September when Brooks' fortunes shifted, it was a horse that did it, and while he did win some money that morning, he would wonder for a long time after if the wager had put him in the right place at the right time or quite the opposite.

Like all pivotal moments in a life, it came about by a chain of events. If he hadn't bet on Noon Shadow in the first race of the day, he would have stayed at the track later. If he hadn't quit after Noon Shadow placed first, he wouldn't have been on the harbor ferry within an hour, nor would he have been on the T when the bomb went off. Blame it on the horse.

Blame it on Hurricane Sonia for flooding most of the Blue Line in 2017 and adding the ferry trip to his travel time. Whichever it was that put him underground on the right train to witness the massacre, it was part of a chain, and who could say where a chain began? Maybe it had *always* been his destiny to be on that train; because what were the chances of a SPECTRA agent being present when some psycho finally found a way to tear a hole in the fabric of reality?

So the big break in a career that had meandered from cop to detective to agent in a supralegal clandestine Intel agency turned on his gambling habit. Go figure. Two paydays in one. But every lucky break comes with a cost. The gambling habit had already cost him his wife, and the cost of witnessing the attack could take years to count— he knew that while he was still in the thick of it. It sure didn't feel lucky at the time, but some people survived because he was on that train, so maybe *they* were lucky. Maybe.

A week prior, he had won and then lost big on the roulette wheel at First Light when red 23 kept coming up longer than it should have. Today, he had balanced the scales at the horse track and quit while he was ahead by reminding himself of a quote he'd seen online, and running it around his mind like a mantra (or a thoroughbred) as he walked to the payout window: *the safest way to double your money is to fold it over and put it back in your pocket.*

He caught the ferry at Wood Island station where the rest of the Blue Line was now growing barnacles under water, and connected to the Outbound Red Line at Kendall. The plan was to stop by the SPECTRA office at Harvard and log a couple hours on the secure network to make up for time lost on Friday when his lunch hour had turned into a bit of a Keno binge. He'd felt guilty about it all morning, and knew he wouldn't be able to really enjoy celebrating the win tonight if he didn't make right at work first. If he balanced the scales, he wouldn't have to worry about how impossible it would be to go in on Sunday with a hangover. But he never did make it to the office, or to the bar after. The kid with the boom box got on at Central.

* * *

Darius Marlowe hadn't deliberated much over his target. Inbound or Outbound? Park Street Station had crossed his mind, of course. The Boston Common could be considered the center of the city, but that made it harder to get out. Harvard Square, on the other hand, was a prestigious locale with more exit options. If he could jack a car at Harvard he'd have a better chance of getting out than if he were hemmed in by the urban labyrinth of the city proper. And striking so close to the ivory tower, beacon of all that was rational in the Western world, well, that certainly scored some points for a man who wanted to rattle nerves. These calculations flitted through his head, and he made his choice almost on impulse.

He sat on the station bench in a multicolored tile alcove with the CENTRAL sign above his head, the boom box at his feet. The dark domed eyes of cameras on poles suspended from the ceiling seemed to glare at the platform with omnidirectional scrutiny. He did his best to avoid staring back, but found his gaze darting toward them anyway, and each time it did he forced it to keep moving, turning his head to rest his eyes on something else. The game reminded him of checking out a hot girl without getting caught. But there were no hot girls waiting for the train, just a white guy about his own age in a Celtics jersey with a ponytail and a lot of leather jewelry. Darius looked past him at a black door beside what looked like a pair of fire hose spigots with red wheels in a recessed aluminum panel surrounded by more of the multicolored tile. There was a metal box with an emergency button, and a keypad backlit with red numbers. A red sign on the adjacent door proclaimed:

This Door Is Controlled &
Monitored By:
MBTA SECURITY
Use Employee I.D. To
Gain Access.

Darius's eyes swept across the dome cameras again. He'd boarded the T at this stop before but had never noticed all these security details. Had he unwittingly chosen a station that housed a higher security presence than most? Charobim had been so intent on instructing him in the science of his mission that they hadn't discussed reconnaissance or even target selection, and Darius had been given no particular orders regarding how to deal with security personnel if they approached him. He recalled an article he'd found on a local news blog while researching. A few years old, it had been written when the MBTA went digital and started tweeting delays and changes of service. The article was pretty inane, but the accompanying photo had raised his hairs, and he recalled it now in vivid detail: a group of men in white shirts and ties sitting at a command console in a dark room, around the perimeter of which ran a curved ribbon of monitors all lit up green with track maps and night vision video feeds of the tunnels. Was he being recorded right now, or only observed? Would they play the feed later to identify the man with the boom box, and if so, was his face in any facial recognition databases already? There was no way of knowing. He was wearing sunglasses, but that wouldn't help much. But he had a minimal online presence, and that just might slow them down.

He felt perspiration in his armpits, even though he'd put on antiperspirant in the morning out of habit. The station smelled of hot brake pads but he knew he wasn't sweating from the heat. He shifted on the bench and turned his back to the cameras, resisting the urge to touch the boom box, pick it up, and angle it away from the digital eyes as well.

A couple more people had gathered, milling around near the wide yellow line: a short Muslim woman in a headscarf dotted with zirconium chips, poking at a smartphone in a bright purple case; and a hipster in thick-rimmed glasses and an army cap, a backpack slung over one shoulder. The hipster looked as fidgety as Darius felt, and somehow watching him as he leaned over the yellow line and searched the depths of the tunnel for the light of a train calmed Darius. *You're going to die in the next ten minutes and you have no idea. You're anxious to get somewhere on time, but you will never arrive, and I know this, and you don't.* If knowledge was power, then the knowledge of the assassin, the executioner, the slaughter man, was very empowering indeed.

Darius took a deep breath at the sound of the approaching train as it rumbled in and glided to a hissing stop.

He stepped aboard and took inventory of his victims. The car was bustling but not full, and he found a seat at the back. He'd chosen one of the rear cars, farthest from the driver. Even with aviator shades on, he noted the details of the car with heightened intensity, and although he intended to survive the dimensional breach, he couldn't help thinking that this must be how a condemned man sees when he steps into the execution chamber. Everything seemed to glow and buzz under the fluorescent lights: the cardboard banner ads over the dark windows, the rainbow patterned upholstery of the seats, even the marbleized rubber floor.

"Nyarlathotep protect me that I may serve well the Great Old Ones," he whispered under the rattle and screech of the accelerating train.

The seats to either side of him were vacant. Directly across the aisle sat a black lady with a leopard-print purse beside a fat white man in khakis and a blue blazer with a white baseball cap. They didn't seem to be together, and neither made eye contact with him. Farther up the train, a Latina in a gray sweater and black skirt was talking loudly into her cell phone about some surgery she'd had recently and how the doctors weren't as good as the ones at Beth Israel. Her nasal voice cut through the mechanical din. There were seats, but she was standing by choice, holding one of the rubber handles. A few seconds of her monologue gave Darius the impression that she was probably afraid to plant her ass on a public cushion. He wondered if she'd sanitized the hand loop with Purell, like some people did with shopping-cart handles. Beyond the loud, obnoxious lady, he could see random swatches of attire shifting around when the car took corners. A pink Red Sox jersey on a young girl with flaxen hair and shallow brown eyes that he couldn't stand to look at; Adidas sneakers on what looked like a grad student with a heavy laptop bag; a plaid shirt on an Asian guy reading a Kindle and wearing black earbuds.

Darius strained his neck and counted the number of passengers wearing ear buds. There was a woman in a pantsuit with a Bluetooth headset, but those didn't count. Aside from the Asian guy, he saw only one other person listening to music—a brunette who looked like a college student with an iPod.

"You're cutting in and out," the lady on the phone said, sounding annoyed, "We're in the tunnel...I'll call you back when we get above."

Darius put his own headphones on now, an over-ear set with noise cancellation that immediately replaced the ambient noise with a white hiss. He could hear the bass drone of the train itself, but only dimly. He longed to hear the black speech when it emerged, but couldn't risk it. Witnessing its effects would have to be enough. He reached into the inside breast pocket of his suede jacket and pressed play on his iPod, filling his ears with the Saturn Movement from Holst's *The Planets*. He took his shades off, folded them, and tucked them into the same pocket. That was when he noticed the red-haired guy who looked like a cop, sitting across and a few yards down, staring at him.

Maybe he *was* a cop. Or maybe just some suspicious-looking Irish fuck from Southie. Well, what did it matter? No earbuds, so fuck him. Darius looked down at the boom box in his lap, tilted it up toward his face, and took one last peek at the pink organ through the black grill. Then he set it on the floor and tapped a button on top.

* * *

Jason Brooks had seen some weird shit demonstrated in the labs at Harvard and MIT in the two years since his security clearance came through with the Special Physics Emergent Counter Terror Recon Agency, but he had never yet witnessed anything like what happened when the kid on the Red Line pressed PLAY.

It began as a sound: a droning guttural chant, like a sutra swirling around in the vaulted heights of a Tibetan temple, far away, as if he were only hearing the reverberations as they ricocheted around stone pillars and filtered through draperies of many-layered silk. It was a sound of myriad voices that were somehow joined like an alloy of molten metals into a single androgynous voice—young and old, male and female, bestial and human, and something more than the sum of these parts, something shimmering with alien harmonics, pulsing with prehistoric sub-sonic sludge.

The two passengers sitting directly opposite the boom box looked up first, the black lady's eyes startled away from the phone in her hand, and the heavy white guy in the sport coat and cap beside her letting his paperback drift closed without marking his page as his hand dropped to his abdomen. It looked to Jason like the sound was making him queasy, maybe even giving him a cramp deep in his bowels.

That *sound*. It was a malicious, sinuous thing, writhing and whipping the tight air in the train with hostile acoustics at the fringes of human hearing. He thought that if a service dog were in the car it would be rolling on the floor, shrieking in pain.

The sound swelled and more passengers noticed it—he could tell by the discomfort dawning on their faces—but most of them didn't seem to know where it was coming from; they weren't looking at the boom box on the floor like he had been when it started.

The device was set beside a mirror-polished metal plate at the end of the row, and as Brooks watched with escalating anxiety, the air in front of the plate wavered, an effect that at first resembled a heat haze on baked pavement, but only for a second before it morphed into a more profound distortion: the boom box, its owner, and the air itself warped into a vortex of liquid chrome. It almost looked like a great magnifying lens had emerged from the reflection of the speaker grill, stretching reality itself. At the center of the vortex the silvered air seemed to pucker and tremble, and the words that formed in Jason's mind to explain what he was seeing made no sense.

Invisible obscenity, he thought. And at that moment the chrome cyclone gave birth.

What emerged might have been sound waves taking on substance, or maybe a gossamer web-work of malignant green light. Maybe it was some other form of matter, something spectral and immeasurable. Nothing in his training had prepared him to recognize it, so his mind classified it with another paradox: *dark light*.

Whatever it was, it spun and twisted in the air like ribbons of ink in water. It shook tresses of tendrils as the passengers turned toward its terrible gravity, too stunned to scream, too riveted to the sight to know if it was beautiful or abominable. The crowd was united on the threshold of uncertainty for a shining moment, enraptured at the sight; the impossible sight of iridescent jellyfish rising like balloons toward the ceiling of the car, and rolling tongues of violet fire unspooling, detaching from the nexus, and spinning in eddies like nuclear dust devils. One of these rotated between the two passengers across from the boom box guy, and the collective trance suddenly broke as the little whirlwind shredded man and woman, fabric and flesh, their forms torn asunder at the cellular level, whipped into a storm of blood and bone fragments and splashed around the car. The overhead lights dimmed, painted with the frothy scarlet sludge. Fractions of a second and they were gone, mice dropped in a blender.

And with that, the screaming began.

Jason had torn his eyes from the lightshow to scan the crowd for an accomplice to the man with the headphones and sunglasses. He didn't see anyone obvious, but he noted that an Asian guy lost in a Kindle and listening to something on earbuds didn't even notice what was going on until the screaming and shoving started.

Tentacles of dark fractal light uncoiled and whipped out in all directions, plunging through chests, and bellies, spooling around throats. Screams choked off. Jason watched in awe as the only standing passenger at the rear end of the car—the attractive lady with the ugly voice whose phone call had been interrupted by the tunnel—was dragged by the throat, choking and flailing, toward the rolling eye of the cyclone from which all other horrors emanated.

Somehow Brooks ended up on the floor, taking cover beneath the bench seats. He caught himself scuttling backward on his elbows and splayed knees like a small animal retreating from a predator. Sweat poured down his neck.

Had someone released an aerosol hallucinogen? It was the only thing that made sense. And if they had, what the hell was really killing that lady who was being eaten alive by a giant squid emerging from a subwoofer?

Bodies hit the rubber floor beside him. He tried not to look at the small one in the pink Red Sox jersey, tried not to see it being dragged by bloody blonde hair toward the ring of teeth, mammoth shards of fractured light shearing flesh from bone.

A polished black Oxford stepped on the splayed fingers of his left hand as someone found the wits to retreat to the other end of the car. Something made of plastic and glass hit the floor and cracked, then slid away on a glaze of blood.

Jason tugged his Sig Sauer P220 from the small of his back, trained it on the center of the maelstrom, and stared in horror at his trembling interlocked hands, the pain from the still crooked fingers of his left barely reaching his brain through the adrenaline and fear.

He sucked in a breath of fetid air, held it, steadied his hands as best he could, and fired three shots into whatever the fuck it was. If they hit bodies maybe they would end misery, if they hit the speaker that had conjured the horror, and woven a nightmare out of thin air, maybe that would end it.

And if the bullets merely passed through to some other dimension, then maybe he would be the next one chewed up here and shat out there.

* * *

With the headphones on, Darius couldn't hear the incantation issuing from the larynx at his feet. It was a cruel consequence of his role as midwife of the gods that he himself could never hear the old tongue, the speech that humanity had lost its capacity for eons ago, now reawakened from crumbling pages and given life with restored anatomy. He yearned to hear it, and to experience what hearing it revealed, but he also wanted to live and continue to serve. And since he couldn't see Azothoth and live, he would have to be content with seeing the effects of the Great One's presence.

He witnessed them now as the train rolled through the dark tunnel toward Harvard with the march of "Mars, the Bringer of War" reaching its first crescendo in his ears, the confusion and mortal dread spreading from face to face on those around him. He could feel the bass vibrations in his shoes, the treble harmonics vibrating the hairs on his head. To hear the unfiltered sound was to experience a shift of not only perception but also dimension, and to occupy the same space as the only tangible gods earth had ever known. The knowledge that these people around him had been blessed with such a sight gave Darius a crackling surge of exhilaration across the flesh of his neck and arms, and he nearly gave in to the impulse to rip the headphones off and accept death for a glimpse.

Darius could almost hear the screams through the noise filter, the pounding of the drums, the stabbing of the brass. Swiveling his head and smiling like an amused child, he saw one, two, three people impaled by invisible anatomy. A woman who had been standing and holding a rubber strap a moment ago was now being dragged across the blood-slicked floor toward him, clutching her throat. Darius stared at her in wonder and watched as her body hitched, convulsed, and disappeared as if down the gullet of a great white shark one bite at a time.

The chaos was in full swing now. It was hard to take it all in. Some people had awakened from the initial shock enough to try climbing over each other, away from Darius and the forces he had unleashed. He searched the car for the one who looked like a cop but couldn't find him in the mayhem.

Three pops. Loud enough to cut through the music and the noise cancellation. Loud enough to compress the air around his head. Gunshots. The boom box sprayed fragments of plastic, tissue, and silicone, and slewed to the side, hitting his foot. Darius grabbed the pole beside him and pulled, rising from his seat and swinging around toward the doors. The cop—lying under the bench opposite—was drawing a bead on him.

Another deafening pop and Darius felt a burning slug punch into his left thigh. He left the damaged device without looking back and tugged the headphones down around his neck, knowing that the gun had shattered the spell, and needing all of his senses now that the cop had identified him as the maestro of the massacre.

The train shuddered to the sound of screaming brakes. Everyone lurched toward the front. Darius wanted to be first out of the car, but a young woman was already pulling on the red T bar with both hands, forcing the doors open. He threw his weight at her, knocking her through the doors as they opened, and falling into the dark tunnel on top of her.

He found his footing in the blackened gravel that lined the tunnel floor and limped toward the front of the train. The wound in his thigh blazed. There was no way to avoid passing through the glare of the headlights, so he put his faith in speed over stealth. He knew the driver would radio the MBTA police and tell them that a man on foot was headed for Harvard station, but maybe he could reach the platform before they did. It was close. The train had stopped just short of the sharp turn in the tunnel where the Red trains always slowed and shrieked before rolling into the station. He prayed to Nyarlathotep with each rasping exhalation. He should have planned more, should have had an exit strategy. But he hadn't counted on an undercover cop or whatever the guy with the 9 was. Darius spared a glance over his shoulder to see if he was being pursued. Not yet. A small crowd of blood-sprayed passengers was pouring out of the train and jamming the tunnel behind him, some of them puking, others shouting about the third rail, still others cursing or praying.

He touched the bullet wound and his hand came away wet with blood. That was bad, but he could walk on it, and that meant the bullet had only hit muscle, not bone. Even if it didn't slow him down much while the adrenaline carried him, it was a major problem to be limping and trailing blood. He might climb onto the end of the outbound platform without being noticed, but he'd be dripping on the wide yellow line and all the way down the ramp.

He wiped his hand on his jeans.

The lights of the station came into view, the curve of red tile on the left. When he reached the platform he scanned the small crowd, looking for MBTA uniforms or neon-striped vests. Nothing. No Boston police either. He heaved his weight up onto the platform, not giving the small crowd a second look, only wanting to make the sharp hook around the wall and run for the exits.

The first shout came from the tunnel behind him.

"Hey! Hold it!"

Darius knew it was the redheaded cop who'd stopped the show. But was he going to shoot toward a platform of innocents? Darius didn't think so. He crawled across the yellow line, the raised traction bubbles rubbing against his chest, putting uncomfortable pressure on his sternum while he swung his legs up to get more of his weight behind the forward half of his torso.

Son-of-a-bitch!

The crazy cop had squeezed off a shot, maybe a warning aimed into the ground because Darius didn't feel so much as a stirring of the hot, cloying tunnel air in response, just heard the earsplitting noise.

So did everyone else: he sensed bodies scattering, heard startled cries, and hoped there wasn't a levelheaded hockey player among them.

He was on his feet now and took the corner, his shoulder bumping against the tile with the first two steps. Then he was limp-running down the sloping concourse toward the main station, toward the Dunkin' Donuts and the Charlie Card kiosks, and undoubtedly into view of a matrix of closed-circuit cameras. To his right, the gap between the upper and lower platforms opened. In a flash he could imagine jumping through and falling onto the lower level, maybe making it onto an inbound train just as the doors closed, like in a movie. No. No good. He'd break both his legs. And soon they'd be tracking him, policing every station. He had to get to the street before that cop made it out of the tunnel and saw which exit he took.

At the turnstiles, he focused straight ahead and put full weight on the wounded leg to blend in a little better, gritting his teeth against the pain. He slowed just long enough for the tinted plastic panel to slide aside, then broke right, knocking a teenage boy out of the way and cutting across the wide floor, his footsteps echoing high and far, as he made for the underground bus terminal.

He heard the rapid report of the cop's sneakers pounding on the ramp. The 66 Bus was idling in the tunnel, passengers milling around the door. The smell of diesel fumes filled his overtaxed lungs as he circled around the crowd.

Daylight flared down the slope, so close, bolstering his confidence.

He'd made the right choice. The ramp would get him to the street faster than either of the proper exits. The stairs would have been the end of him. Still, he was leaving a trail of blood and video.

He patted his jacket and felt the comforting bulk of the ritual dagger. He was going to need it when he reached the street.

* * *

Brooks jumped the electric gate, slipped on a drop of blood the size of a half-dollar, and pelted down the ramp toward the bus terminal. The perp was already out of sight, but he'd gone this way. Brooks didn't know what the train driver had called in after throwing the emergency brake, but he wasn't going to make his own calls unless he failed to grab this fucker by the collar.

In the bus tunnel, bodies milled around, beginning to board.

Someone shouted. Brooks held his gun aloft and yelled as he ran, "Police! Police! Move!" He wasn't police, but at least people got out of the way. It was the on-foot equivalent of a siren and flashers, and he sure as hell couldn't yell "SPECTRA." Covert agencies with stupid acronyms made shitty battle cries.

He came up into the daylight, his pounding steps faltering as he crested the ramp at Mt. Auburn Street. Panting and spinning on his heels, scanning the buildings, the cars, the trees...nothing. No sign of the guy. *"Shit!"* He stamped the pavement, caught himself squeezing the butt of his pistol too hard and re-holstered it. He took his phone out and tapped a speed dial key.

"It's Brooks," he said, catching his breath. "Terrorist on foot at Harvard Square. Last spotted leaving the bus tunnel. Get MBTA and police in full force to lock down the square. We have…I don't know how many dead on the Alewife train."

The agent on the other end of the call was firing off orders in the DHS Command Center and telling Brooks to stay on the line, but he was only dimly aware of the man's voice as he let his phone hand drop from his ear (still ringing from the gunshots he'd fired in the subway car), his eyes drawn to the sky like ball bearings tugged by an industrial magnet.

Something had shot past him in the tunnel while he'd been in pursuit. Something big. It had been moving too fast to focus on, spinning and radiating what might have been violet streams of plasma. It had blown past the station platform and kept going straight down the tunnel faster than any train and almost as big. He'd been too focused on the terrorist to get a good look at it (or maybe that was an excuse, maybe the *last* thing he wanted was a good look), but he remembered thinking that it might have been expanding in flight. And now, looking at the sky over Cambridge, he knew it had shot out of the tunnel somewhere farther down the line. It pulsed and wavered high in the sky above the descending sun, and all he could think was that someone had punched a black hole through the powder-blue atmosphere, a pitch-black void with a corona of undulating violet rays.

He scanned the foot traffic around him: Harvard students, skater punks, and tourists. Not a single one was looking up in terrified awe. He put his palm out against the chest of the next oncoming body: a tall, thin, middle-aged guy with a goatee and glasses, wearing a Pink Floyd T-shirt. Brooks wrapped a hand around the man's shoulder and turned to stand beside him, pointing with his other hand at what he was already thinking of as the *black-hole sun*. The guy's eyebrows scrunched, and he almost broke away, but then he seemed to decide to go with it long enough to find out what it was about. Maybe the cop vibe told him he wasn't about to get pick-pocketed.

"You see that?" Brooks asked him.

The guy shook his head. "See what?"

Chapter 12

Sleep had wiped the memory of the cavalcade of military vehicles from Becca's mind, and the image didn't come back to her until she was standing in almost the same spot again in the cold light of a wind-chilled morning, holding the leash while Django sniffed the ground. The waterfront streets were oddly quiet for a Sunday morning, even for her disaster-zone warehouse neighborhood.

She turned the TV on while making toast and tea, but the toast went cold, unbuttered and uneaten, while she stared at the newscasts and flipped through the networks.

Cable news wasn't in her budget. She had a digital antenna for the networks and got most of her news from the Internet. Soon she was sitting on the futon with her laptop, her attention divided between the two screens as she tried to sift speculation from fact. But no matter how often she refreshed the browser or flipped the channels, there were no definitive answers about who was responsible for the massacre that had rocked the city. The newscasters seemed to share her frustration that the authorities wouldn't commit to classifying it as a terror attack or an accident. The former seemed likely, judging by the grainy surveillance camera pictures they kept showing, depicting a "person of interest" wanted for questioning: a young man in a suede coat and sunglasses with dark hair and headphones around his neck.

Had he set off a bomb? That seemed to be the most popular theory among the experts parading before the cameras, but if it *was* a bomb, no one seemed to know what kind. And if you watched the reporting long enough and tuned your attention to what *wasn't* being said, the omissions painted a more frightening picture than the stark fact of seven dead and ten injured on the Outbound Red Line. No one was calling it biological, chemical, or dirty radioactive, and no one was outright denying those possibilities. There was no mention of shrapnel, but there was talk of severe trauma. And while most of the passengers had apparently survived the event, none of the witnesses were being interviewed on TV.

Had some stomach-churning facts been redacted to prevent mass panic? The MBTA was in lockdown for the day. On social media she found a link to a video of some people in Hazmat suits patrolling part of the Green Line with handheld devices. It had provoked a comment flame war, debating whether or not these were Geiger counters. Becca bookmarked the clip, but when she tried to pull it up again twenty minutes later to send the URL to Rafael, it turned up a 404 error. That was when she realized she'd been soaking up paranoia for a good three hours of escalating anxiety. The caffeine from the tea she'd been refilling wasn't helping either. She turned the TV off, tossed the now stale toast into the trash, and curled up on the floor and spooned Django until she shut down from stress and fell asleep.

When she woke, she was ravenous. By the shadows on the floor, she guessed she'd been out for a little over an hour. The sun had passed its noontime zenith, and she still hadn't eaten anything. Nor had she taken her medication for the day. Not good this time of year, with the city sliding toward apocalypse.

She made a peanut butter and jelly sandwich and tried to eat it at her computer, but she ultimately had little more than two bites once she started clicking through the photos from the mill, nervously scratching at the scab on her arm.

Blood, grime, and arabesques of alien anatomy.

She couldn't force herself to view them at more than thumbnail size for more than a few nauseating seconds, and eventually realized that she was merely sorting them to identify the best examples of the phenomena, and that she was doing this to shoot a few over to Neil Hafner. "Uncle" Neil, who had given her her first camera lessons at

Catherine's request, who had written her a letter of recommendation for art school when she bombed her SATs because she was too depressed to deal, and who now owned F-Stop Camera Shop, off of the C train in Brookline.

Becca wanted to see Neil in person, wanted to watch his face when he first looked at the pictures, and most of all wanted to hear his calm, good-humored voice as he teased her about them and explained how they could have come to be. But with the MBTA shut down, an email exchange would have to do for now. She opened a new message, attached the three photos in the largest resolution her mail provider would allow, and typed:

Hey Neil,

Hope all is well with you on this crazy day, but you probably know more about what's going on than the rest of us, given your old crime lab contacts. As for me I'm pretty freaked out, but hey, guess what? I adopted a dog. Well, rescued one, anyway. I'll send you a pic soon. Meanwhile, would you please take a look at these photos I took yesterday that are *also* kinda freaking me out? They're digital infrared from the modified Nikon. **I have not photoshopped them for any effect**. This is how they came off the card. So WTF are we seeing anyway? When I shot them, they were of blank walls. You can still see the brick in one and the sheetrock in the others, but there was no sign of whatever that crazy pattern is (tentacles?) during the shoot.

Call me please, after you've had a look?

Thanks,
Becca

Now that she was finally confronting the photos on her big screen, they sucked her in. She even thought of it in those terms when she glanced up at the clock on the menu bar and saw that almost four hours had passed. *Sucked in.* Was that what had happened to Moe Ramirez? Had he been sucked into a wall?

Impossible, right?

But she had grown up with the impossible. Didn't like to think about it much, didn't care to look at it straight on, but it had always been there in the periphery of her life. Whispered snatches of conversations she'd caught as a child after sneaking out of bed and hiding in the dark at the top of the stairs. First in the home she barely remembered, where she'd eavesdropped on her parents, and then, after her mother was gone and her father was drinking and looking toward the mountains, spying on her grandmother who had been in some ways more secretive and in others...less. As an adolescent, she had been so angry at them all for keeping secrets from her, so determined to one day uncover the truths that had shattered her family.

(Do not call up what you cannot put down.)

Now, grown and sensing darkness on the fringes of a forgetful life, she didn't want to know the answers.

Was it that she didn't *want* to know, or that she *couldn't* risk shattering what little stability she had built for herself one brick at a time? If those bricks now formed a wall against the past, then so be it. The mural she'd painted on it was more comforting than the reality it kept at bay. It was certainly better than ending up in an asylum like her grandfather.

And yet, she couldn't entirely silence the part of her mind that was too smart for total denial, the part that was good at making connections. That part of her was busy just below the surface, tying strings between the oddities of her childhood and those emerging now. *Hello darkness my old friend.* Her mother had loved that song. Well, she'd played it a lot, anyway. There were days when the only sound in the house was that damned song, and then she was gone, and the fighting in hushed tones after bedtime was gone, and Becca was left with what Paul Simon had been promising her for weeks through a phonograph needle at her mother's prompting: the sounds of silence.

She stared at the image of Maurice's cardboard crown. That one was the worst. The crown in a puddle of blood. The others she could almost chalk up to interpretation. It was easy to ascribe biological features to complex patterns, like seeing faces in a water-stained ceiling. Heaven knew she'd often sought out such features of old buildings for that exact effect. Looking for meaning in the mold. But the crown, and the fucking Burger King logo...that was more than a pattern extrapolated from complex chaos. And if the crown was real, did that mean the other...*things* were also real?

Mold and water stains were real, but that didn't make the faces they resembled real. And if some interference in the infrared spectrum looked like a fractal, and that fractal looked like it was made of tentacles, and the suckers on those tentacles looked like eyes…that didn't mean that when you stared into the abyss the abyss was staring into you.

Suckers. Sucked in. Poor Maurice. She blinked and her eyes burned from staring at the damned screen. She pressed her palms against her closed eyes. The pressure felt good. Violet splotches bloomed in her mind, and she could hear the beating of helicopter blades.

Across the apartment her cell phone was ringing, but it was soon drowned out by the sound of the rotors. She went to fetch the phone and saw a black helicopter flying alarmingly close to the big windows. It wasn't one of those bubbly traffic or news choppers either, but a long, angular military looking type. It swept out and away, circling around the building. The caller ID on her phone read: NEIL HAFNER. She took the call and jammed the phone into her ear to hear him over the noise. "Hey, Neil, you got my email?"

"I'm sorry, Becca."

"What?"

"I'm sorry. I tried to tell them you have nothing to do with this."

"Who?"

"Is that a helicopter? Listen to me, they're coming for you and you need to just go with them. Don't be scared."

"Neil? You're scaring me. Who are they?"

"SPECTRA. You've never heard of them, but I made the mistake of forwarding your email to somebody. They would have caught the keywords anyway, so maybe it's better that I contacted them—"

"Wait. Slow down." He was talking so fast she couldn't keep up. He sounded panicked. It was a tone she didn't associate with his voice at all, and she realized that she doubted it was really him on the other end.

A double bang echoed through the warehouse from above, and she suddenly felt like she was inside a giant steel barrel that someone had decided to use as drum. Her heart rate jumped and her mouth went dry. Staring at those photos had primed her for paranoia, and a black helicopter landing on the roof did nothing to alleviate the feeling.

"Is this Neil Hafner?" She asked.

"Yes, Becca, it's me. I asked them to let me bring you in, but they wouldn't. I'm just a retired forensics geek. But they won't hurt you, okay? I'll come to you, I promise, I'll find you."

Jackboots echoed in the stairwell. "Find me where? Where are they taking me? Neil? *Neil!*"

"You have to understand that they're scared too, Becca. They're in crisis mode... high alert...fucking DEFCON 2."

Django was barking now, going into territorial-defense mode and sounding a whole lot bigger than he really was. Becca plugged a finger in her open ear. "This is because of the pictures? My pictures? You said something about a keyword. What word?"

"Tenta—"

The call cut out.

The door burst inward and rebounded off the wall. Men in riot gear flooded into the loft, rifles cocked on their shoulders, eyes boring through scopes. Black Kevlar vests and helmets and Velcro pockets bulging with tech and weaponry. They were shouting orders at her and each other and reporting into headsets. Django was holding his ground between her legs and barking at them through an almost tangible cloud of testosterone, Becca desperately holding him by the collar to keep him from lunging and biting. Later she would wonder what she would have done if she hadn't had the dog to deal with, to protect. Maybe she would have put her hands up or curled up in a ball on the floor in the kitchen. But with Django trying to defend her all she could think about was keeping him from getting shot. It would be so damned easy, so justifiable for them to just shoot him and be done with it.

The armored men (and one woman, she could now see) surrounded her in a circle. A short, stocky one with a soul patch was yelling at her, spittle flying in foamy white bubble drops: "*Shut that fucking dog up! Shut it up now or I will shut it up for you!*"

She went down on her knees and wrapped her arms around Django, shaking her head, and feeling heat welling up in her face, unsure if it was fear or anger or some sickly blend of both. Django's emaciated body lurched with every aggressive bark, and she couldn't calm him, couldn't break his fixation on the threat he perceived, and sure as hell couldn't shut him up, but she could cover him enough that they'd have to put a bullet through her to get one in him.

A tall man with eyes the color of a chemical ice pack was telling her to put her hands on her head, and he sounded calm enough now that he was closer than shouting distance, now that he could see that it was mostly an open living space, now that his scouts were shouting, "Clear!" from every partitioned area, and it was becoming apparent that they were dealing with a solitary, skinny girl.

But Soulpatch hadn't calmed down at all. He was towering over Django trying to stare him down and only making him escalate, and now she saw him remove a can of mace from a vest pocket.

For one crazy moment she didn't think about all of the guns pointed at her. The world contracted to just Django and the man with the mace, and she punched him hard in his armored gut, rocking him backward on his heels.

Something snapped in her wrist, a bright, jarring pain twanging up her arm. There was a chorus of ratcheted weapons and a tightening of the bodies around her.

The calm, ice-eyed commander put his gloved hand on Soulpatch's chest to restrain him from retaliation. Becca fell to her knees and wrapped her arms around Django as he snapped and barked and tried to break free.

"I'll let you cuff me, but you have to *let me crate my dog first!*"

"Where's the crate?"

"By the TV."

"Copeland, bring that dog crate over here and make sure it's empty."

"Yes sir." One of the men closest to the living room slung his rifle across his back and carefully removed the blanket from the crate as if he hadn't ruled out the possibility of finding a bomb in it. He brought the crate over, set it down at Becca's feet, and opened the cage door.

She guided Django in and latched it, still kneeling on the floor, then put her hands on her head. She could feel her body and mind shutting down as they pulled her hands behind her back and cuffed her, and ransacked the apartment.

They went for the studio first, where they pulled the partition walls and tapestries down before unplugging and packing her computers and hard drives into metal attaché cases. They sealed her SD cards and USB memory sticks in Ziploc bags, checked the scanner bed, and packed up her cameras and notebooks.

The last thing they bagged was Becca Philips. They didn't read her the Miranda, just zip-tied her wrists and slipped a black bag over her head, and marched her up the clanging metal steps to the rooftop where they shunted her into the helicopter, strapped her down, and lifted off in a whirlwind.

* * *

When Becca came to, she wasn't wearing the bag anymore, but the room she lay in was dark. She figured she must have passed out from the reduced oxygen. The bag had smelled like stale coffee. The room reeked of disinfectant. It was either in an empty building or one that was well soundproofed. She felt around in the darkness and found a cushioned pad that she might have been placed on, and might have rolled off. She was still dressed in her cargo pants and favorite black TOOL T-shirt. The only visible feature of the room was a thin rectangle of light, a little thicker at the bottom, delineating the door. She got up and went to it. Tried the handle just for a laugh. It was of course locked. But the attempt earned her the attention of the guard on the other side. The lights came on—florescent bars behind a cage in the ceiling—and the door opened. A kid with a crew cut blocked the opening. He was dressed in khaki fatigues with a shoulder patch that said SPECTRA BOSTON, the heel of one hand casually resting on the butt of his sidearm.

"Glad to see you're awake, ma'am."

"Don't call me that."

"I'll let them know."

"Water. Please."

"You got it."

He closed the door. She looked around the room. There were no chairs but she didn't want to be sitting on the floor when they came in, whoever *they* were, so she leaned against the wall facing the door, knee cocked, arms crossed. A closed-circuit camera on a ceiling-mounted bracket watched her from the corner.

When the door opened again, the crew-cut kid came in with a pair of folding chairs and set them up in the middle of the room. Behind him was a redheaded guy with a bit of a grizzled look. He didn't have fatigues on like the kid, but a shirt and tie—sleeves rolled up, a titanium watch on his wrist among the ginger hair and freckles.

He didn't smile but handed her a cold, perspiring bottle of water and said, "Rebecca Philips, I'm Agent Jason Brooks. Please have a seat."

Becca ran her thumb around the top of the water bottle. The cap was sealed, and she didn't feel any pinprick holes from where they might have put a syringe in it, but that probably didn't mean much. They could easily have put a needle in her arm after she'd fainted, anyway, so she cracked the seal and took a gulp.

Brooks sat and flipped his tie out of his crotch. He looked like the kind of detective who would never get used to wearing one. Becca sat down facing him, elbows on knees, bottle dangling between them. She was exhausted, even though all she'd done since waking up was write an email and get abducted at gunpoint.

"What the fuck is SPECTRA?" she asked, "Is that some kind of new surveillance arm of the government?"

"SPECTRA?"

"The patch on Opie's shoulder. Looks like the Pink Floyd logo."

Agent Brooks laughed, and for a second she could imagine him hanging out at her favorite bar and buying a round for everyone when the Sox hit a homerun. She didn't want to like him, but that was probably why they'd sent him in here first, because he had some charm he was about to use on her like some kind of interrogational jujitsu. But the whole situation was absurd anyway because she had nothing to hide; she was nobody and knew nothing. They had bagged the wrong girl.

Tentacles. She almost said it aloud when she remembered the call from Neil, but stopped herself. Why would that word trigger such a heavy-handed reaction? She decided she wanted to at least hear some questions before she started blindly tossing out answers.

Brooks ran his thumb and forefinger across his stubble, still grinning. "Yeah," he said, "I don't really get it either. Covert agencies have logos now. I guess the lawmakers like to see something for the money."

Becca nodded. "What does it stand for?"

"Wouldn't make any sense to you."

"Try me."

"Special Physics Emergent Counter Terror Recon Agency."

"That's a mouthful. So...you think I had something to do with what happened on that train. Well, I didn't even hear about it until I turned on the TV today."

"We've been through your camera cards and computers and there are quite a few photos of subway tunnels. MBTA stations that have been closed since the flood, station gates where the locks have been removed with bolt cutters. Doesn't look good."

Becca crinkled the water bottle in her hands. She suddenly felt the need to tread very carefully. There had been stories over the years about people—sometimes the *wrong* people, sometimes American citizens—getting lost in the labyrinth of the War on Terror. The word *Rendition* floated up from the back of her mind like a warning written in red light.

She needed support from outside. She needed people to know where she was. She thought of Rafael and wondered if he too was in an interrogation room. The possibility filled her with both hope and dread: that he might be in the same building, that he might not be free to find out *she'd* been taken and tell someone. Tell who? The media?

She felt sweat beading at the base of her hairline as she realized she had no idea where this room was. They'd taken her by helicopter and she had no idea how long she'd been blacked out or if they had drugged her. Was she even in Boston anymore? Massachusetts? Was it even the same day?

In spite of the water, her mouth was dry again. She opened it and spoke in careful, measured sentences. "I think I'm here because of my friend, Neil Hafner. He had a career in law enforcement. Do you know him?"

"We'll get to that. Why the pictures of subway features, Ms. Philips?"

"Urbex."

"That sounds about as meaningful as SPECTRA. What's URBEX?"

"Urban exploration. Google it. It's like...part hiking, part exploring, part archaeology, only in modern cities. My friends and I do it mostly for the photography. It's sort of an art school thing."

"Trespassing in restricted areas of public transportation is art now?"

"We're not even vandals. You have all my pictures, so you know I shoot all kinds of abandoned places, not just the T."

"We are analyzing your photos, yes, and I'm sure we'll have many questions about them soon. But let me ask you something.

Your answer will determine how this is gonna go for you, so think about what we already know and what we will know by the end of the day before you try to lie to me."

Becca raised an eyebrow.

"We're getting to know each other here. I belong to SPECTRA. You belong to URBEX. Do you also belong to the Starry Wisdom Church?"

"No."

"Then why do you have photos of the leader of that organization on your computer? Photos of the Reverend John Proctor taken at Allston State Hospital on what members of that church consider to be a holy day?"

"I photograph anyone who looks interesting."

"Yeah. So do we. We read their web sites too, and these people happen to believe that mankind's greatest accomplishment was raising the sea level a few feet to make coastal cities more comfortable for their dark gods. They want to *sacrifice* us all to their dark gods. Sound familiar? Have you visited any of these web sites? Don't fuckin' lie to me, it'll take me five minutes to find out."

Becca turned the cap of the water bottle back and forth: clockwise and counter, bit her lip, and said, "Think I'm gonna need a lawyer."

"We're not the police."

"So I'm not being detained?"

"Ms. Philips, this city is in the grip of a National Security crisis. You don't get a lawyer until it's too late for him to save you from the consequences of the choice you make right now to help or hinder."

"What's your name again, Agent?"

"If you're going to help me, you can call me Jason."

"Jason, you're barking up the wrong tree. I'm not a cultist or a terrorist, okay? I take pictures of fucked-up, abandoned places because I'm fucked up and abandoned. I'm just looking for beauty in the cracks."

Brooks took a device from his pocket—about the same size as a phone, but with a hooded lens. He swiped through some options on a touch screen and the lights in the cage overhead went dark while the wall to Becca's left was illuminated with a crystal-clear slide projection of one of the fractal tentacle shots she'd taken at the mill.

"Is this the kind of beauty you're taking about?" he asked her, the image shuddering slightly when he couldn't keep his hand perfectly still. "Because that looks pretty fuckin' ugly to me. What is it?"

She gazed at the photo in awe. Seeing a picture she'd taken of a wall now projected on another wall, she could finally ascribe a sense of scale to the writhing anatomy. It shallowed her breathing. "I don't know," she said. Her voice sounded hollow in her ears, and she was grateful for the darkness in the room masking the vulnerability she felt when confronted with a power that made the full weight of the government seem meek in comparison. "And you know I don't know because you've read the email I wrote to Neil, and that's who I want to talk to."

"Not happening."

"Get me Neil and send someone to feed my dog. Otherwise I'm not talking."

The image shuddered across the wall and disappeared as Brooks threw his metal chair at it. Becca flinched and held her hands up in front of her face. She could feel him towering over her in the dark as he shouted. "You do *not*. You do *not* get to make the rules, and we are *NOT FUCKING AROUND HERE!* People died in that tunnel. I was there, and *kids* died. *Parents* who are never going home to their kids died. I don't give a shit about who you want to talk to and I sure as hell don't give a shit about your damned dog!"

He drew a ragged breath and waited for her to dare reply. The silence and darkness welled around them.

"You're wasting time on me," Becca said. "Neil knows how to read photos and he's the only person I'm talking to."

When the lights came up Brooks was already at the door. He left without looking back.

Becca sighed. She probed her right wrist with her left thumb, gingerly flexing the joint, and feeling for shattered bones. It hurt like hell from the impact of punching the Kevlar vest.

Chapter 13

Brooks stepped into the hall, into the gray wash of cloud-attenuated sunlight spilling in from the windows overlooking Government Center and Faneuil Hall. He stepped up to the glass and looked down on Congress Street, scratching the back of his head and thinking about how Becca Philips had no idea how close to home she was right now. Just a few miles to the east across the Channel, they were still taking her apartment apart, searching for anything she might have kept off of her computers: a handwritten journal or little black book of contacts tucked away behind a vent grill, under a floorboard, or inside a mattress. *Wouldn't it be nice if she really was a conspirator?* But he already didn't believe she was, just as he knew he was going to have one of the guys over there feed the damned dog.

He had lost it in there and needed to regain his composure. The kids on the train had shaken him. He'd held it together until now, but the clock was ticking on catching this monster. He would need to try another tack with Philips. He couldn't shake the feeling that she knew something or suspected something that she wasn't willing to give them. And why should she be holding back? Well, Blue Team would be rounding up the entire congregation of the Starry Wisdom Church presently, and within two hours everyone would be talking about everyone else, hoping to cut a deal. Then he would see if Ms. Philips was still singing the same song.

Reluctantly, Brooks raised his gaze over the gray buildings, the silver and black shimmer of the New Waterfront, and let it drift to where it always did now whenever he could stand to let it: that corner of the sky where the black sun pulsed like a migraine. It was still there, but he'd known that as soon as he'd approached the window. It was almost always in his peripheral vision when he was near a window or on the street. And always in the same region of the heavens. The sun and moon moved through their courses, but the black star remained fixed at what appeared to be low altitude. It did not orbit, and if it rotated, it kept pace with the earth, with the city. Didn't they call Boston The Hub? If it was, then this damned thing was a playing card stuck in a spoke.

"What are you on about Brooks? Playing cards?" Dick Hanson had emerged from the monitor room and taken a place beside him at the window. Shit. Had he been talking aloud? This was exactly the kind of thing that made him worry that the event in the subway had scrambled his brain. Was he cracking? Didn't people with tumors sometimes experience weird ocular effects? Brooks wondered if he should take a leave, get an MRI, tell Hanson he was seeing shit that wasn't there.

And leave people like Hanson and his cronies at Limbus to protect the city? To protect my daughter?

"Huh? Playing card? I said 'this case is hard.' She's a hardcase, this young lady."

"So far, sure. You think she knows something, has some involvement?"

Brooks squinted at the horizon. "She probably just stumbled into it. Probably doesn't really know shit. Wrong place, wrong time."

"So why is she pushing back?"

"Oh, I don't know…anger at being abducted? Maybe cooperating with authority just goes against her grain."

"Well, the only connection we can find to the church is that photo she took of the reverend. She doesn't seem to have many friends, but we'll drag her teachers in here if we have to, and they'll at least care about losing their jobs. We're also trying to track down the guy who shows up in her phone records the most. Rafael Moreno. Might be a boyfriend."

Brooks looked from the black orb in the sky to Hanson and back again, but the man clearly didn't see it dripping darkness in thin swathes upon the city, like ribbons of oily black incense smoke that flowed down instead of up.

SPECTRA had found most of the people who had been in the train car, all of the survivors. Some were still in ICU at MGH, but the rest were being held in this facility under the auspices of a quarantine. They had been told that if the weapon were found to contain a biological agent, there could be a risk of contagion. While the idea had shaken them and made them harder to interview, it had at least kept the lawyers and the ACLU at bay. It didn't keep the media away, though, and some of the survivors' names had already been leaked. The government couldn't hold them much longer. They had all tested negative for radiation and infectious germs, but they didn't need to know that just yet. And Brooks' superiors had made it clear that the real risk of releasing them was that their stories (or worse, their *perceptions*) might be contagious, especially given the number of reporters ready and willing to expose the general population. Brooks wasn't exactly sure he understood these concerns. He'd heard of ideas going viral but had never taken the metaphor as literally as some of his superiors appeared to.

He knew only this: The subjects in holding all reported seeing the same weird shit on the train that he had. Except for one man and one woman who had been wearing earbuds and listening to music at the time. Those two had only seen the effects of the violence—people being ripped apart by invisible things. There was a possibility that those invisible things had not seen the Vietnamese engineer or the young lady student either, because neither had been harmed. Statistically that was well within the realm of coincidence because they weren't the only ones left unscathed, but the others were mostly people who had been positioned at the other end of the subway car when the shit hit the fan. The two who had been wearing earbuds when it started had taken them out once they became aware of the massacre in full swing, but even then they hadn't been able to see what was causing it.

Brooks had lied at his debriefing, claimed he'd been listening to his iPod as well and hadn't been exposed to the sounds that started it all. He'd made the snap judgment to lie mostly on instinct when the pieces of the puzzle were still coming together, but he hadn't regretted his choice yet. In the past twenty-four hours he'd only heard things that confirmed his gut decision. Like the suggestion from one of the Limbus operatives that they could wipe out the witnesses with an *actual* bio-war germ if it became necessary to make that the official story. Brooks hadn't told anyone about the black sun he saw over the city, but when he'd visited a critical patient at Mass General, and realized that the man's room was on the Western side of the building, he had pulled back the curtain and asked him if he saw anything. The man, an English professor at Tufts, had described the thing better than Brooks ever could.

The suspect with the boom box had been wearing high-end noise cancellation headphones, apparently as a prophylactic against what he'd unleashed. Like some kind of drug, the sound opened a new level of perception in those exposed. And somehow this expanded perception made them vulnerable to attack from what they saw. If the director found out Brooks had been exposed, he'd be sitting in one of the soundproofed rooms ten floors down with the rest of the cattle, waiting for a verdict.

Hanson was still talking. Brooks tried not to stare at that damned spot in the sky, tried to stay present.

"Sorry?"

"You don't look so hot. You get any sleep since it happened?"

"No."

"You should go get some before you pass out on your feet."

"Not until we catch the guy. I'll sleep then." He couldn't help glancing back at the sky and following the lines of two black tendrils that had become more prominent than the others. One of these led to the John Hancock Tower, the other (thicker and blacker) dripped behind that sci-fi looking building at 111 Huntington Avenue near the Christian Science Center.

"Without a lead, that could be days," Hanson said.

"You think it will be?" He balked at the prospect of sitting around waiting for a lead. He needed a reason to get back in the field where he could make up for his losses on the train.

"No. The facial recognition software's come a long way, and he's in the database somewhere. Everyone is now, thanks to social media. He'll turn up on some gas station cam. Just a matter of time. And the geeks dissecting his device will come up with some kind of explanation. Or a theory anyway. A foothold for what we're dealing with."

"Well, I'm not good at waiting. I'd like to try something."

"What's that?"

"The witnesses. The 'mass hallucination group.' Let's get some of them out of the basement and ask them if they see anything else that we can't. Take them up to the top of the Pru and see if they can spot any residual weirdness anywhere. It just might lead us to the guy or his associates."

Daniel Northrup, SPECTRA's own top spook, had joined the conversation, lit a cigarette, and planted his shoulder blades and the bottom of one shoe against the wall. Smoking was supposed to be illegal in the government building, but Northrup was a law unto himself. He'd been staring at the veined marble tiles that covered the lower half of the walls and listening to the exchange between Brooks and Hanson. Now he swiveled his head in their direction and Brooks found himself marveling, as usual, at the perfect frosting in the man's sideburns and temples, and wondering if anyone could be so vain as to dye gray *into* their black hair to get that distinguished effect.

Northrup poked the air gently but emphatically with the burning cherry. "We are *not* taking them out in public. You can have three at a top floor window of this building."

Brooks nodded.

"Well? Get on it," Northrup said, exhaling a drag.

* * *

Becca swallowed her pride and asked the guard to bring her an Ibuprofen and an Ace bandage for her wrist. That was the last contact she'd had for what felt like two hours, but at least it had brought enough relief to keep her idle mind from dwelling on the injury and how stupid she'd been to attack an armed soldier, or cop, or paramilitary goon. Whatever. When the door opened again, Jason Brooks was holding her army green camera bag, presumably with her Nikon in it.

"You ever do any aerial photography?" he asked.

"Can't say I have."

"First time for everything." He handed her the bag. She took it without thinking, and a sharp pain shot through her wrist. She shifted the bag to her left hand and wondered if she could even operate her camera with the injury. Brooks frowned at her and raised an eyebrow at the Ace bandage.

"It's from hitting one of your thugs," she said. "I don't know if I can hold my camera with it. Damned brick of a thing. What do you want me to shoot, anyway?"

"The city. From a helicopter."

Becca laughed.

"What's funny?"

"Uh, don't you guys have all kinds of satellites for that? Are budget cuts so bad that you need an art student with no zoom lens?"

"I want your infrared images. Whatever it is you normally do to get the pictures."

"Well, I doubt I can do much good with a sprained wrist in a moving helicopter."

"I'll get you a brace. If you do this, I'll get you that talk with your so-called uncle too, deal?"

"You're gonna have to do better than that."

"Your dog's been fed. I saw to it."

"So your guys are still raiding my underwear drawer?"

"No, they're gone. And you could maybe be home tomorrow if you cooperate."

"I doubt that. Did you catch the guy yet? The guy who bombed the tunnel?"

"I can't talk about that. And nobody said it was a bomb."

"Can't talk about it or can't talk about it with a suspect in custody? 'Cause that's what I am right?"

"Look, I don't really need you, now that I think about it. I'll go fetch a tech to fly with me and use your camera while you sit here and stew."

Becca raised an eyebrow. *"My camera?"* She set her jaw and shook her head. "Not without me."

* * *

They gathered on the roof, a crew of four: the pilot, Agent Brooks, Becca, and a squat, pudgy, bald guy with two-days of stubble on his face. She thought he might be another military type, but he was dressed in jeans, a plaid shirt, and sneakers. Her next guess was I.T. guy, and maybe he *was*, somewhere, but not here at Government Center. He gave off a nervous vibe, and then it clicked, and she realized that he was in custody, too.

Brooks introduced them. "Becca this is Tom, Tom, Becca. He's the eyes and you're the lens, okay? Tom has a special kind of...*perception* that will guide us to the sites I want you to photograph." The pilot started the rotors. The bird was a big military type, and she wondered if it was the same one they'd brought her here in, but having had a bag over her head for that ride, she couldn't say for sure. She'd only seen it briefly through her window on approach.

Brooks gave her a hand climbing in and gestured to a seat. Becca buckled up and examined her camera, checked the settings and the card. They hadn't replaced it with a blank; she could still see her last set of photos. Brooks took the seat beside the pilot and passed headsets around. Tom stared at the sky, his gaze fixed on something only he could see, his fingers knotted in his lap, knuckles white. She wondered if he had a fear of flying or if his stress was all about the "special perception" Brooks had mentioned. Becca tried smiling when he glanced at her, just a tight little one, nothing too generous, but his gaze slid over her and back out the window beside her.

Becca feared heights, but planes had never really bothered her. Something about not being able to fall out of a plane. But when her Urbex friends went up on rooftops and water towers, she hung back. Edges with drops scared her. Nina had suggested that this might have to do with a fear of her own self-destructive urges and some impulse to jump whispering in the base of her brain. She'd had to admit that sounded about right. Nina wasn't too damned shabby as a shrink.

But helicopters, well, she'd not been exposed to them much before the past twenty-four hours, so she wasn't sure how she felt about them, though they seemed fundamentally untrustworthy. Flying in a machine that couldn't glide to a landing in an emergency had always struck her as unnatural, and she wondered as they lurched off the pad if she couldn't maybe have one of those black bags over her head after all.

Her stomach dropped when they crested the edge of the building they'd been perched on and she saw the little figures of people and their shadows on the plaza below. Then the bird tilted and swung over the city, past the gold dome of the State House, skirting Beacon Hill to the right, and soaring over the yellow and russet swatches of the Boston Common in fall splendor. Leaving the park behind, they were soon moving among the skyscrapers of Copley Square.

Tom leaned toward his window, his breath fogging the glass, his eyes wide with terror or awe at some empty spot in the sky. Brooks was looking at it too. He turned to Tom, and Becca heard his voice in the headset asking, "What do you see?"

"Same thing we saw from the window. Black smoke dripping from the black moon down to the ground, only now I can see exactly where it's going."

"Where?"

"The Hancock Tower. It's like a magnet for it. But it's not as heavy there as it is beyond the Prudential."

Brooks sat back in his seat. To the pilot he said, "Veer right and go wide of the Hancock, then pass between the Pru and one-eleven. Can you do that?"

"Yes sir."

Becca stared at the blue-mirrored surface of the John Hancock Tower, the tallest building in Boston. All she could see were several strata of cloud cover reflected in its blue façade and the black speck of the helicopter passing across it like a fruit fly buzzing a glass of ice water. No black smoke.

She gripped her seat as they passed between the Prudential Tower and the thing she'd heard referred to as the R2-D2 building. Brooks was instructing the pilot to drop lower, and damned if he didn't seem to be looking at something as he gave the directions. He sure wasn't consulting Tom, and she wondered if the first and only consultation so far had been for the purpose of confirming something he could see for himself. For a moment there was the feeling of passing through a corridor of steel and glass, and then they were soaring over the Christian Science Center, their shadow traversing the vast silver rectangle of the reflecting pool.

The water rippled, and at first Becca thought it was from the wind until she noticed a pattern coalescing around the center of the pool. For a fleeting second she thought the helicopter was causing the disturbance, but when they had swept across the water and arced around over the great stone church, she craned her neck and saw that the water was still agitated, just in that spot. There were a few people strolling beside the pool and sitting on the edges of the stone planters that ran along Huntington Ave. Some of them were looking skyward at the helicopter, but she couldn't tell if any had noticed the ripples.

"What am I supposed to be shooting?"

"The water. Get a bunch of shots of the water and some of the sky above the pool," Brooks said.

"The sky?"

"Just pretend there's a rope going from the middle of the pool up to the sky and…try to get a few shots of it."

"Right, shoot the imaginary rope. You G-men are fucking nuts."

* * *

Nereus Charobim walked down Mass. Ave and gazed skyward at the black helicopter circling above. He drew no particular attention from his fellow pedestrians on this brisk autumn afternoon. Just a black face in a black overcoat on his way to some business or other. No one noticed the viscous black strands like marionette strings running from his shoulder blades skyward, or the pulsing orb they were tethered to. His destination was marked by a thicker emanation from that dark star, and as he neared the place where it touched down, he could sense the grand design coming into focus.

The entire complex was an architectural marvel, a set of grand monuments to a philosophy that had seen its zenith and was now on the wane. But so were all the faiths of men. Perhaps one day these grounds would be overtaken by the new faith, which was really the oldest faith, and the buildings would be graven with the iconography of the Great Old Ones, and the survivors would attend his sermons in the vast domed cathedral between this library and the pool. When that day came, when the great men of this city saw him in his true form and called him by his true name, *Nyarlathotep,* he would have the giant Van De Graaff generator moved from the Museum of Science across the river and installed on the dais of this church, and the revelations he would espouse at the birth of the new aeon would be *electrical!*

It was coming now. He could smell it on the air like ozone and low tide.

Darius had done well. The device had given voice to a language that had long eluded the pharaoh. All these years he had been consigned to the shadows, speaking only to the unhinged through dreams and mirrors, misplacing his hopes for a suitable servant in failed mystics and artists: de Sade, Crowley, Manson. But in the end science was his salvation.

Opening the portal in the bowels of the city had breached dimensions, brought Azothoth through, and set his nuclear chaos as a new star in the sky, visible only to the few who had heard the invocation. And now that black star was drawing the gods from the other side, pulling them through into this world in places where the boundary was thinnest, the membrane porous. Mirrors and waters become windows and doors. Mirrors and waters. And this pool was both.

The dark energy that had rained down on the city for a day and a night was gaining substance and gathering mass. It had clothed him in flesh, and what his apprentice had wrought in a lab was now organically manifest in his own throat. His heart, lungs, larynx, and tongue were no longer astral, but true flesh. And through them, he could move molecules, mountains, and moons. He could utter the black speech again and shake the pillars of the earth.

He was an artist of the apocalypse, an engineer of the end. And he had come to sing his song.

He entered the library and passed through the Hall of Ideas, where projections of words seemed to surface from the center of a fountain, glide across the floor, and climb the walls. Only a handful of people were gathered around the bronze-and-glass sculpture today, a giant bowl in the center of the marble floor. A pair of children and their mother dipped their fingers into the glassy water, the little girl trying to catch the blue words as the miracle of technology swept them over her fingers and spilled them out onto the floor. As Charobim passed through the room, the words *WISDOM, KNOWLEDGE, POWER* stretched and fractured over the coarse black wool of his overcoat. The family did not look up from the fountain at his passing, but the mother rubbed her arms as if chilled.

High above, a parchment-colored lamp glowed in the form of a globe girded by iron latitude and longitude lines, its equator encircled with a calendar ring, giving it a resemblance to Saturn. Two squares were illuminated in the concentric grid: SEPT. and 21. The Equinox was nigh, and the alignment of dimensions was now like two great glass lenses sliding together, overlapping, and moving into sync as they brought two worlds into focus. In just a few days, the people of this seacoast city would meet their masters. It would be like seeing the shapes of zebras or chameleons emerging from the camouflage of their surroundings. And the seeing would be mutual. But today, in this place, there would be another preview for the lucky few.

He approached the Mapparium, heard the hushed chatter of tourist voices through the door, and paid his six dollars for admission.

He entered, delighted to see that the marvel had drawn a fair crowd. The Mapparium was an enormous stained-glass globe, three stories high, bisected by a thirty-foot bridge. Standing on that bridge in the center of the sphere, one could view the entire Earth, based on a 1934 Rand McNally map. It was a beauty to behold from within, lit from without, blue light falling on the faces of the crowd from the world's oceans, or swatches of orange and green from the countries. Moving through the crowd, he couldn't help sparing a glance at the approximate place in the South Pacific where Cthulhu lay dreaming in sunken R'lyeh, nearing the end of a long season of slumber, in an octopus's garden in the shade.

"*Cthulhu R'lyeh wgah'nagl fhtagn,*" he whispered. He felt the crowd part around him, and raised his eyes toward the interlocked pentacles at the apex of the globe. There was a restless silence as everyone waited for the show to begin, an audio program with LEDs to indicate points of interest. He had disabled the electronics with a wave of his hand upon entry—all but the main lights that encircled the stained glass on the outside.

Now he reached the center of the bridge and cleared his throat. The globe had the unique acoustic property of returning a voice to the speaker's ears with such clarity that it created a sensation of murmuring into one's own ears. For those standing on opposite ends of the thirty-foot bridge, a mere whisper was enough to be heard loud and clear.

Nereus Charobim inhaled deeply, and began to drone the overtone chant which turned the tumblers in the locks of human consciousness like a silver key, and as he did so, he reveled in the symbolism of the globe, the feeling that all the hollow places of the Earth were touched by the sound of his resurrected voice, that all of the people and beasts of the planet trembled with the vibration of it.

The screaming commenced a few seconds before the globe shattered and heavy shards of stained glass rained on the crowd in the blinding white glare of a ring of halogen lamps. Where seconds ago the soft colors of the rainbow had painted the faces of the patrons, now they were bathed in stark red on a bridge slick with blood.

* * *

From the helicopter with her headset on, Becca couldn't hear the screams, but she could see people running and bleeding and passing between the buildings, some toward the reflecting pool, fleeing God only knew what. And then, behind them, walking slowly and somehow driving them down the lane like lambs to slaughter, came a man in a black coat. His face was a smudge of darkness, as if the air in front of it were distorted by heat. She trained her camera on him and started clicking. "You getting him?" Brooks asked.

"Yeah. Is he the guy from the train?"

Brooks didn't answer, just stared at the figure, entranced. Becca glanced at Tom and found him equally enthralled by the increasingly turbulent water of the reflecting pool. She released her seatbelt, turned in her seat, and took a few shots of that as well. She'd passed the pool a few times when walking from Back Bay to Copley Square, and she knew it was only a couple of feet deep; now that a whirlpool was forming in it, she was shocked that she couldn't see the bottom of the vortex.

She shielded the LCD window of her camera with her left hand and clicked back to look at the image she'd just shot. When the infrared image appeared, it revealed something like a giant curved tube of piebald flesh rising from the ring of agitated water, something with bony spines like hooks.

Motion caught her eye and a flash of black metal. She looked up from the camera and saw Brooks rising from his seat with his gun in his hand. "Put your belt back on," he said, edging between her and Tom, and grabbing the handle to slide the side door open.

Becca obeyed the order. She wanted to tell him what she'd captured, but he wasn't wearing his headset anymore, and then the wind was blasting in through the open door and he was leaning out, half sitting on the floor and reaching for the rail with his foot. The pilot spared him a glance and maneuvered in a wide, gentle orbit around the man in black below. Was Brooks really going to shoot him? Becca tried to see past Brooks' shoulder. The man in black didn't appear to be armed, but she could only catch a glimpse before he was gone again as the helicopter struggled to gain a steady trajectory that would keep him in sight for more than a few seconds. Now they swept wide and away from the plaza to realign and give Brooks a long enough line of sight on approach. Becca unbuckled and found a looped strap to hang onto with her left hand. The weight of the camera in her right caused her wrist to scream in protest, even with the brace on. She craned into the wind behind Brooks and wished she'd packed a zoom lens.

They were going in low now, racing over water, stone, and fleeing people, toward the black smear of that rippling man. His face took on little detail as they approached and she had the crazy idea that the distortion was being caused by something he was singing.

What did Brooks see that she couldn't? And could she afford to only see the dangers around them on a delay, after shooting and checking the infrared? Fuck it, how could she photograph things she couldn't see?

She pulled the headset off and dropped it on the seat behind her, then leaned into the wind, into the waves of ultraharmonic song and watched the sound take form in an iridescent web emanating from the walking man. As she absorbed his song and watched it oscillate in the air, she saw black tentacles writhing from his shoulder blades.

Gunshots punched the air, and the shimmering web was shorn along the paths of two bullets from Brooks' weapon.

The walking, singing man jerked and staggered from the hits, paused in his advance, but only for a moment, then kept coming.

Gripping the strap with her left hand, Becca leaned out beside Brooks, shutter button half depressed. She let the autofocus find the man, wishing she had both hands free to turn the barrel and fine-tune it. She snapped a quick series, then, still hanging out the side door of the helicopter, shot the reflecting pool, the destination of the walking man, whose tentacles seemed to be gesturing at it in some indecipherable semaphore.

Now she could see the thing in the whirlpool with her naked eye. It rose from the pool into the sky, dripping sheets of water that bystanders stared at in confusion. Others, the ones fleeing the singing man, scattered in terror at the realization that he was driving them toward an abomination. But the two groups were becoming one, as those who had been at the pool before the arrival of the singer were exposed to the song. Becca saw the change in their faces, like people waking up to discover that they had been sleeping in a burning house. She could still feel the strangeness of her own transformation, the sense of a drug altering her perceptions, turning myriad keys in the spaces between synapses.

The creature in the pool was like nothing she had ever seen or imagined, an insane hybrid that seemed to defy terrestrial biology by a union of the great and the small. The bulk of the body was a colossal tube of mottled flesh sprouting rows of sharp, yellow spines from ridges where its pink and brown pallor was tattooed with veins of angry red tracery. The tube terminated in great petals of ripe meat, falling in flaps and sprouting a bouquet of gray tentacles that squirmed and thrashed with a speed that belied their size and made a mockery of physics — Becca's stomach rebelled against the sight with dread so forceful that it almost overpowered her. She tilted forward, nearly dropping her camera into the water and tumbling after it, but Brooks caught the lurching motion out of the corner of his eye and flung an arm out to catch her.

Becca steadied herself and tightened her grip on the hand strap. Tom was yelling at her, *"Get back in! Get away from it!"* but she could barely hear him through the wind and song, the screams, and the shuddering pulse of the rotors above her head slicing and fracturing that horrible sound into a staccato assault on her sanity.

The base of the creature rose from the water ahead of the giant trunk, and she saw legs like a scorpion's, plated with chitinous armor and crawling on an array of spiked claws, the torso tube swaying at the rear where a scorpion's stinger would be, while the legs scurried with sickening speed to the edge of the pool.

A smell of maggots flooded Becca's sinuses, and she felt her bile rising as her tongue tried to crawl back into her throat, retreat from the taste of death on the air. Her eyes watered, and she held down the shutter button on the camera, taking a rapid flurry of shots and hoping she was aiming near enough at the creature to get most of it in the frame. She tried to gulp a breath of cleaner air from the interior of the helicopter, and held it when she turned to look back at the plaza. The monster had seized a man from the scattering crowd in one of its foreclaws, and the nest of tentacles had parted to reveal a puckered maw with a chattering beak at the center.

Becca couldn't watch. She tossed the camera into the bay of the helicopter and scuttled in after it. Tom was pressed against his seat as if he hoped to merge with it. He wore the wide-eyed look of an animal locked in the slaughter chute at the instant it comprehends the reek of blood and shit.

Brooks climbed in behind Becca and edged into his seat beside the pilot, pointing at Mass. Ave. The pilot nodded and steered away from the pool. Becca tumbled in the open compartment, crawled on hands and knees to her seat, and was almost strapped in when a pair of tentacles slammed the front window, throwing the helicopter sideways. She saw the tips of the tentacles chopped off by the rotor blades before the cathedral came into view at a wrong-looking angle. In a panic, she fumbled with the buckle until by sheer, clumsy luck it latched. Her muscles tensed for a crash, but the pilot had regained control and the bird gained altitude, the buildings dropping away in a grid of gray squares...giant fans, AC units, and rooftop gardens where the reflecting pool had been seconds ago.

Brooks had his headset on and was directing the pilot. Becca clawed at her seat, her heart pounding as they circled over Symphony Hall and touched down on the vacant top level of a parking garage on Westland Ave.

The landing shook the cabin, and Brooks was out and walking before the blades stopped spinning. Becca and Tom sat paralyzed, still gripping their seats and catching their breath.

"You stay here. Both of you," Brooks said, jabbing his finger and walking backwards down the car ramp. Tom seemed relieved at the order, and Becca was willing to bet that if Brooks had *wanted* Tom to follow him to street level, he would have had to march him there at gunpoint. Tom's jaw trembled on the verge of speech, but none was forthcoming, just a thin whine. His gaze kept drifting back to the slime smeared across the windshield.

Becca couldn't read the pilot's face under his helmet, shades, and beard, but she had an idea and wanted to test it. Leaning forward, she pointed at the glass and asked, "How did you see through that shit to land this thing?"

"What shit?"

At her question, Tom sank deeper into his seat.

Becca unbuckled and climbed out of the helicopter, camera in hand. Brooks gestured for her to stop. "I can't lose you in the city. Don't make me cuff you to the helo."

In reply, she merely held up her camera.

He shook his head and continued walking down the ramp. They were almost in the shelter of the garage, and she hurried to catch up with him. "I have a job to do, right?"

He stopped, turned, and sized her up, obviously restless about the time she was forcing him to waste in dealing with her. "Whatever you got from the air is good enough. Go back. If I have to track you down again for the pictures—"

"I'm not gonna run."

He scoffed, but before he could argue further, screams and car horns cut the air and the concrete garage shuddered beneath their feet. Brooks ran to the edge and peered out at the street below. When Becca came up beside him, she was already looking through the viewfinder.

The creature was crawling down the center of Westland Ave., postulant slime oozing from the tentacles severed by the chopper blades, claws sending shockwaves into the pavement with each step. The street was far from crowded, but people were emerging from the doors of apartments and shops to see if there'd been an accident. Two cars and a delivery truck were mashed together on the sidewalk, and a few people were running frantically, some trying doors to see if they were locked, others pushing past the residents in the doorways, knocking them down to reach cover. It dawned on Becca that those who hadn't been at the reflecting pool, who hadn't heard the chanting, would be looking through the creature at their equally confused neighbors across the street, utterly blind to the abomination among them.

The sight of the creature galvanized Brooks. He either no longer cared about losing Becca or had decided that the cost in time and effort wasn't worth it. Without sparing her another glance, he sprinted down the spiraling ramp, his weapon drawn in spite of its likely impotence. Becca took a few more pictures, then hurried after him.

On the street she found a mixture of the terrified and the befuddled. She made her way among them, scanning the crowd for Brooks, and saw that he'd made it almost to the intersection of Hemenway on the trail of the thing, which had to be moving at least thirty miles an hour. Already its bulk was disappearing as it crossed the street, and she felt an unfamiliar nausea as she watched a stream of cars passing through the titanic claws and the base of the mottled trunk without crashing, as if they were passing through a projection. Looking back at the crashed delivery truck on the side of Westland, she wondered again at the difference between those whose senses had been opened like her own, and those who remained untouched. Had the drivers swerved to avoid the monster or had they only been reacting to the panicked people in the street who had seen it and were running pell-mell away from it?

Deciding she didn't want to be there when Brooks gave up the chase and returned, she cut through a passage in the apartment tower across the street from the Christian Science Complex. Horns bleated at her as she ran across Mass Ave., but she ignored the cars, scanning the crowd for a man in a black overcoat, a man with tentacles writhing from his shoulders. She didn't see him, but now, surveying the sky from the ground, she did see a black orb floating behind the skyscrapers. It dripped ribbons of darkness onto the city, one of which extended down Westland in the wake of the creature. The fens lay in that direction, and she wondered if the thing was headed for the boggy creek that ran through there, looking to burrow in the tall reeds until night fell.

She knew she should get out of the Back Bay by whatever convoluted path might make her most invisible to the authorities. She was now only one of an ever-growing number of civilians on the street with what she was thinking of as *the sight*, but she was probably the only one with photographic documentation of what lurked beyond the visible spectrum. She needed time to think and examine the photos before committing to a course of action.

She needed to get away, but her boots were carrying her back to the reflecting pool. They seemed to have an agenda of their own, and, as she neared the scene of the killing, where the only evidence of the creature was a cloud of blood spreading in the water, she realized that she needed to see the place where the thing had emerged, needed to look into the pool and see either a portal or the flat bed of impenetrable stone that had always been there.

Crossing the open ground she felt horribly exposed, but chaos hung in the air like a poison gas and no one paid her any attention.

Someone was in the pool—a man, lumbering under the weight of water-soaked clothing, struggling to rise from his knees to his feet. He wasn't wearing a cardboard crown, but she recognized him.

Becca set her camera bag in one of the concrete planters and climbed over the rounded marble edge of the pool. The cold water sluiced around the tongues of her boots and soaked through her pants. Maurice was close to the middle of the pool, where the vortex had been, but she saw no sign of it now. The water was settling into stillness, and she could see the bottom. Even with her new perception she spotted no fissures in the stone, no hole to account for the whirlpool or the emergence of the monster. At the north end of the pool, the blood cloud now floated in tatters.

Maurice trudged through the knee-high water, dragging his wet trench coat behind him. He seemed even more dazed than when she'd last seen him, searching the sky with faraway eyes.

"Moe?" She had to repeat the name louder to get his attention, but when his eyes slid sideways and fixed on her, they kindled with recognition, even while the lower half of his face maintained a grimace of pain.

"Hey, shorty. Thought I might see you again."

"I thought you were dead," she said, and wished she hadn't.

"Not yet, sugar. Soon, though…soon."

"You passed through a wall at the mill and came out here with that *thing*." It wasn't a question, and he nodded in reply. And then she saw that his hand was in his coat like Napoleon's, and it was dripping blood into the water, little hemoglobin roses blooming between them.

"Oh God, we have to get you help."

"No help for me now."

"Don't say that. There's a helicopter less than a block away. I'll get them to take you to a hospital. You just…just hold onto me." She wedged her shoulder into his armpit, smelling the dirt and sweat and death of him, and trying to take his weight, getting his blood on her khaki pants where she could see the stains, and on her black shirt where she couldn't, and as she walked him forward the scarab amulet swung on the chain around her neck and caught the fire of the sun, sending reflections darting like minnows through the dark water around them.

"I'm done. Been through the veil and seen the cogs. I told you we was at the…hub," he said, the last word delayed when he swept his gaze up her body to look into her eyes and caught sight of the scarab dangling just inches from his nose, flashing like Morse code on his ashen cheeks.

"*Praise Kephra,*" he whispered.

Having led him to the edge, Becca looked for someone with enough muscle and wit to help get him over the rounded marble border where water rolled into a grate, but before she could hail anyone his legs gave out and he slid off of her. She grasped at the trench coat and managed to ease him down so that he landed with his rear end on the marble, his feet still in the pool. She knelt beside him and steadied him. Someone was going to have to keep him from falling over while she went to get Brooks or the pilot. She wasn't going to let him drown in two feet of water. Scanning the shell-shocked witnesses, fear climbing her chest with icy fingers, she realized that there actually were cold fingers touching her, the delicate probing digits of Moe Ramirez touching the beetle and lifting it for a closer look.

His face was a mask of awe—eyes blazing, nostrils flaring with the stilted rhythm of broken lungs, death indistinguishable from ecstasy.

"You have it," he said, "*The Fire of Cairo.*"

She touched the beetle, her fingers folded around his, and she drew his hand away from the pendant, squeezed it gently in an effort to get his eyes to focus on hers. He was delirious, but she needed to reach him if she was going to keep him in this world. *Keep him in this world.* The words echoed in her mind as soon as she'd formed the thought. He claimed to have been out of this world mere minutes ago, in some parallel dimension. And somehow she didn't doubt it.

"It's true," he said, his face contorting with anguish, "The gem is gone, the flame is lost."

"I don't know what you're talking about, Moe, but you need help."

Now he met her eyes. "No, *you* need help." His eyes welled up with tears. "And I won't be here to give it to you."

She shook her head and squeezed his hand harder.

He steeled himself, winced, then straightened his shoulders, locking his eyes on hers with new intensity. "You hear me now, girl. You're gonna hafta cover your ass carrying a totem like that. You hide it, now. And keep it hidden."

Becca tucked the beetle back under the wide neck of her shirt. When it was out of sight, he breathed a ragged sigh.

"I can pass easier now I've seen it. But we shoulda had more time." He coughed, a violent wracking spasm that sprayed specks of blood over his coat. "I'm sorry…so much you need to know and I can't help you now…." He blinked, heaved, and his eyes lit again like a dying flashlight given a smack. "There's a book…*Mortiferum Indicium*. You find that…might have a chance."

He slumped. She slid aside and let his head rest on her thighs, stroking his coarse hair with her fingertips and thinking that this was what it was like to comfort a sick child or a dog on the euthanasia table. She felt a strong urge to argue with his resignation, to get help and lift him over the side, to run for the airlift, but the feeling was diminishing with every labored breath he drew. She couldn't see his face, but could feel the flutter of his blinking eyes transmitted across his scalp each time she touched his temple and dragged her fingertips to his hairline. One of these blinks would be the last, a shut with no open.

A sudden thickness formed in her throat. She barely knew the man, but she felt for him. He was a misfit like her, and before today her affection for him had been inspired by the fact that he seemed crazier than her. But no, her breed of crazy was an inability to reconcile her internal chemistry with the facts of the cosmos, the cycles of Earth and Sun. His, on the other hand, was a kind of stark-raving sanity, an acute awareness of deeper, more profound cosmic truths that few could bear to even consider. He'd made the bold pursuit and confrontation of them his life's quest. But the quest had cost him his life, and there was no time now to ask him what he'd hoped to achieve, or what he'd learned.

"I'm glad I get to die under this sky instead of the other one," he said.

Becca watched a tear fall from her face and land in his dusty hair, a drop of water in which the salt of her body now mingled with the pollen of some unfathomable hell.

A sound from above—the cries of geese—drew her eyes skyward, and she watched a flock rising from the fens and winging over the city in a strange formation. They were heading south, following the Earth's magnetic field to warmer climes…in the shape of a five-stemmed branch.

Chapter 14

Jason Brooks was back on top of the parking garage surveying Westland Ave. through a pair of high-powered binoculars. For a moment he trained them on a flock of migrating geese that resembled a symbol he'd seen in the graffiti Becca Philips had shot and the hair on his forearms rose. But the passing form was a minor oddity in light of all that had just occurred, and the flight soon resolved into a more traditional V. He refocused on the street below.

The bedlam there was settling a bit as panic-stricken *seers*— those who had seen the monstrosity—were absorbed into the consensus reality of the majority who hadn't been at the reflecting pool. Neighbors, relatives, and coworkers had at least figured out there wasn't another bomb exploding or somebody with a gun popping people in the street, and were now leading their gibbering fellows indoors or into cars bound for hospitals, or simply wrapping arms and blankets around them while asking questions.

It would take time for the general population to process the commonalities of this "mass hallucination," but within a few hours, with the help of the media, the city at large would begin to see the pattern. It wasn't like the subway tunnel. It couldn't be contained. Already the crowd was a mixture of seers and their first listeners and no team could round them all up or quarantine the entire neighborhood. That made Rebecca Philips just one of many...almost. She alone had willingly infected herself with the sight, and for what? To get a better photo?

Sweeping the pavement and the building entrances with his binoculars, Brooks felt an increasingly heavy weight, knowing that despite her sworn promise, she had no plans to let SPECTRA benefit from her sacrifice.

He could hear the Director's baritone already: *One of many, Brooks? How about the only one who captured it on fucking film?*

He wound up—knee and elbow raised—and dashed the binoculars onto the concrete at his feet.

The damned things didn't even give him the satisfaction of breaking. He wiped his cupped hand over his chin and mouth, felt his stubble prickling in his palm. What were the odds of spotting her from the air if she didn't want to be found?

Pretty shitty without those binocs.

He plodded toward the helo, then turned and went back for them, scooping them up by the strap and feeling like a jackass. Flyboy and Shellshock were silent as he strapped in.

"Take us up and circle the area," he said, examining the lenses. Damned things weren't even scratched.

* * *

Samira Fanan was half a block away from the Starry Wisdom Church on Beacon Street when she saw the black armored vehicles. Her hand went to the pocket of her long wool coat, and someone bumped her from behind as she clicked her phone on. Murmured curses reached her ears as those she had blocked by stopping short flowed around her. She turned her face away from the church and shuffled sideways into the shadow of a shop awning. Reaching for the phone had been an instinct, but now, hearing the drone of a helicopter, she folded it into the palm of her hand and let her arm drop to her side. She scanned the street. Anyone could be moving among the pedestrians, watching her, scrutinizing her reactions to the raid in progress. She steadied her breath and tucked the phone back into her pocket. She'd known this was coming, just hadn't known when.

No familiar faces on the street.

She took her bearings and remembered a gap between the apartment buildings that led to one of the public alleys. Would the alley be swarming with agents and police? Maybe not this far out. She didn't have time to deliberate. She shoved her hands into her pockets, tucked her head down, and slipped through the gap, the rough red brick scraping against the shoulder of her coat.

Stepping into the broader alley behind the building, her head cocked toward the church, she didn't see the figure emerging from the shadows to her right until a leather gloved hand wrapped around her mouth, pulling her backward down a concrete stairwell.

She was sure it was an agent, so when her abductor whispered into her ear, it came as a shock to hear the voice of Darius Marlowe.

"It's okay, Samira, it's me. They've arrested Proctor. You're not going to scream if I take my hand away are you?"

She ticked her head to the side and back, a sharp, assertive no. The gloved hand loosened its grip and came away from her face, taking its sweaty, chemical smell with it. She quickened her breath, widened her eyes, and turned to face him.

She'd never seen him unshaven to this extent before; he looked feral, yet simultaneously smug, grinning at her with...was it an air of pride? She let her eyes dart from side to side in a facsimile of panic, glancing across his hands and the pockets of his black jeans as well as the shadow of the last step below them in what appeared to be the rear entrance of a vacated apartment. No visible weapons.

"*Darius.* Are you crazy? What are you doing here? I saw you on the news. They'll catch you. Your face is everywhere."

He nodded, but said nothing.

"Was it you...at Harvard?"

"I started it. I opened the way for them."

"The Great Old Ones." She whispered it.

He nodded again, then craned his neck and looked skyward. The helicopter was getting louder, and he waited for it to buzz across a white patch of sky between the buildings before continuing. "I couldn't let them take you in, Samira. Proctor they can have. He isn't committed to the apocalypse. You'll see that now. Others, too. They say they want it, but they're too comfortable with the status quo. If we'd been more oppressed it might have been better. There would have been some unity, some conviction…."

"Why you, Darius?"

He flinched, and his eyes darted from the sky to her face, scrutinizing her, wounded by the question. "What do you mean, *why me?*"

"I mean *how*? How did you do what could never be done before? Who helped you?"

He smiled, and she wondered how long it had been since he'd last brushed his teeth. "Not out here," he said, and nodded across the alley to the neglected back of another brick apartment building, where a small, rusted barbecue grill stood among the weeds. "Come on, I've set up a safe house. The others are waiting."

Their faces were close in the cramped stairwell, his breath and the humidity of dank concrete mingling in a stale miasma. She ignored it and put her hand on his chest, not to push him away but to connect with him, to fix his shifty, darting eyes on hers. Leaning in closer, she spoke softly, forcing him to tune his ears to her small voice and away from the urban background noises, any number of which might represent an encroaching threat. "You've done it, Darius. You've unseated the reverend and asserted your power. You can take his place when this blows over and everyone will follow you. *I'll* follow you and serve you…." She squeezed his breast through his clothes and watched his Adam's apple bob as he swallowed. "But maybe what you've already done is enough for now," she said. "If you go too far, overreach…."

His eyes narrowed, hardened.

She leaned into his curls and whispered, "There's so much we haven't done yet, Darius. This is all happening so fast, and I'm afraid for you. Maybe we should let sleeping gods lie for now. You can't lead the church from prison."

He gripped her bicep, pulled her to her feet and up the stairs. He shot a look at her, and she thought he looked like a man on fire: radiant and dangerous, the muscles of his face roiling with myriad emotions, too many for anyone to take full form—wrath, vengeance, exhilaration. She let him guide her across the alley to the fire escape, where he bent and laced his fingers to give her a leg up. She hesitated, and, looking up at her, he said, "You'll see. This whole city will be my church. You'll see."

She scanned the backs of the buildings, the gray clouds reflected in blank windows, then stepped into his hands and reached for the bars above her head.

When she stood on the first level, he jumped, grabbed hold of the creaking, swaying structure, climbed past her and took the lead, confident that she would follow. At the third story they came to a cracked window, through which she saw a dingy white curtain. Darius tapped the glass once, paused, then tapped three more times. The curtain rustled against the glass and one tap came back in answer. Darius hiked the window up and pulled the curtain aside for her.

Samira poked her head in to survey the room before climbing leg first through the window. It was a vacant apartment, apparently undergoing renovations between tenants. White splotches of spackle marked the walls, and masking tape ran along the door and window frames where someone had started cutting in a new paint job, but the tape was peeling and yellowed, as if the painter had been called away, never to return. Seven members of the congregation had assembled here, and she recognized every face. Five men and two women—most, but not all of them, young. Some sat in folding metal chairs, or on what odd bits of renovation equipment lay about: a stepladder, an overturned bucket. Others leaned against the walls.

They were a grim bunch, their faces anxious and weary. Most probably hadn't slept in days. They nodded at her and a couple murmured her name upon entrance, but none came forward to greet her. Only Kristina Meawad visibly brightened when they made eye contact, and Samira was surprised to see her. The girl had never seemed like the radical type; her brother Stefan had probably put her up to it. A police scanner sat on the paint-speckled floorboards, plugged into an uncovered outlet. It hummed and crackled but transmitted no voices.

Another device sat beside the scanner, unplugged. It looked like a conventional radio, a boom box with some exposed circuitry where a plastic panel had been cut away, and looking at it she felt her heart drop into her stomach. She stepped to the side of the room as if casually joining the group and awaiting instruction from Darius, but she chose an angle that afforded an escape route through what appeared to be a kitchen, judging by the linoleum floor and white countertop. A few groceries were scattered amid paper plates and plastic utensils, and she thought she could smell spicy take-out hanging in the stale air, emanating more from the pores of these sweaty, paranoid men and women than from any containers that might be festering in the trash.

"Is this everyone?" she asked Darius.

He nodded. "You're the last."

She knew everyone in the room, and that begged the question she'd tried to ask him in the alley: Who was helping him? Or was he the leader of his own cell?

She turned around to face him. "Your mentor. Is he here?"

Darius grazed his thumb across her cheekbone and, with condescending reassurance, said, "Don't worry. There will be no more secrets. I'll explain everything."

And with that he moved to the center of the room, cleared his throat, and issued his manifesto to all who would hear it.

"Now that we are all gathered, I would have you hear the good news that comes down to us from The Messenger, through me, his right hand and, until recently, his voice in the world." Darius paused for dramatic effect to let them absorb this pretentious introduction. They shuffled and squirmed, sensing that he would soon be demanding sacrifices of them and wanting to have out with it, to hear the price before the pitch. He met their eyes, each in turn, and to a man they cast their eyes downward like subservient dogs. Even Cyril. This was not the Darius Marlowe they had known before.

Satisfied that he had their full attention, he continued. "We here were born at the right time. We stand on the precipice of a new world. It has been ages since the Great Old Ones walked among men, breathed the same air.

"Long have they slept, and the keys that would synchronize the orbit of their world with ours had been lost. Lost to the degradation of our species from the ur-race that once spoke their true names, vibrating the sands of Sumer and Acadia, Phoenicia and Kemet. They sometimes stirred, and they have always been among us, but we lost the ability to see, hear, and touch them, and they us. The interface of our race to theirs was lost to the amnesia of our minds and the dumbness of our tongues. But I have *restored the ancient speech*, and wiped the glass clean so that we may know them again, and they us! They walk among us even now, and our *Reverend* is blind to their presence!

"Not through *his* tutelage have I come by this knowledge, rather it has *come to me* by initiation at the hand of the Black Pharaoh himself, Nyarlathotep!"

A harmony of indrawn breath swept the room, and the bodies seemed to sway like the reeds of the Nile at the passing of a great beast, a black crocodile, a python, or a jackal.

"The stars are right. The worlds align to make a window, a door, a portal. And only just in time."

Darius's voice dropped into a delicate, somber tone. "Because man unchecked, left to his own devices, ruled by his greed and arrogance and amnesia, will destroy this majestic planet and all of its inhabitants. You know this. We have lamented it, but until now we have been powerless."

Heads nodded, bodies swayed. They were falling under the hypnotic rhythms of his rhetoric.

"Man has no regard for the life forms he *can* see because they lack his intellect. As if intelligence were a requirement to earn his compassion. As if a child of low mental capacity were worth less than one of average intelligence. Less worthy of existence without suffering. Man has climbed to the apex of the earth, and gazing from his silver spire has deemed all other creatures inferior and therefore unworthy of mercy. And so he poisons them, slaughters them, enslaves, or devours them. Always forgetting that he may yet meet his superior in the cosmos. And what mercy might he expect then?

"He justifies this brutality with the myth of the Garden, his fairy story of dominion over the beasts and birds, the creatures of air, land, and sea. But there is an older myth that is no myth. And the gods who once trod upon the ocean floor with their heads in the heavens care for mankind as little as he cares for the ants beneath his boot.

"His lust, his addiction to power, to a wealth of tawdry baubles and neon amusements vomited from the putrid maw of his feeble dreams. His *conveniences*, which sicken the Great Mother Hydra. His gadgets and trinkets, his plunder and pollution, his overpopulation of a globe strained to the breaking point with more and more bipedal parasites craving the same flat, materialistic pleasures, the same empty status symbols, devoid of depth and vision and spiritual awe at the titanic grandeur of the cosmos. He is a pestilence to be washed away by a cleansing tide. And I am the warden of the flood."

Darius let the statement hang in the air. He surveyed them, and Samira followed his gaze around the room. He had their rapt attention. The contrast between the socially awkward Darius Marlowe they had known before and this commanding and eloquent presence had confirmed for them his claim to divine inspiration. He was channeling something far greater than himself, and for this, she also saw the fear in their faces. No one had the courage to speak up and ask what he had done in the tunnel. No one dared ask what he planned to do next, or what he expected of his compatriots. Was there a spark of doubt among them? Samara wondered if she could blow on it just right to kindle it without putting it out.

"People are telling reporters they saw things they can't even describe," she said. "Something in the sky. Have any of you seen it?"

They looked at her like she had intruded on a dream. Slowly, eyes were downcast, body weights shifted, as if they were ashamed to admit that, no, they had seen nothing in the sky.

Cyril said, "I heard a guy on the radio saying that he watched a monster crawling down the street in Back Bay. But the broadcast cut out as soon as he started to describe it. I think they're cracking down on witnesses, trying to cover it up for as long as they can."

"So why can the infidels see what we can't?" Samira asked the group.

"To see the gods...," Darius said. "If you can see them, they can see you."

"And?"

"If they can see you, they can touch you."

"Have *you* seen them, Darius?"

His gaze seemed to turn inward as if examining some powerful memory. A feeling of electricity charged the stale air. At last he said, "I have seen their works. My invention gave voice to the old keys. I awakened the Lord of Chaos and brought him through, but I took precautions and denied myself the sight."

"Precautions?" Samira asked. "What were you afraid of?"

For the first time today he turned a withering gaze on her, and she felt the room scrutinizing her in the spotlight of his contempt. Was she pushing too hard?

"I believe they will recognize us as their sworn servants and spare us," Darius said.

Cyril asked, "You believe...but you don't know? He didn't tell you?"

"In the tunnel, it was the first time, and it wasn't a suicide mission. I still have work to do. Gathering you is part of that."

Kristin spoke up, her voice thin and cracking. "What does the pharaoh say about a place for us in the new world?"

"My Lord has not told me everything, and my studies are ongoing. This is why I've been careful." His gaze pierced Samira again as he said, "All of this would have been easier if I'd been trusted by the church leadership, if I'd been given access to the archives. I would have more answers for you now. But I'm afraid the *true* brethren is only forming here and now in this room, piecing together what facts we can. Maybe it was meant to be this way. At least it keeps them from rounding us up like the figureheads down the street. I won't lie to you and tell you I know everything. But if you trust my link to the pharaoh, as I have trusted him, then I believe you will be in the right place at the right time to shepherd in the new aeon, to form a new race, to inherit the Earth."

Several questions overlapped now:

"How will they know us?"

"When can we meet him?"

"What do they see in the sky?"

Darius answered the last and loudest. "The Lord of Chaos, Azothoth, hangs over the city now like a black sun with many tendrils. His emanations are spreading like a web of night and reaching into any suitable portal, any reflective surface, to draw forth the pantheon. Azothoth has laid his blessing upon Nyarlathotep and restored the messenger's voice so that he can assist in opening those gates." He pointed at the boom box. "And with *this*, we can help."

"How?" Cyril stepped forward and Samira thought he looked like a man heeding a call to action. Until today she would have said that he possessed the charisma Darius lacked, but no more. And if Cyril were following Darius, the others would fall in lock step.

"We will call forth the Goat with a Thousand Young and ride her offspring to the other side." He swept his eyes over their awed faces. "It will be our initiation and empowerment. Afterward, we will move between the worlds freely to do the master's bidding."

The room seemed to lose oxygen as they all sucked it in. Sensing that her devotion had been judged thin, Samira spoke up now with ardor in her voice, *"To be a midwife of Shub Niggurath...I would kill for the honor."*

Darius smiled. "Good," he said, "You may have to. Your cloaks and lamens are in the backpacks in the hall. Daggers, too, if we need them, and a few guns. We go on foot and don the robes at the site."

"What *is* the site?" Samira prodded gently. The others were already flowing around her into the hall, willing to follow their Pied Piper wherever he led them and find out if it was crawling with SWAT, BPD, and DHS snipers when they arrived, but their heads turned back toward Darius when she raised the question. Again he reveled in the suspense, the attention he had never garnered before today.

"The biggest mirror in Boston."

They set about strapping on the backpacks Darius had prepared. He pointed out one with a gun in it for Cyril, and one with a smaller robe for Kristin. Samira stepped up beside her and asked, "Bathroom?"

Kristin gestured to a door on the left at the end of the hall.

Samira ducked in and dropped the hook on the doorframe into the eyehole. She fished her phone out of her pocket and texted SPECTRA while running the sink.

Watching the spinning icon and the low bars and waiting for the message to send seemed to take an eternity. She slid the phone back into her pocket, flushed the toilet, and opened the door, startled to see Darius's face. He stood in the doorframe, blocking her way, and turned his palm up. For a heart-stopping second she was sure he was demanding that she hand over the phone, and her reeling mind simply couldn't process the word he'd spoken until he repeated it: "Keys. I need your church keys."

"Why? You can't go in there without getting arrested. Those agents will be picking through the place for hours if not days."

"I don't know if you and I will be separated in the crossing, but once I can pass freely between this side and that, I plan to emanate in the church to retrieve a few things from the hidden crucible. You know they won't find that unless they torture it out of Proctor."

"How do you even know about it?"

Darius laughed bitterly. "He never trusted me. Never initiated me into his inner circle, but my master knows *all*."

"So you know about—"

"The rods and the map to where the box is buried? Yes. And if those agents are still searching the church at midnight, I'll be in and gone before they hear the flagstone fall." He wagged his fingers. "*Keys.* Please."

Chapter 15

The helicopter was already soaring east over the sunken Aquarium, approaching Government Center when the text came in. Brooks had mounted his phone with a strip of adhesive Velcro onto the console in front of him. He carried swatches of the stuff in his kit and in recent years had attached the battered device to more dashboards than he could count, knowing that the bone-rattling vibration of a Humvee or helicopter would invariably override the vibration of a phone in his pocket but a lit screen would get his attention.

The text wasn't specifically for him. It was going out to several units within range and called for armed agents and armored teams to move in. He could ignore it and return to the station, but that would mean having to account for losing the photographer sooner. Not a prospect he was eager for. It also meant sitting in a debriefing room when he could be in the heat of field action. The pilot's sunglasses kept swiveling toward him and back again, waiting for a prompt. Soon the question would come and he'd have to decide.

Action called, but it wasn't Darius Marlowe's face he saw while he considered jumping in. The MIT student had been sifted from a facial recognition database, and Brooks knew he had a better chance of recognizing him in person than any of the other agents and cops, having already seen him from multiple angles in the flesh in the subway. But the face in his mind now was Heather's. His daughter was only a few years younger than Marlowe, and she was down there somewhere. Maybe safe in her apartment in Jamaica Plain, maybe not. The greatest battle he'd fought since obtaining his security clearance was the one waged in his own mind over whether or not to have her tapped and tracked. He had friends at the NSA who could do it for him, but he'd chosen to honor her privacy and keep her blind trust at the expense of sleepless nights and bad digestion. It was a decision that was getting harder to live with every minute of this day. He wanted to direct the helo to her rooftop, strap her into the seat Becca Philips had vacated, and fly her out of the city, away from whatever shitstorm was brewing in the psychedelic light of that black sun.

"Agent Brooks? You with me, sir?" the pilot's voice crackled in his ear, a narrow band of frequencies boring into his head.

"Yeah."

"What's it gonna be, sir? Back home or out to Copley?"

"Copley," he said.

He rummaged in his kit bag for Kevlar and extra magazines.

* * *

As the sun marched west, the cloud cover that had hung over the city throughout the day was coming undone like rotting gauze. Patches of cold blue and ash gray moved across the glass face of the John Hancock Tower. The declining sun was still more gold than pink, and few lights had come on in the tower to break the glossy perfection of the great grid of windows. Sixty stories and almost eight-hundred feet of monolithic minimalist architecture hovering over the Romanesque masonry of Trinity Church and swallowing it in shadow. And now, moving in that long shadow, noticed at first only by a few pigeons roosting in the arches of the church, came a formation of nine black-robed and hooded figures wearing engraved copper plates on chains around their necks. The copper flashed as they walked, sigils strobing out of the shadows in a geometry of orange fire.

Three of the company had set censers in the bushes on the south side of the stone foundation of the church, and wisps of smoke, musky and resinous, curled around their robes as they strode across the grass toward St. James Ave.

Their hands moved in an elegant choreography of mudras: fingers crossed and wrists twisting, elbows rising and arms undulating in some primeval precursor of tai chi, raising and directing an invisible force, a viscous bioelectric substance which they summoned like dew from the soil, like smoke from the sky.

Knives flashed now in the dusky light, and the dancers stepped forward in synchrony, stabbing the air, tearing a membrane that separated the pedestrian world of the skyscraper from a dark heaven, a nocturnal paradise whose alien constellations stretched their razored rays down to form the crown of a prodigal prince, the man at the head of the triangular formation.

And now they chanted a drone that rumbled like storm waves pounding a beleaguered shore. *IÄ! SHUB NIGGURATH! IÄ! SHUB NIGGURATH! IÄ! SHUB NIGGURATH!*

Scraps of cloud scudded widdershins around the bowl of the sky, a ragged shroud unwinding around the mirrored tower. The pigeons took to the sky and, wheeling over the black-robed figures between the stone church and the glass skyscraper, scattered at the appearance of a dark, malignant wood marching toward an impossible horizon in the towering grid of windows—a forest that existed only in reflection—and the silhouette of some lumbering beast moving among the gnarled branches. Beating their wings to push away, they cast themselves into the turbulent wind of a descending helicopter, caught between Scylla and Charybdis.

* * *

The helo touched down on the grass at the center of Copley Square between the Boston Public Library and Trinity Church.

Brooks had his vest on and his 9mm at the ready. He took a last look around the bay as he climbed out. Tom looked sick and fatigued. The poor fucker. Brooks wished he'd try to get up, get out, get lost, like Ms. Philips had done. He had taken the guy along as an excuse to fly toward the black streamers that only the initiated could see, without having to spill the fact that he himself was one of them. Now he'd dragged him all over town while the number of roaming seers had grown.

"You can go," Brooks said. "Tom.... Hey, Tom, look at me." He clapped his hands, startling the man out of his paralysis. "I said you can go if you want to, you can hoof it back home. You've done your part to help."

Tom's eyes showed the white of glaring fear. *"Leave?"* he said, "Aren't you going to take me back to headquarters where it's safe?"

"If you sit tight in the helo, we'll take you back when we're done here, yeah. But you're free to go if you want. You have family in the city?"

Tom nodded.

"Well, it's your choice. But you might want to get out of here before the shit goes down."

That was all it took to get the man to unbuckle and climb out. Brooks checked his sidearm one last time and tucked it into its holster. He looked at the rack of automatic rifles and considered taking one but decided against it—didn't really believe bullets would be much use against whatever they faced here. He gave the pilot a quick salute and turned toward the church.

Armored vehicles were lining up on Boylston and Dartmouth. Helmeted men with assault rifles. It was a reassuring sight, but he didn't join them. He could fall back among them if he needed cover, but instinct told him to take advantage of his independence, to go ahead as a scout and see if he could find Marlowe, or Agent Fanan.

The plaza offered little cover. He skirted a line of trees across the street from the Fairmont Hotel, but at its end came to a wide open space that he had to sprint across before he gained the shelter of Trinity Church. The street was nearly empty of people.

Most had cleared out of the square at the approach of the armored cars and helicopter, to watch from between the statues of Art and Science that flanked the library steps: two bronze women, robed and enthroned, one gazing at an orb in her hand, the other holding a brush and easel. Brooks wondered what dark arts and sciences were at work here, and what they might soon unleash between the church and the tower. The whole scene was taking on a mystical resonance for him, and he felt that gambler's intuition that there were patterns and meanings, vectors and probabilities lurking just below the surface of things, and that if he squinted at reality the right way, if he relaxed his focus and let his peripheral vision lead his eye, he would see the opportunity to win when it emerged.

Edging around the rough-hewn stone, he sensed a wrongness in the glass façade to his right. Something vast moved in there, like the shadow of a leviathan below a surface of blue water. And when he gazed into the mirrors, trying to use them to see what lay around the corner of the church, he saw not a reflection of Trinity, but of a dense, vine-entangled forest. Trees like those didn't even belong in the new growth forests of *western* Massachusetts. They belonged in the Grimm's Fairy tales his mother had read him — they belonged to the dark heart of old Germany.

Blind to what he would find around the corner, Brooks drew his gun and sidestepped with his back to the church. He could hear the chanting now. He crouched low, weapon aimed at the ground, and stalked around the corner, but before he cleared the building and reached the grass, he saw them: a group of robed figures marching across St. James Ave. toward the Hancock Tower. They moved in synchrony, like dancers, their hands tracing gestures in the air as they went, some holding glimmering blades, the leader carrying a black box by the handle.

Brooks thought of the device on the train and almost fired at the figure with the box, but the hoods made it impossible to see their faces. It might be Darius Marlowe, but what if it was Agent Fanan? He raised his pistol, hesitated, and then they were across the street and passing between the small oak trees rising from the concrete islands that sheltered the skyscraper from car bombs. He sprinted across the street and into the shadow of the tower. Looking back he saw an armored car trolling up Clarendon alongside the small lawn between church and chapel.

Brooks was aware of vast shadows shifting in the glass beside him, and when he looked into the mirrors, the brain-shattering sight of a forest again nauseated him. The mirage lacked the stark clarity he'd glimpsed at a distance, and it crossed his mind that maybe it was akin to a projection on a movie screen. Up close the boles of the great black oaks resembled pillars of greasy smoke rising in such slow motion that the vapor took on a bark-like texture. The ground on the other side of the glass was littered with a bed of what at first appeared to be fallen leaves but upon closer inspection turned out to be pieces of ash the size of human hands.

He gazed up the vertiginous plane of the tower at the pale sky high above and saw the same oily black cord they'd flown under on landing, connecting the tower to the black orb. He was reminded of an umbilical cord. His stomach churned, and he wanted more than anything for the building to just be a building and for the sky to cradle a solitary yellow sun without that malignant black twin.

But if none of these things were what they should be, were the cloaked figures really men and women? Would they bleed and buckle over if shot, and if they pulled their hoods back, would he see human faces, or something…else?

He passed between the planter islands and onto the triangle of concrete that skirted the main entrance, the bank of doors now coming into view. No security guards emerged to confront the cloaked cultists, and Brooks was stone cold certain for a moment that none of the tenants of the Hancock Tower were in this world any longer, despite the fact that the building stood perfectly intact. Were they lost in some parallel dimension? Roaming a forest of black-smoke trees and obsidian columns where rivers of blood wove between ruined temples and stepped pyramids erected in alignment to stars unmapped by man? He swallowed, and his throat reopened with the slow stickiness that came with lack of saliva. All of the moisture in his body seemed to be flooding to his armpits and the slick palms on the grip of his gun.

The cultists came to a halt in a triangular formation, mimicking the shape of the concrete slab on which they stood, their heads and hands upturned toward the mirrored monolith. The chanting reached a crescendo, a discordant human drone iced with electronic harmonics, swelling and cresting, and crashing against the glass in a wave that caused the building to *waver* as if the walls were made of water or dense vapor.

Something was gathering in the surface, something was coming through, and now Brooks realized that the creature stalking the impossible forest beyond the glass had a name, and was being called forth by that name from one world to another.

IÄ! SHUB NIGGURATH! IÄ! SHUB NIGGURATH! IÄ! SHUB NIGGURATH!

Lightning flickered in the glass, delineating a jagged horizon of shale crags and conifer spires. A shockwave rolled over the shadow forest and stirred the heavy wool of the black robes, flooding Brooks' sinuses with musk so rich with piss and peat and the sexual secretions of that lumbering beast that he retched and felt his knees buckle.

He turned away, drew a breath, and held it for as long as he could, then moved in, searching the ground for the boom box.

A giant cloud of oily black smoke floated out of the glass trailing myriad cycling limbs with tufts of coarse fur...*or were they wisps of curling vapor?* There was a clattering of hooves on the concrete, and the cloud revolved to reveal its massive head, black and goatish, with a snout the size of a car and horns like curved swords forged of serrated bone. But the worst of it was the eyes, rows of eyes the color of congealed milk lining the snout and brow of the thing, rolling along divergent paths, scrolling black hourglass pupils.

The boom box was nestled in one of the concrete planters, aimed at the glass. The cultists were in front of it, now approaching the creature—some eagerly, others with tentative steps. Brooks had caught sight of the copper disks dangling from their necks, each engraved with a different letter of some arcane alphabet, encircled by asymmetrical symbols. Did they aid in the summoning, or were they protective devices that marked the cultists as forbidden meat? And if they *were* wards of defense, would the one Samira was wearing be enough to protect her? If the disc provided her with a kind of immunity, then maybe she had a better chance of surviving the encounter than he did with his gun.

The reeking black mass was moving into the center of the concrete triangle now, wisps of it breaking away through a perverse process of mammalian fission, the hooved tendrils forming pseudopods and then detaching into blind offspring: tumorous bubbles bucking and braying around the central cloud.

Brooks heard boots and checked the street again. The first unit was crossing St. James Ave., but the lead man had stopped running and stood wide-eyed in the street, making the sign of the cross as his comrades bumped his shoulders and flooded around him. He'd heard the chant, could see the beast, and was raising his assault rifle.

Brooks looked back at the tower and saw a man and a woman in business dress exiting one of the main doors. They saw the black-robed figures and stopped dead in their tracks. Brooks didn't know if they could see the monsters, but having spotted the flashing knives and the approaching tactical team, the man pulled the woman back into the lobby.

One of the cultists tugged her hood back, spilling long black hair, and turned to look over her shoulder: Fanan. A shot crackled past Brooks and two of the blue windowpanes shattered. A shriek cut the air from the now-exposed lobby. Gunmen were kneeling around the planters, aiming their rifles at the cultists, but the lead man, the one who'd heard the chant and seen the goat creature, had fired into the black cloud and taken out the glass. One of the shooter's team members was now pushing the muzzle of his gun down toward the pavement and trying to usher him to the side of the road. Brooks turned back to the tower as two of the cultists drew handguns and fired. Bullets sparked off the concrete planters but the police didn't return fire impulsively, now acutely aware of the glass building.

One of the gun-wielding cultists took a headshot from a rooftop sniper and crumpled under a mist of blood.

Fanan drew her own gun from her cloak and dropped another cultist. Brooks sprinted toward the planters where the riflemen were taking cover, seized the boom box, dashed it to the street, and fired a slug into it. The air seemed to lose an electrical charge when the chant cut out, but the wrecked device had already served its purpose. Spinning around he came face to face with Samira Fanan, the roiling black mass charging her from behind. Her eyes bulged as a ridged horn tore through her robe, impaling her.

Brooks cried, *"NO!"*

With no chant to fill the air, he could hear a thin whistle emanating from her throat, laced with a crackling gurgle. The beast jerked its head back, and Fanan's body was swept away with it. Before Brooks could recover from the sight, Darius Marlowe, mounted on one of the mammoth goat's offspring, charged into the space where Fanan had been, leading a procession of six riders. God only knew what the riflemen saw coming at them. Most wore helmets that covered their ears. Were they now watching cloaked figures on invisible steeds running them down and jumping the barriers? A couple of them fired shots in panic. Another window shattered, this one on the third floor.

The great beast passed into the street, its many hooves cycling, but not touching the ground, and even if the Special Forces guys couldn't *see* the monster, it seemed they could smell the fetid wave of poison fumes that wafted from its black fur and gaping maw. One vomited, others clamped their gloved hands over their mouths and noses. Brooks squinted against the acrid musk, eyes burning.

The riders' cloaks blended with the black fumes rising from their shaggy mounts, and soon they too appeared to be made of greasy smoke. Brooks recovered as the procession passed, and looked up at the rooftops bordering the square. He could make out the silhouettes of snipers training their rifles on the street and the church grounds. Their infrared goggles flashed in the sunlight as they pivoted, but no shots were fired. The cultists and their steeds were too close to the glass, too much a chaos of rolling smoke.

Tactical vehicles screeched around the square behind him. He could hear and feel the pounding of boots on the pavement, could sense the crosshairs of the riflescopes passing him over from the rooftops. And then, just as the great black goat had emerged from the mirrored plane of the tower, so did it pass back out of range into that malignant mirage beyond the silver panes, leading the black-robed riders on its spawn.

Chapter 16

Watching the front door of her warehouse apartment, Becca thought there was no way of getting in without goons jumping her and throwing her into a van with blacked-out windows. She didn't see such a van on the street—not even one of those fake delivery vans with a bogus company logo on the side that agencies like SPECTRA used, if TV was to be trusted—but she knew it would appear, jumping the curb, side door sliding open, and men in Kevlar giving her the cable-tie-and-bag-over-the-head express service to Government Center for the second time in two days if she were to walk up the steps and fish her keys out of her pocket. She could feel it.

Maybe she was paranoid, but she thought Maurice would approve.

The cabbie, a balding white guy with an ample beer gut and bushy sideburns, was getting antsy. "Time to shit or get off the pot, sweetheart" he said.

Becca sighed. If she told him to go around the block one more time, that alone would be enough to draw attention to the cab. She rolled her window down and listened to the air outside. The neighborhood was quieter than usual at nightfall; most people were indoors, heeding the Governor's advice.

A plane droned overhead, and gazing up she saw a contrail but no helicopter blades on the rooftop. She couldn't hear Django barking, either, and that was what she was listening for. Would Rafael have checked in when he couldn't reach her by phone? Would he have used his spare key to tend to the dog? With an apocalypse in its opening overture, she felt that having robbed the dog of his freedom to run from it, she was at least responsible for not consigning him to starvation. Maybe that was a little out of balance with so many human lives at stake, but for her it was a simple emotional imperative. There might not be much she could do for the city, but she could at least rescue the dog again.

And yet, another voice was vying for space in her head beneath the platinum wig she'd picked up along with a clean pair of jeans walking through Copley Place Mall before hailing the cab: *Bullshit, there's nothing you can do for the city. You may be the only one who can do something, if you don't get caught here. Is that what you're doing? Trying to get caught so you don't have to shoulder the burden and deal with the pressure?*

"Fuck it, why save myself if I can't even save a dog?"

"You talking to me?" the cabbie said, swinging an arm over the seatback.

"No." She handed him a crumpled twenty. "Give me a five-minute head start and then drive up to the courtyard and I'll hop back in, okay?"

"Why don't I just drop you *there* and wait for you?"

"Just do it like I said." Then she was out of the car, forcing herself to walk, not run. They had to be inside the building if they were here. Most of them, anyway. Whoever was watching the street would probably radio the ones inside to announce her arrival.

She approached the door, keeping pace with a silver SUV, hoping it wasn't the vehicle of the recon guy, and then using it as cover to duck into the weedy courtyard. She'd left her army bag in the cab—it was too much of a giveaway—and now she reached into her jacket pocket and found what she needed, the one tool she'd transferred.

It was fast work, and no doubt sloppy, but she was coming back out of the courtyard right in time for the cab; and before anyone knew where the blonde had gone, or that her cab wasn't just leaving but picking her up again, she was in the backseat, lying low, and telling the old man to get her out of there, not too fast.

Her fingers trembled with adrenaline as she dialed the prepaid cell phone. She could so easily imagine Rafael looking at the unfamiliar number and deciding to blow it off. Just when she thought he would, he answered, his voice uncertain.

"It's me," she said. "Just listen, I'm okay. I need you to take care of the dog for me. His leash is hanging on a hook in the kitchen. Take him to do his business in the courtyard. Use my headlamp; it's on the same hook as the leash. Walk him before you put him in your car. I don't know how long he's been crated. Then take him to your place and feed him. The bag of food is in the cabinet by the fridge. Can you do that for me, Raf?

"Becca, where are you? Are you in trouble? Some spooks took me in for questioning about you and I was freaking out, but I told them you would never hurt anyone. They weren't even cops, they were like…I don't know. What's goin' on, Becca? What kinda mess are you in?"

"I can't talk. Promise me you will do exactly what I asked, please."

"Okay, I promise, I'll get the dog. My landlord will wig if he sees him, though. Then we'll *both* be living on the street."

"Walk him first, Raf. He likes to pee in the same spot every time. It'll comfort him." And with that she hung up before he could ask any more questions and forget the particulars of the favor she'd asked of him.

* * *

Rafael let himself in with the key Becca had given him when she'd needed him to water her plants over the week she'd spent on a road trip in May. He'd been wondering when she was going to ask for it back but hadn't mentioned it because he didn't really want to know if she trusted him that completely, or if she'd simply forgotten he had it. He was surprised when it worked. He figured the men in black would have changed the lock. When it did work, he hesitated, expecting to be grabbed as soon as he entered. But looking around the entryway, he saw no one and decided to take the elevator instead of the stairs. It was a cage-type, and he figured at least he'd have a better chance of seeing the agents through the grate when it reached Becca's floor. If they wanted to grab him, they were going to grab him and there would be little he could do about it. It was the anticipation that made him crazy. The feeling that he was being watched. He just wanted to have out with it and confront them. But maybe the spooks had bigger fish to fry now that the shit was hitting the fan. He'd seen some of that on the news, but the broadcasts felt choppy and censored. Seeing national network reporters standing in front of Boston landmarks wasn't all that strange anymore; there'd certainly been plenty of that during Hurricane Sonia. But they seemed to have an especially anxious vibe this time, as if there were men with guns and national-security orders just outside the frame, watching to make sure no tongues slipped.

In light of all that, maybe the girl who saw it first was no longer a high priority, and her dog sitter even less of one.

Besides, they had already dragged him in for questioning, and let him loose. It hadn't been too hard to convince them he knew nothing, because it was mostly true. Still, they'd made him sit long enough to get tired and careless in his answers, had called him a vandal and threatened to deport him. When it brought them no closer to finding Becca, they'd let him go. Even gave him his knife back, the one Becca didn't know about that he kept in his boot. It had been the source of the most tension in his interrogation until the polygraph spelled out for them in tight little scribbles what he'd been swearing all along: that he couldn't say where Becca was because he hadn't heard from her, and he didn't have the slightest affiliation to the brineheads of the Starry Wisdom Church.

"We get it: you're not a brinehead, just a chucklehead. Whaddaya need a nine-inch knife for?" The agent had slapped the sheathed blade against the table, making Rafael jump. His untouched water cup sloshed a dollop over the side.

Rafael glowered at the Irish prick. "Me and Becca explore some of the same places skinhead junkies hang out. Maybe you're familiar with their position on mixed race couples?"

"So you're a couple, you and Becca Philips?"

In retrospect, he realized he must have shaken his head with enough dejected disappointment to clarify his role in her life for them.

The elevator shuddered to a clanging stop, and the cage bounced a little under his feet. He pulled the gate open and stepped into the hallway where Becca's photos lined the eggshell-white wall, including a candid black-and-white portrait of him, now indecipherable in the dark with the high windows all black above. He would have preferred to be running this errand in daylight, but there was less of that with each passing week. He felt for the other key on the ring and turned it in the door of Becca's apartment. A near-perfect silence was broken by Django's growls and barks, and Rafael breathed a sigh of relief at the assault on his ears. At least the mangy mutt was still here and healthy enough to give an intruder hell.

He switched on the lights and made his way across the broad wooden floor to the crate. Before he'd covered half the distance, the barking had ceased, replaced with whining and the thumping of the dog's tail.

"Hey buddy," he said in a soothing tone meant partly to calm his own nerves. "You remember me, huh? 'Fraid I ain't got any jerky for you this time, but I am here to feed you."

A quick look around the room only made him aware of every object an agent could hide behind: the futon, the bamboo screens and tapestries Becca used as room partitions, the bathroom door. But Django hadn't barked until Rafael entered the apartment, so if anyone was lurking here, they'd kept quiet long enough for the dog to forget their presence, and that didn't seem likely. Django probably had a good enough sniffer to keep track of anyone within a good thirty yards.

Rafael began to relax. He knelt and unlatched the crate door, and Django bounded out, tail swatting Rafael's calves as he circled, snuffling and whining. Rafael let the dog lick at his chin while he scratched the back of its head. "Okay, buddy, it's okay. *Fique tranquilo.* Your mama will be back soon. I hope. But I'm taking you to my place till then."

Django followed Rafael to the kitchen where he found the bag of kibble in the cupboard under the counter and fed the dog a handful. He rolled the bag tight and took the leash from the coat hook where it was draped. Becca's headlamp fell off onto the floor. He'd almost forgotten it.

The courtyard hadn't looked pitch black, and he was pretty well accustomed to finding his way in dark places, even without the flashlight he'd left in his kit at home. But then he noticed a strand of Becca's long, brown hair caught in the elastic band of the headlamp, and he thought of how the sweat from her brow was in the band, collected on explorations they had taken together. He slipped it over his head and slipped the dog collar over Django's. With the leash in one hand and the bag of kibble in the other, he left the apartment, locking the door behind him.

He felt a wave of relief tinged with guilt when he reached the elevator. He hadn't searched the apartment to inventory any damage the police had done or to take anything else Becca might need, something she might not mention on the phone. While he'd been in there, he'd felt a strong urge to get what she'd asked for and get out quick. Before what? It seemed a little absurd that the people who had already grilled him about her and turned the place upside down would now put the heat on him again when all he'd taken was her dog. But what about the other side? If the government was interested in her possible connection to a terror cult, might not the cultists also be looking for her?

He almost went back in while he still could, just to see if he'd missed anything she might want him to find, but something in his gut told him he'd been lucky so far and shouldn't push it.

Django whined at the elevator gate, and that decided him. He pulled it open and stepped in with the dog at his heels.

Outside, the air was colder than when he'd entered. His breath fogged in front of him, a white cloud in the beam of the headlamp when he turned it on. A few flickering stars shone through the thin gauze of cloud. A sliver of moon hung like horns over the squat buildings to the east. Django was tugging at the leash, sniffing at the sidewalk and pulling him toward the courtyard.

Light spilled over his boots from an approaching car, and he trotted along behind the dog, letting the leash pull him into the shadows before the car came nearer.

Weeds brushed his jeans. Broken glass crunched underfoot. The pale beam from the headlamp splashed over the brick wall in front of him, contracting from a flood to a small spotlight as he approached it.

Django lifted his leg on a mound of crab grass, then sniffed along the wall until he found a brick he liked and hosed that down as well. Rafael swiveled his head to aim the light into the far corner of the courtyard, but the shadows were too deep there and the weak light too far away to illuminate that most likely hiding place. He knew his nerves were getting the better of him, knew that if anyone were hiding here, Django would have already launched into one of his territorial barking fits.

What if Becca *is hiding in here somewhere?*

The thought made his heart skip, but the dog would have smelled her, too, and would have dragged him over to her, whining.

Django was at his side now, staring up expectantly, like he wanted another handful of kibble for having finished his business, the second urine stain sinking into the porous brick wall behind him, fading from black to gray, and steaming in the pallid light.

"Don't have to poop, huh?" Rafael asked. "Guess that figures if you haven't been fed yet." He rubbed the dog between the ears and recalled the time Becca had shown him the piss stains in the UV light at the asylum.

He reached up to the headlamp, not daring to hope, and put his finger on the button, then paused, turning to look back at the passage to the street. No silhouettes there, and the building across the way was dark. He wondered if there were agents behind those dark windows with zoom lenses or night-vision goggles. He sighed, turned back to the wall, shielding it with his body, and clicked the headlamp from white to ultraviolet.

Becca's neat, slanting handwriting glowed across three bricks: *Pick me up at X1 at 10:00. Bring Django. Ditch your phone.*

It took him a minute to figure it out, but X1 had to be the site of their first expedition together. He wondered if she organized the photo files that way. The men looking for her would have been through those files by now, and if they had already found this bit of neon graffiti with their own forensic flashlights, they might be picking her up right now. But he thought she wouldn't have bothered using a code if it was one she'd used before. This message was meant to be something only he would understand. He covered the light with his hand, switched it off, and looked over his shoulder.

"C'mon, Django," he said with a tug on the leash, "Time to go rescue the nice lady who rescued you."

Chapter 17

Nina Rothkopf was on the edge of her seat when the phone rang. In her left hand she held a glass of Pinot, in her right the TV remote. She kept forgetting she was holding the glass, but then her onyx bracelet would chime against the stem and recall it to mind and she would take a sip, only dimly aware of the way the light from the TV tinted the pale gold liquid with a chlorinated hue. The second floor of the brownstone was dark, as she'd also neglected to turn on the lights when the daylight had drained from the windows.

The object of her fixation was a 36" flat screen in a mahogany armoire. On a normal night, its doors might never be opened. She liked the cabinet more than the technology it housed and preferred reading to television. She watched movies and news occasionally and certainly could have afforded a bigger screen if she'd wanted one, but she'd been happy to surrender the big wall-mounted unit in the divorce, happy to buy a smaller one and stow it behind dark-wood panels. The idea of orienting an entire room of her home around a shrine to the idiot lantern repulsed her. But tonight, she was kneeling at the altar, tonight she was riveted to the word from on high: the apocalyptic sermons of the sages of cable news.

She was so entranced that at first she didn't hear the phone ringing. If the intrusion had been sirens, her ears would have been tuned to them, and she might have gone to the window to peek through the curtains. She had stood at the window after pouring the wine and had watched the black armored cars rumbling down Beacon Street at dusk.

According to the talking heads, there had been another terror event, this one at Copley Square, and again few details were being relayed, but that hadn't kept the commentators from filling hours with guarded speculation and dire predictions. If anything, the lack of specific details made the coverage more compelling. Nina understood the psychological dynamics of this better than most viewers, but the rational knowledge that she was being strung along with mystery, suspense, and omission hadn't kept her from falling under its spell.

Her phone sat on the end table at her elbow. Earlier she'd found a photo on Twitter, posted by a bystander at Copley. Apparently the horrors this person had witnessed defied description in a series of 140 character tweets, but the photo had depicted bloodstains on the concrete skirt of the Hancock Tower. It had been taken through a shattered widow on the third floor, and the profile of the tweeter indicated that he worked there. The tweet before the photo post read:

> Bullet just took out a window on our floor and hit the ceiling. No one hurt. Looks like police in combat gear down there. #CopleyTerror

The tweets following the photo suggested that the intrepid phone reporter on the scene had photographed the bloodstain only after watching how it had come to be there:

Something just impaled somebody. Body lifted off the ground. too slow to be gunfire that burst the chest. #Copleyterror #holyfuckingshit

There is something INVISIBLE down there killing. Ppl in blk robes just dispeared. #CopleyTerror

Nina had searched the hash tag #CopleyTerror, but it hadn't caught on yet, and returning to the feed of @Benjamins_Boston she had found the tweets deleted and the photo purged.

After that she called her daughter and made her promise not to leave her apartment. It was tempting to try to drive to her, but Nina reminded herself that impulsive action tended to make things worse. They would weather the storm in known locations, and things would look different in the morning.

The wine might have helped calm her nerves if she could remember to drink it, but most of what she had swallowed since setting the phone down was a distillation of disinformation and doublespeak issuing in harmony from all available channels. She was well acquainted with the dialect from her failed marriage. But a few facts for civilians were repeated like a drumbeat: The MBTA was in lockdown. Copley Square was off limits. Highways were not closed yet, but roadblock checkpoints were being erected. Citizens were urged to shelter in place and avoid all nonessential travel.

Nina realized that her gaze had wandered from the television screen and settled on one of the carved ebony tribal masks mounted on the wall beside the armoire. She wondered what agency lurked behind the mask of the media in Boston tonight.

Her marimba ringtone finally caught her attention, and she turned to the little rectangle of light beside her. Setting the wine glass down and picking the phone up, she didn't recognize the number. Probably a patient. It was a wonder they weren't *all* placing emergency calls to her tonight. Most of them were paranoid on a good day.

"Nina? It's Becca Philips."

"Becca. Are you okay?"

"I don't know." Her voice carried a tone familiar to Nina: the sound of someone who has been holding it together, keeping anxieties wound up tight, and now at the simple invitation of a trusted counselor, is finally breaking down.

"Is it the news? Or did something happen to *you?*"

A pause, a long mucousy drag of indrawn breath, then: "It's the same, Nina. I'm involved in this."

That made her sit up straight and put the wine glass down. But then, troubled people often believed they were at the center of epochal events. "Involved *how*, Becca?"

"Um...I have client confidentiality, right?"

"Of course you do. But do you understand the limits of that?"

"No. What are they?"

"If you intend to harm someone. If you're involved with terrorists."

"I'm not going to harm anyone...." Becca hesitated. Nina could hear a burst of breath distorting the phone speaker as the girl sighed out her resolve. She waited it out.

"You know the dreams I was having about monsters?" Becca said.

"Yes, of course."

"I started seeing the same kinds of things in my infrared photos."

"Becca...that could be like looking at an inkblot. Humans have a great capacity to see meaningful patterns in chaos."

"No. Listen. The government seized my camera and computer, my hard drives, because they wanted to see what I saw. They were looking for the same creatures, expecting them to break through—"

"Break through?"

"—because they saw it happen on the train. They saw something break through from that *other layer*, and some people can see it without dreaming, some can see it without a special camera, and some people *want to see it*, they *want to see the monsters*...." Becca's voice was brimming with barely constrained hysteria, but she regained control before Nina could ask who wanted to see the monsters.

"I know it sounds crazy. *I* would think it was crazy if I heard it a few weeks ago. And I did, I met a man, a homeless man who was spewing this same insane shit, but then I took a picture of a *thin place* where they pulled him through, or he walked through, or *cut* his way through with a goddamn cat laser…." She laughed. It might have mutated into a sob in the distortion of her breath through the speaker. "Oh, shit, I'm not helping my case here, I know. But this man who knew, I found his diary and I think he might have even been a student of my grandmother's books…. Anyway, I saw him again. I saw him come back out in a different part of town, wounded and dying."

"It's an incredible story, Becca. What do you need from me? Are the authorities looking for you?"

"They let me go. Well, not really. They wanted me to take more pictures of what's happening. But all hell broke loose and I got away. I don't know if they care about me anymore. But I think they want my camera. I don't know. They'd probably lock me up again if they found me, just because that would be simplest while they sort things out."

"Where are you now?"

Becca ignored the question. "It all reminds me of the stories my Gran told me when I was a girl. I think she would have known what this is, and I'm starting to wonder about her death. Was it really natural causes, whatever the fuck that means? Was she a threat to someone? And I know I sound like I'm raving paranoid, I do, I *know* I do. But if you'd seen some of the shit I've seen, Nina, you would be too. I'm sorry…I don't know why I called you. It's good to be able to talk about it with someone who knows me, someone…objective."

Silence on the live air between them.

Nina said, "It seems like a remarkable coincidence that your photos would capture an occult phenomena your grandmother studied. That is what you think happened, yes? That your process accidentally documented something she speculated about?"

"Yeah, that was what I was thinking. But now that you say it, I wonder if it *wasn't* a coincidence. She encouraged my interest in photography. She used to talk about how it was an almost sacred modern art because it was all about light and shadow and perception, seeing reality from certain angles...I used to think she was a bit off her rocker, you know, it all sounded the same to me after a while, growing up with her and her metaphysical rambling. But she introduced me to my first mentor, and now I wonder if she wanted him to teach me alternate processes because she knew that if they ever came through, they would appear first at the edges of the visible spectrum—"

"You lost me there."

"—and in the dreams of certain people. Cultists who trained themselves for it, artists, madmen, maybe even people with a genetic predisposition...."

"Becca," Nina said cautiously, "I'm not judging you. I hope you don't feel that I have in the past. In fact, I encouraged you to explore your dreams and try to get to the bottom of their meaning. I only prescribed the medication to stop them because you were suffering."

"I think the dreams meant exactly what they looked like. The monsters don't symbolize anything."

"You think they're real."

"So do the men in the black armor. Look out your window. Turn on the TV. Of course they're real."

Nina felt a frisson pass over her scalp. Some animal part of her resonated with the simplicity of the statement. These were not clinical conditions. The wine, the darkness of the room, the furtive, redacted tone of the newscasts she'd immersed herself in. She was losing her objectivity.

"What do you want, Becca? Why did you call me?"

"I *want* you to judge me, Nina."

"What do you mean? Judge your sanity?"

"No, my ability. I keep going back and forth between thinking I should turn myself in and let other people handle this, and thinking that I might be the only one who can solve it because of something my grandmother left behind for me."

"What's that?"

"I can't tell you. And I don't know how much of the way I'm seeing this has to do with my Seasonal Affective Disorder, but it seems like my family's fingerprints are all over this, and I feel like I might owe it to my Gran to stop it. And I just need to ask you to forget for a minute that this sounds insane and pretend I'm asking you about a challenge you can believe in, because I need to know if you think I have it in me to face monsters."

The doorbell rang. Nina jumped, almost dropped the phone.

"Becca, I practice psychotherapy, not sorcery. You're asking me to endorse a quest?" She regretted the words as soon as she said them, but she couldn't take them back. The doorbell had jarred her and snatched the honest reply before she could utter it: *I believe you are much stronger than you give yourself credit for.*

"I shouldn't have called. I'll let you go."

"Wait.... You've reminded me of something I read in a journal. There was a study done recently. A pharma company in Cambridge. I think they were a subsidiary of Limbus; they were working on an insomnia drug that ended up inadvertently causing hallucinations. It started with all of the trial subjects having similar dreams, and then, at higher dosages, hallucinating while awake."

The doorbell chimed again. Nina rushed her words, "They abandoned the sleep drug and changed tack, hoping to develop an anti-psychotic. I don't know if it panned out, but I'll look into it. It's probably not something I could get without enrolling you in a study, but maybe in a week or so when the emergency's over—"

"Goodbye, Nina. I don't need blinders. I'm sorry I bothered you."

"Wait." Nina stood, pulled her robe tighter around her T-shirt, and started down the stairs. "Becca, you need help. Let me help you. Call me in the morning so I know you're okay, and if the city isn't in lockdown, I'll see you. Where are you staying tonight? Are you with anyone?"

Nina was at the door now. She peered through the leaded glass in the side panel. Shit, it was Jason. What the hell did he want? The phone was silent, but the display showed the timer still running. Becca hadn't hung up.

"How can I help you if you don't trust me, Becca?"

"I'm going to try to get out of the city tonight. I need to look for something at my Gran's house. I'll call you."

"Be careful…."

The timer stopped. The call ended.

* * *

Jason Brooks could see a distorted figure in the glass. On any other day he might only be annoyed by it, not unnerved, but today it reminded him too much of Copley, the creatures, and their way of shifting in and out of some parallel place. But then the door opened and his ex-wife's face appeared in the narrow gap above the chain. She was holding her cell phone close to the hollow of her throat, and he wondered who she'd been talking to. Had it been Heather, who wouldn't take her own father's calls? A man? Or was there a man upstairs—the reason for the chain still on the door?

"Nina. Why the chain?"

"Well, the city is under siege by some kind of terror cell for starters, but I'm sure you know more about it than I do."

"Come on. You saw it was me through the glass. May I come in? *Please?*"

"What do you want, Jason?"

He looked at his shoes, at the chain, and stuffed his fists into his long, black trench coat. The temperature had taken a dive with the sun.

She closed the door and he had one of those moments he'd had often as a cop when he thought it wasn't going to open again, and in this case it wouldn't be okay to kick it in. But she was only undoing the chain, and seeing as there was no space for the two of them to share in the foyer, he knew that letting him in the door meant letting him into the apartment. He closed the door behind him and followed her up the stairs. At the top they came to a dark room illuminated only by the cold light of the TV flickering on the west wall and the ceiling. Nina swept her palm over a switch and a pair of opaque white sconces lit the stairwell and most of the den.

Something brushed his leg. It was Verily, the cat, arching her back and curling her gray tail. Well, at least *one* of the females in his life didn't hold a grudge. When she jumped onto the banister and stretched her neck toward him, he rewarded her with a scratch at the base of her skull, knowing as he gave it that he'd be picking downy fur off his coat sleeve for days.

Nina sat on the hassock, her hands on her knees, but she offered him neither a seat nor a drink. The message was clear: *Get down to it or get out.*

He shot a glance over his shoulder at the TV, hoping she'd turn it off. She didn't, but it was muted, and that was all the concession he was going to get out of her.

"I'm here because Heather won't take my calls. I need you to get her out of the city."

"Why?"

He waved a hand at the TV without looking at it.

"Use your words, Jason. You're a big boy."

"You know I can't talk about it."

"Right. So I'm supposed to flail around blindly and protect our daughter without any details to guide me."

"You both should have left after the flood. Coastal cities.... *You* know it's only a matter of time before the coast is in fucking Worcester. Why wait? Why not get out after the first disaster? We've been over this, Nina. Too many times."

"You're saying this is about the sea level? I thought it was about terrorism."

"I'm saying you could have made arrangements over the past year. It's not like I haven't warned you, but here's the next state of emergency and you probably don't even have a kit packed for it. Do you?"

Nina sighed and shook her head in dismay.

"What does that mean?" he asked. "What are you shaking your head at?"

"You want to save us? Is that it? Like in some action movie? You think that will make Heather forgive you?"

"I just want to know she's safe. And you, too."

"Because it's dramatic, whatever the hell it is we're even talking about—some act of terror—is dramatic, so you want to be a hero. But when we lived together...Jesus, James."

"What? When we lived together *what?* Just say it, go on."

"You didn't lock your gun up, you didn't change the batteries in the smoke detectors, you didn't have a plan for the kinds of everyday dangers that actually take lives. And unless there's a suitcase nuke in Boston right now, I'd say our chances of getting caught in the crossfire are pretty slim. She's staying in until it blows over. She promised me."

"She promised you."

"Yes."

"She's nineteen. Think of the things you promised *your* parents when you were her age."

"You *would* tell me if there was a nuke in the city."

He dragged his fingers through his hair. "You have no idea. *That's* the bar I have to meet to get you to listen to me? A nuke? Why can't you trust me just a little?"

If she knew there were drones headed for Boston right now, talk about taking out the city with a micro warhead, she'd do whatever I asked. And this apartment is probably bugged.

"I lived with *you* long enough, and heard you comment on the news enough times to do some deduction," she said. "*Something* went off at Harvard Square, but the city's still here, so I figure if they had something big they would have used it first, right?"

He had to admit that she was throwing his own kind of logic back at him, borrowed from days when she'd scared easier and he'd learned how to reassure her. "It's not that simple," he said, "Something is changing, and it's starting here, in Boston. The people who are exposed to it may never be the same. The way they see the world, see reality, will be fundamentally changed. Not for the better. It makes you vulnerable. It's hard to explain."

Nina's face had changed while he spoke, and he knew he wasn't doing a very good job of explaining, probably *couldn't* even if he were allowed to be more explicit, but for a second, before she guarded it, he was tempted to think she believed him.

"What is it? What have they unleashed?"

"I don't know, honey." He almost flinched at the word as it left his mouth. This talk about mortality was erasing years.

She was standing before him now. He didn't know when she'd risen from the hassock. One of her slender hands reached for his face; slowly, the way a hand goes toward a potentially dangerous animal, one that might bite. He was looking away from her at the floor when she said, "You've seen it." It wasn't a question. She would have made a good interrogator, but she was a better shrink.

She touched his stubbly chin, grazed her thumb over the dimple there, the one she used to like. He wanted to get out, almost regretted coming here, and at the same time, he wanted to pick her up and carry her into the bedroom and fuck her and somehow he knew that she would let him. A tear ran onto her fingertip, bridging the distance between them even as it was born of the knowledge of the void that yawned between their respective worlds now—hers the ordinary one they had once built a life in, a life he had wrecked; and his, a realm of monsters.

He swallowed and cleared his throat. The sound was loud and harsh in the silent room. "Heather should have a choice," he said. "She shouldn't have to see things she'll never be able to *unsee*...shouldn't have to live in the world I'm living in now without even knowing she had a choice."

Nina took her hand away and looked at the water on her fingers.

"It's not contagious," he said, "Not contagious except by hearing. I don't know how fast it will spread, but it's starting here. If you listen to me, you'll have a head start. Go anywhere. Just get her in a car and go."

But Nina wasn't listening anymore. She was staring over his shoulder at the TV as if she'd seen a ghost. Brooks turned to the muted screen, and there was Rebecca Philips in a box beside a news anchor. One of the self-portraits SPECTRA had pulled from her hard drive? If so, it was one of the few that wasn't a nude with ghostly exposure trails and weird shadows. Maybe a friend had taken it. She stood in front of a graffiti-stricken wall, the hint of a smile almost lighting her haunted face.

Agent Brooks met his ex-wife's eyes and recognized the glare of the guilty. "You know her, Nina?"

Chapter 18

Becca slouched in the back seat of the Jeep Cherokee Rafael had borrowed from a drummer friend who'd been happy to go a few days without parking tickets, her head against the foggy glass, Django sleeping in her lap.

She had finally stopped searching the night for flashers and had been drifting in and out of consciousness, lulled by the drone and vibration of the road, only hanging on because Raf had no idea how to get where they were going and had ditched his GPS-enabled phone before picking her up at the abandoned school.

They had followed Route 1A up the coast and found that, away from the highways, the warnings of roadblocks were baseless, at least so far. There weren't many cars on the road until they joined Route 128 and encountered something of an exodus to points north. But before long, they were alone again, wending their way through streets familiar to Becca, coming into Arkham along the Aylesbury Pike.

Django perked up and crawled across Becca's lap to sniff at the cracked window where the sulfuric low-tide reek of the Miskatonic wafted into the vehicle. As they dropped around the shoulder of Hangman's Hill, the town opened before them: huddled rows of slouching gambrel rooftops punctuated by the rising spires of several churches, bisected by the silvered black curve of the river and frosted by the glow of a cloudbank reflecting the lights of the surrounding mill towns. Arkham appeared to have tucked itself in by midnight, except for the iron lamps lining the paths of the Miskatonic quadrangle.

Becca leaned between the seats and directed Rafael to take a right onto Boundary, followed by a left onto Crane, a quiet lane of mostly renovated houses, many owned by the university and leased to tenured faculty. She felt the tension in her weary body finally beginning to uncoil when they pulled up in front of number 19, a modest, cream-colored house with black shutters and a central brick chimney. Gran's house.

Becca passed Django's leash to Rafael and dug around in her army bag for her key ring. "I hope my uncle hasn't changed the locks yet. He's probably too cheap for that, but he might have just to keep my dad from crashing here."

She found the key and slotted it into the lock, turned the knob and gave it the same old lift as she opened it, a time-worn habit to minimize the noise of the ill-fitting frame, a remnant of days when sneaking in at midnight would have woken Gran.

It had been apparent from the street that the house was dark, but stepping inside, Becca felt a wave of grief wash over her at the cold emptiness of the place. Somehow the vacancy of the house she had grown up in made the loss more visceral than the body at the funeral had—that cosmeticized shell that didn't quite resemble the woman she had loved. Here, in the silent interval before a realtor removed the scuffed furniture and the wax-stained carpets, before the painters changed the color of the walls just as the embalmer had changed the color of her Gran's complexion, there was still a sense of the woman's soul in the musty air. Here, where Becca had memories attached to the scuffs and stains, she could still smell the woman who had been a mother to her, could almost hear her voice.

Drawing the mingled perfume of moldy curtains, old incense, and baking spices deep into her lungs, she knew that this was the smell of home. And it would soon be sold to pay off debts.

She set her bag on the couch and flicked a switch by the door, filling the room with warm illumination from a lamp on an end table—an orange and yellow beaded globe suspended from a curling iron arm. A star pattern of stained-glass diamonds set amid the beads and plaster gave the lamp a Turkish vibe. Gran had acquired it on one of her travels, and it had always reminded Becca of a sunrise in miniature. There were similar lamps and hanging globes in other rooms. Becca recalled the cool blue and purple glow of the one on Gran's desk in her study. The woman had abhorred plainness and had brought the rich cultures she'd studied into every room of her home. Rafael was turning on his heel, taking in other adornments: the African statues, the framed illuminated manuscripts, the Persian rugs and jade carvings.

Becca felt a tingle of relief at their presence. That her uncle Alan hadn't yet cleared the place out and boxed everything up for sale was an unexpected blessing. She had been under too much stress since the funeral to even begin to confront and process her feelings. She had come here in search of something—that was true, there was an objective to the visit—but she realized now that she had also come seeking refuge, seeking a sense of Catherine's presence. Maybe what she sought was still here. She collapsed onto the couch with a bone-weary sigh.

"You grew up here?" Rafael asked, taking it in.

"It seems a lot smaller after living in a warehouse. Or...with her not here."

They had risked stopping at a convenience store on 1A, and now Rafael found the kitchen and set a bag of food and a six-pack of Sam Adams on the counter. Becca watched him across the opening in the wall through which she had so often talked with Catherine while the older woman cooked. Rafael opened and closed drawers until he found a bottle opener. Becca knew he'd succeeded when a sound like a spinning coin winding down reached her ears.

Django, finished sniffing out the living room, jumped onto the couch and laid his head in her lap. She stroked the downy fur around his ears. Rafael returned and set her beer on the end table beside her. She pulled herself up, opened the end-table drawer, and fished around for a coaster. There was a cash-register receipt in the drawer, penciled with a list of words in Hebrew and Greek distilled to numeric calculations. Becca felt a pang, as she removed the cork coasters, passed one to Rafael, and slid the drawer shut on the scrap of paper. She had grown up surrounded by similar notes; they'd been more common than grocery lists.

"Cheers," she said. "To getting the hell out of the city."

Rafael laughed. "You make it sound like a weekend getaway." Clinking his bottle against hers, he said, "To not spending the night in custody."

After a long pull on the bottle, Becca got up and retrieved the dog food from the jeep. She poured some into a Tupperware bowl, filled another with water, and set the pair down in a corner of the kitchen. Django, who had tracked her every move, took to them with relish.

Rafael waved his hand at the table where he'd set two plates: one with his own plastic-wrapped Italian sub, the other with a sad-looking peanut-butter sandwich and a banana for Becca.

"Thanks, Raf." She scratched the back of her head and her stiff hair failed to fully resettle. She knew she must look a wreck and hardly had the energy to even eat. She wanted a hot shower and sleep, but to stay the night here would be risky. If SPECTRA still considered her a priority, they would pay a visit to her prior residence sooner or later.

"Sit down," Rafael said, "You gotta eat, girl."

She nodded but didn't sit. The idea of lingering was making her nervous.

"What? You already have your peanut-butter quota for the day? Guess I should have got spaghetti—the other thing you eat," he teased.

"No, it's good, it's fine. I just need to check the study first."

"You said she had a lot of books, right? Could take a while. At least have a bite, or take it with you."

She shuddered theatrically. "Handling books with peanut butter on my fingers? Gran would have another stroke. I just need to know they're still there. Then I'll eat."

Rafael unwrapped his sub and dug in with an enthusiasm to rival Django's. The dog sniffed the air beside the table, and when no cold cuts were forthcoming, turned and trotted after Becca, his tail swishing against the narrow walls of the hallway.

At the top of a steep staircase Becca came to the hushed, carpeted sanctum of the second floor, Gran's domain. When she'd lived here, Becca's bedroom had been on the ground floor, and every trip up the stairs to the old woman's bedroom, private bath, and study had brought a feeling of crossing a threshold and passing into more rarefied air. Voices were kept at library volume here, and doors were to be knocked at before entering. Knowing that Gran was gone and never coming back did little to diminish Becca's sense of reverence for the woman's domain, and as she paused at the bedroom door, she almost raised her hand to rap her knuckles gently against it before pushing it open.

The room was dark, the bed made. The green globe lamp sat on a white doily where it always had. The same wood and stone artifacts still congregated around the bed: guardian figures rendered in plaques on the walls, statuettes on the bureau. The Sumerian Marduk hunting the winged dragon Tiamat with his arrows and thunderbolt trident; the Archangel Michael brandishing his flaming sword and grinding the serpent beneath his boot heel; the thousand-armed bodhisattva, Chenrezig, his limbs fanned out like spokes in a wheel of weapons and gifts for the protection and aid of all sentient beings. As a girl, Becca had heard the tales of these heroes and countless others. And now, with one foot in a wedge of light from the hallway, she offered up a silent prayer to the retinue of protectors who had watched over her Gran through all her nights of dreaming, and petitioned them to accompany the great lady on her final journey through the deepest dream of all.

At the end of the hall, she came to the carven oak door of the study, and for the first time in her life, found it ajar. Something squirmed in her stomach. She pressed her fingers against the wood, and watched it drift inward with a rising whine.

It was dark, but as she stepped over the threshold from the Persian carpet runner onto the hardwood floor of the study, she knew from the echo—before her eyes could even adjust to the faint streetlight through the window—that shelves laden with leather and cloth were not absorbing her footsteps.

The curator of the university library had already been here with his movers. Uncle Alan or Catherine's attorney had let them in, ushered them up the stairs, and in accordance with the late scholar's last will and testament, granted them access to her most private room.

Becca found the light switch. Ripping the shadows from that room was like pulling a shroud off of a naked corpse. The bookshelves, all of them, were bare.

* * *

Django was waiting for her at the bottom of the stairs, sitting on his haunches and swishing his tail. She had told him to stay, and to her surprise, he had. Maybe training him would be easier than she'd hoped. Or maybe he was afraid of some lingering vibe on the second floor. Becca could well remember being afraid of the study herself when she'd been small. The door had seemed to tower above her, locked more to keep abominations in than people out. Had she acquired that vague notion through an accumulation of things Gran had said to keep her curiosity in check? Or from scraps of conversations with colleagues over tea in the den? Had Becca *seen* things she had thrust into the dark recesses of her mind? Things that would have made it impossible for her to grow up sane if left unrepressed?

The smell of old leather and parchment lingered in her memory. And incense. And ink. And something...else. Something fishy. She patted Django and went to the kitchen for her sandwich. Peanut butter didn't exactly go great with the taste of beer in her mouth, and she wanted to finish the beer more than she wanted to eat at this point, but she knew she needed the sustenance. She took an ice pack from the freezer for her aching wrist and carried it with the sandwich into the den, where she found Rafael kneeling in front of the fireplace, positioning chunks of firewood from the iron ring around some balled up newspaper, his boxers hanging out of his jeans.

"That might not be such a great idea, Raf."

He looked at her over his shoulder, eyebrows raised.

"Having the lights on is probably risky enough, but if someone sees smoke from the chimney, we might draw unwanted attention sooner."

"It's cold in here, Becca. I tried turning on the heat, but it didn't kick in. You think they shut off the gas?"

"I don't know. But I'm not sure we should spend the night here. And I sure as hell don't want to burn the place down." She settled on the couch, and took a tug on her bottle. "For all I know the chimney could have a bird's nest in it. I don't remember Gran *ever* having a fire in that thing."

"Ever? There's firewood."

"Pretty dusty firewood. Seems like it's been there forever. I think it was just for show."

Rafael stuck his head into the fireplace and peered up the chimney, as if he had any chance of seeing an obstruction in the dark channel. Kneeling, with his arms akimbo, he looked over his little teepee of wood and paper, then sighed and got up, fetched another beer from the kitchen, and joined Becca on the couch.

She laid her head on his shoulder. "I really miss her."

Rafael took her hand and squeezed it.

"Of course you do. She raised you. It's gonna take time."

"It just seems wrong, being here and not hearing her voice. After I moved to Boston, when I visited, I'd always hear her voice calling from the kitchen. So excited to see me. And when she hugged you, she'd squeeze the hell out of you. So strong for her size."

"She sounds cool."

"She would have liked you. Would have made you tea and told you stories all night. And she would have wanted to hear all about Brazil. Would have told you things your grandparents believed that you never knew."

"So your dad, he just took off after your mother died, and dumped you with her?"

"It's complicated. He was afraid."

"Of what?"

Becca sighed. "My mother couldn't deal with my grandmother. At all."

"She sounds pretty easy to get along with."

"As a person, yes, if she liked you."

"And she didn't like your mother?"

"Not really. I was probably too young to be a reliable source on that, but you pick stuff up. Gran was into some dark things...her research. I know if she were here, she'd understand what's happening now. She'd be able to tell those agents something about the nature of it, maybe even how to stop it."

"Maybe someone at the university, whoever has her books now, you know, maybe a colleague could help. But what does it have to do with you and me? Maybe we should just get on the road and drive. Get away from it."

"That's what my dad did. He ran away."

"From what? You think something your Gran...*called up* is the cause of what's happening?"

"No. She used to dabble, I think, to test the validity of her theories. But that was before she realized just how serious the consequences could be. Before my grandfather went insane and my mother killed herself."

"*Jesus.*"

"I try to forgive my dad for not forgiving Gran. I try to remember what he lost."

"No. Fuck that. *You* lost the same, and then you lost him too. He should have put you first and stuck it out, or taken you with him."

Becca sighed. It was the same old black hole in her heart, and nothing new to be said about it. The same unresolved loss and abandonment, shrouded in the mystery of having been so young at the time that everyone had tried to keep her in the dark, to shelter her. As if that were possible.

"You think your mother saw something?"

She nodded.

"When you lived here did you ever see anything? Any kind of supernatural manifestation?"

Becca sat staring at the inert firewood, sifting her memory. She put her fingers to her lips and laughed. The sound startled Rafael.

"What? You remember something?"

"Yeah," she said, smiling, "But it's a good memory. I'd forgotten all about it." She pointed the neck of her beer bottle at the hearth. "The only mythical creature I ever saw evoked in this house was Santa Claus."

"Huh?"

"For real. It must have been my Grandpa because I was young enough that he wouldn't have been in the asylum yet. Fucking Santa Claus in a red suit with the beard, boots and all climbed out of that fireplace one Christmas Eve while I was crashed on the couch with the tree all lit up. I totally forgot about that until now."

"You sure it wasn't a dream?"

"I'm sure. They set it up to trick me somehow. I think they let me sleep on the couch just so I'd see it. And it was *perfect*. The sack came out first, and then Santa. How awesome is that?"

Rafael was squinting at her with a half smile. Then he committed and the smile kicked out into a skeptical smirk. He shook his head, his dreadlocks swaying. "There's no way a man *and* a sack could fit in there. He had to be crouching with his ass in the fireplace, waiting for you to wake up."

Becca sat up with a jolt.

She slid off the couch onto her knees, crawled on all fours to the fireplace, and started tossing the split logs out onto the rug. She uncrumpled one of Rafael's newspaper balls and laid the sheet on the hearthstone to keep the soot off her clothes as she crawled into the black aperture. On a typical expedition she didn't give a damn if she got dirty, but on the run without a change of clothes and the possibility of her picture on TV, she didn't need to be marked in any way that would attract attention.

She ran her fingertips over the bricks at the back and realized that the black coloration didn't come off. It might have even been spray-painted on to create the illusion of long use, but for all she knew there had never been a fire set here. Ever. The newsprint was more likely to blacken her hands and pants than the stones were. She swept the paper away and crouched in the brick frame.

It was a large fireplace, probably larger than most, but Rafael was right—it was too small to contain a man in a fat suit. She ran her fingers over the bricks, pushing on each in turn, and feeling a little silly. Wasn't that the device always used in old movies? The key brick in a wall? She ran a finger across the seams—top, bottom, and sides, felt around behind the hearth frame, and *there:* a cold metal lever, rough with rust or oxidation. She jiggered it, unsure of how to turn, push, or pull it, and then getting a finger underneath what felt like the short branch of an L, she jogged it, and with a thump, the brick wall at the rear shifted and settled. She gave it a push, and it swung inward on invisible hinges.

A door. A patch of darkness delineated only by the light of the table lamp falling on dust motes caught in the gossamer cobwebs billowing gently around the tunnel mouth on a faint draught from below. Somehow she knew that the stale air she tasted came from below and not behind or above. This was not a doorway onto a recessed room hidden in the architecture of the ground floor, nor a stairway leading to the second floor or attic. It led down to a basement she'd never known existed, a hidden cellar with no other door. She *knew* this as she stared into the blackness. Before the stairs were even lit, she knew they were there.

Rafael, beside her, closer than she'd realized, said, "I'll grab the headlamp."

But before he could stand up, Becca had found a chain of brass beads and pulled on it gently, afraid it might break in her fingers. A bare, yellow bulb came on, revealing a tight, winding, stone-and-mortar stair. She shuffled in, feet first.

Rafael put a hand on her shoulder. "Let me go first; make sure it's safe."

She shook her head, staring into the tunnel beyond her boots. Then she tilted her chin up and planted a quick kiss on his lips over her shoulder before using his momentary surprise to slip out of his grip and push her butt off the floor with her hands braced behind her.

Django darted into the space between them, sniffing at the musty air, and then Becca's feet were on the stairs, her upper body and head clearing the doorframe, and passing the faux brick wall with its artfully cut fragments. She scraped down the first three steps on the seat of her pants like a half-awake child bobbing down a staircase on Christmas morning, until the ceiling was high enough for her to take the remainder standing.

The curve of the stairs prevented the dim bulb from illuminating the room at the bottom, and again she groped in the dark, feeling along a beam at the obvious height for a light switch. Her fingers found the edge of a metal plate mounted on a two-by-four. With an indrawn breath to brace herself and a click, a small stone cell lined with crowded bookshelves flickered into existence.

The chamber was furnished with a small desk and a solitary folding chair. The stone and mortar of the stairs gave way to a smooth cement floor covered in elaborate chalk diagrams: multi-rayed stars, sigils, and names rendered in a thorny, arcane alphabet. Becca put her hand out behind her into Rafael's stomach and whispered, "Watch where you step." The whisper felt right for the place, though she couldn't have said why. It was a solitary, unoccupied room.

On the table lay a short stack of books and one large tome open to a page somewhere in the middle, a glass magnifier perched on the right-facing page. Beside the open book, a black silk cloth lay draped over a globe-shaped object the size of a child's skull. All was lit by a frosted white orb in an iron cage anchored in a high corner, one of the only spaces not covered with sagging bookshelves.

Becca wondered how her grandparents had furnished the small cell, how they had fit everything in through the narrow stair. Her grandfather had been a handy sort of man, and she could picture him building the shelves and table in the same room where they would remain, but she had a feeling that the secret chamber predated her family's residence at 19 Crane Street. Miskatonic was one of the only universities in America renowned for occult studies. So why did Gran need a secret room with a hidden entrance? What authority had she been hiding this aspect of her work from? The second floor study had seemed sinister enough. Was there some lore that was forbidden even at Miskatonic?

Becca tiptoed over the chalk lines like a superstitious child avoiding cracks in the sidewalk, heard Django whining from the mouth of the fireplace above, and was grateful that he hadn't followed them down—his paws would smudge the protective circle. Clearly that was its purpose. But whether Gran had drawn it to keep things out or in she didn't know.

There was so much she didn't know as she settled into the creaking chair and looked over the open book. The text was handwritten in fine, ornate letters. She lowered her eye to the magnifier, but it did nothing to clarify the arcane script, which appeared to be in the same mode as the names traced on the floor. Gaining confidence, Becca flipped the left-facing pages and skimmed. The book was rife with abstract diagrams that blurred the boundaries between art, mathematics, and pornography. Triangles of stacked numbers, columns of those thorny letters, and cross sections of marine biological blasphemy.

The paper felt like living tissue between her moist fingers, and she let it fall back into place. She eyed the black-shrouded sphere and felt a chill course through her. She tried to remind herself that this room had lain beneath her bed for years, and that her dear, sweet Gran had been its mistress. But even a kindly grandfather's wood shop can be a lethal chamber of blades to a child untrained in their proper handling.

"*Damn,*" Rafael whispered behind her. "Creepy shit."

The faded spines of the stacked books drew her attention next, one in particular jumping out at her and causing her heart to beat wildly: *Mortiferum Indicium.* The book Maurice Ramirez had pointed her to with his dying words. She pulled it out of the stack, and another book clattered onto the desktop with it, a Moleskine journal, Catherine's notebook of choice.

Becca set the *Mortiferum* atop the broad, open page of the book with the diagrams and took the journal in her trembling hands.

She slipped the elastic band off, opened it, and fanned the pages beneath her thumb, watching as dated entries flickered past, giving way to blank pages at about the three-quarter mark. One phrase lingered under her eye long enough to read when a page snagged on her thumb for a fraction of a second: *have seen him in the depths of the glass, a slender man with no face, nearer each time I look.*

When she reached the virgin pages at the back, Becca snapped the journal shut. She felt a surge of guilt that breaching the secret room had failed to arouse. Maybe it was the familiarity of the neat script, which had filled years of telephone notes and birthday cards. She was reminded of her own journals documenting dreams, nightmares, and the living nightmare of her recurring depression, and knew that she wasn't ready to dive into the private diary of Catherine Philips.

It's not a dead woman's privacy you're worried about; you're afraid of her dark side. You know it's deeper than your own. It drove Grandpa insane and made Mommy kill herself and Daddy run to the bottle and the needle.

Becca drew a shuddering breath and slid the journal away from her.

"You okay?" Rafael asked.

"Yeah. You want to go watch the street? I don't know if we should stay much longer, but I found the book."

"I feel it too. Someone will come looking for you here. Take it with you to read later. This place is weirding me out."

She looked up at him and felt a weak, nervous smile forming on her dry lips. Lips that had kissed him what felt like a year ago, though it had only been minutes. "My fearless urban explorer is creeped out? After the abandoned asylums and tunnels, this is what finally does it for you? Chalk on the floor and musty books?"

He tried to smile back, but it went sour.

She squeezed his hand. "Yeah, me too," she said. But he was staring at the bulging black silk, spilled across the desk like a puddle of India ink. "It's that," he said, "I don't like it."

"Don't touch it."

He nodded and stepped away, retreating to the stairs but not climbing them. He sat on a tread. Django whined again and took a few tentative steps down. Rafael scratched the dog's lowered head.

Becca opened the white leather cover of *Mortiferum Indicium*, turned a blue-and-gold marbled endpaper, and came to the title page where she found the credit:

Translated from the Latin by Dr. Catherine Philips

She flipped the pages and took in a few lines:

> *The tongues of old are lost now to the corruption of the species. Even in the Black Pharaoh, the Vox Dei has been silenced in retribution for his sins against the Elder race. And so he bides his time, that usurper who came forth from the desert clothed in the robes of priestcraft. He who gave ill council to the heretic king Akhenaten and wrought calamity upon his kingdom, who unleashed a plague upon the royal family to seize the throne.*

Why was this book so important? She didn't have time to read it whole, and doubted her ability to make sense of it. Why had Maurice been so sure that she could gain something vital from these pages? She considered taking it with her back to Boston. It might fit in her bag. But she couldn't bring herself to pick it up. It seemed somehow safer for it to remain here, hidden from those who might have already sought its secrets and failed to find it. As long as the room remained hidden....

"Raf, can you close the back wall of the fireplace without locking us in?"

"Lemme see."

She heard him shuffling up the stairs, and Django skittering around in agitation, worried that their pack might be dividing. Rafael soothed him, and said, "Go see Becca, go to Becca."

She closed the tome and opened the journal again, deciding that a further invasion of Catherine's privacy was her only hope of narrowing the focus of her investigation. A note about what she had been working on at the time of her death, a reference to certain page numbers or passages in the *Mortiferum* might at least give Becca a point of entry into the book.

The contents of the journal both soothed and unsettled her, a sweet-and-sour feeling oscillating in her nerves. The handwriting was a balm for her grief, but the sense of the notes, scrawled urgently with jagged haste, made her stomach quiver as she read.

> *For the first time in my career I am crossing the line and dealing with a black-market trader. The path that led me to this man, an Iraqi refugee I will call Mr. K, has been fraught with peril. I wish I could deceive myself that my intentions were pure and that I planned to donate the artifact to the university once I obtain it, but to tell my colleagues of the acquisition would be to sacrifice my tenure, my retirement, and my reputation. Even at Miskatonic there are taboos. It wasn't always so, but certain lines of inquiry have left stains upon the university that no endowment of funds, no prestigious awards, and no revisionist history can remove. To study such things in the abstract, while frowned upon, has never been cause for expulsion; but if it were known that I have passed into the realm of practical experimentation, I would be blacklisted. And yet, how am I to test my theories if not by empirical trial?*
>
> *The theories of any science are not intrinsically good or evil. It is only through application that we may judge the morality of such forces as electricity and atomic energy. So it is for the powers of the spirit.*
>
> *But a folklorist is not expected to experiment with the theories of the primitives she studies. How is it any different, I ask, from the modern mathematician or physicist applying the formulae of Pythagoras?*
>
> *Sadly, I am between a rock and a hard place. To the world outside of academia, I would be a laughing stock, a delusional new-age charlatan, were I to publish my theories of a dimension parallel to our own inhabited by sublime forces, ancient and intelligent. And yet, among those who know*

enough of the occult history of our planet to connect the dots as I have, my desire to plumb the depths and put my theories to the test is anathema. To them I am worse than a witch. But can I blame them? I fear the price of the knowledge I seek, but I fear that ignorance of our unseen neighbors will one day cost us more.

Becca thumbed the journal open to a later entry:

...seen inside the stone. He has waited these long aeons for some reckless fool to stir him from the slumber of his exile, and now I have. God help me—if only I could believe a benign and merciful lord ruled the universe. I should never have acquired the black mirror. I should never have chanted it open. Some keys are best lost to history.

The entries became harder to read as the journal progressed, the hand and mind of the writer growing visibly more distressed. Becca could imagine those old hands: every gold ring, every blue vein in the liver-spotted, translucent skin. Another line drew her eye, glimpsed at random as she perused the final entries before the blank pages:

I finally understand Oppenheimer, now that it's too late to learn from his warning. I should have remembered him before it came to this, but I rue the hubris that seduced me, that led me like a lamb to slaughter by the tether of my damned curiosity. When he beheld the fire in the heart of that first mushroom cloud, he thought of Vishnu in the Bhagavad Gita, revealing his wrathful form to Arjuna. "Now I am become death, the destroyer of worlds." And now I am become death. Forgive me, Peter. If you can see me now, I beg you forgive me.

The image of her grandfather standing vacant and wraithlike in the asylum common room, staring at the courtyard flashed on Becca's mind.

What I came here pretending to be, I am becoming.

She could sense Rafael and Django pacing the floor behind her now. She knew she would take the journal with her, but she needed to see Catherine's last entry, to know her last thoughts, before closing the cover and leaving.

The final page was scant on narrative and long on equations, consisting mostly of an example of an art her grandmother had once explained to her in brief when Becca had asked her about the scraps of paper that littered all the surfaces of the house.

It's called Gematria, dear. In some languages every letter has a number value, and scholars like your grandmother like to amuse ourselves by puzzling out the value of a word.

Becca had only dimly grasped this at the time, but it had made her think of her mild-mannered Gran as a kind of secret agent with a decoder ring. The image had made her smile, and had stayed with her.

If you know the number of a word, and you find another word that has the same value, then you can meditate on the relation between them.

The oddness of the idea had also stayed with Becca. That different words could have an invisible affinity or resonance with each other based on a number they contained. Math wrapped in language like jewels hidden in fruit.

At the top of the last page, Becca found Catherine's final note:

הַגָּדֹל הַמָּאוֹר = 294
Genesis 1:16, The Greater Light.
Solomon, the architect employed by the Brotherhood of Solomon, built a stair to the sun with as many steps, at the hub of the wheel.
But where did you hide the Fire of Cairo, Peter? After you banished the beast their dread St. Jeremy called up, where did you hide it?

Something moved on the desk at Becca's elbow, and she startled. It was the black silk shroud sliding sideways. She grabbed at it but too late. Django had the end of it in his teeth, was pulling on it, growling. Becca, her mouth agape in helpless horror watched the cloth fall from the edge of the desk, exposing the object it had concealed. Django dropped the silk and erupted into a battery of barking. He sounded bigger than he was, bigger and wilder, a guardian bracing to make a stand, and Becca was staring into a perfect circle of polished black glass, tilted up at her like a mirror on a vanity.

A faceless man in a red robe with blue fire in his hair stared back at her, and she didn't know how a man with no eyes could stare and scrutinize, but she knew in the depths of her bowels that he did; he saw through every layer of her skin, through every cell like an x-ray, and his omniscient gaze somehow narrowed to a focus that she could feel by its coldness on the white-gold beetle that hung between her breasts.

The legs of the metal insect twitched, the wings fluttered, the pinchers clicked, and she watched the man in the mirror turn to another portal, another circle, a window to another place, and the shape of his jaw wavered as he spoke to someone there.

Soon, he would turn to face her again, and what would happen then? Would she go insane? Would she get up from this chair, this desk, this cellar vault with a single imperative screaming in her veins—to spill out her own blood by whatever means presented itself? She thought she just might.

Suddenly she knew that the battle of wills this faceless one had fought with Catherine Philips had been a protracted campaign; but with herself, in whom that strength of mind was diluted, it would be brief.

And now the dark face was turning to look at her again, but she couldn't make a sound in her throat, couldn't make her hand seize the silk, couldn't make her eyes look away. The beetle burned into the skin of her chest like a brand, and she felt rage emanating from it, felt a vengeance in the metal to match the sound of Django's barks, and knew that this was the opposite polarity to the coldness she had felt under the dark man's gaze, this heat emanating from a sentient creature, a guardian awakened in the presence of an enemy.

Becca reached out, put her hand behind the obsidian disc, and slammed it to the desktop just as Rafael threw the black silk at it, covering both her hand and the artifact in a single sweep. She withdrew her hand from under the fabric, kicked the chair back from the desk, and stood up, her heart pounding, the heat in the beetle fading. She stared at Rafael, eyes wide with horror.

Between them Django growled at the desk, the fur along his spine standing up.

"Someone saw me. Someone in there saw me."

"*In there?*"

"Yes. It's like Skyping with the devil or something. We have to get out of here. Now."

He looked up the stairs. "Becca, I don't know. We were lucky to get here without being pulled over. This little Anne Frank setup might be the best bunker we could hope for if someone shows up. I mean, the jeep out front isn't registered to either one of us. We could turn off the lights upstairs and no one would even know —"

"Did you hear that?"

"Hear what?"

"*Shhh....*"

Rafael looked at the ceiling while Becca knelt beside Django, cupped a hand over his muzzle, and stroked the back of his head. The dog was still growling, but too low to be heard in the house above.

Rafael said, "What did you —"

Becca cut him off with a raised finger. "We need to get out of here," she whispered. "If the man in the mirror sent someone, we'll be trapped."

Rafael shook his head. "No one could get here that fast."

As if to prove him wrong, a loud *crack!* resounded from above, like the sound of a door being kicked in or a gunshot taking out a lock. Django erupted into another territorial outburst, and Becca felt her heart drop in her chest, the whole situation tilting out of control, like a table tipping toward the floor, spilling everything her grandmother had entrusted her with, everything she'd managed to find on her own, and every faint hope that a dying man had put on her.

It was all going to end here in the dark.

She stuffed the journal into her bag and clutched the white leather-bound tome to her breast, thinking that, heavy as it was, it would still make a poor bludgeon.

She didn't know who was upstairs, but she felt sure it was the faceless man himself come to take what he wanted from her, and in a flash she knew just what that was: the scarab that dangled from her neck. Surely if he'd wanted the books, he could have come here before to claim them; but it had been the sight of her and the talisman she wore that had roused him from the depths and spurred him to action.

They needed to climb the stairs. Now. Fast. They needed to make a break for the back door of the house and use Django's teeth and any weapon they could seize to get out before he grabbed them. But what weapon could help against an entity that could spy you from a sheet of black glass and appear at the door a moment later?

She grabbed Rafael by the bicep and pulled him toward the stairs, but he only rocked on his feet, staring dumbly at the far wall and the darkness beyond the pool of light around the desk. Django was pacing, ears flattened against his head, unsure where to direct his aggression—toward the stairs and the sound of an intruder, or toward that patch of darkness that held Rafael's gaze. Becca squinted at the darkness and saw a pale green light wavering above an elaborately adorned chalk triangle. It reminded her of the northern lights, a curtain of luminescence, gaining solidity with each passing second.

Something was forming deep within the shifting veils of green light, something bestial. An acrid stench flooded the room, accompanied by a scuffling sound of many heavy limbs scratching at the concrete floor. The sound betrayed the anatomy before it was even fully formed: a percussion of hooves and claws.

Becca was pushing Rafael up the stairs with Django at her heels when her eyes finally made sense of the shape now manifest in the chalk triangle.

A man in a black cloak sat astride a goatish monstrosity with arachnid limbs protruding from its chest, covered in bristling gray fur, and terminating in serrated black hooks. The rear legs were goat-like, angular, almost skeletal, and the horns on its head spiraled through a range of lustrous shades of black and gray as they dwindled to lethal points that Becca had trouble taking her eyes from.

Now Rafael was tugging on *her* arm, calling her name, trying to shake her from her death trance. Something gleamed, like moonlight on a dorsal fin, and she saw the wide, curved blade the rider held in his fist, pointed toward his hood-framed face, a face she now recognized: the wanted man from the Harvard attack, the MIT student she had seen on the news sites, Darius Marlowe.

He dismounted the creature and strode forth, the symbols on the floor doing nothing to constrain him, his face a rictus of gleeful blood lust.

Rafael was scrabbling at the latch at the top of the stairs. Becca felt her throat constricting. They were trapped between the man with the knife and whatever might be waiting on the other side of the fireplace. Django was barking at Marlowe and the spider-goat behind him in full rage, froth flying, his voice pushing into a range of distorted volume she'd never heard from him before, but then the fireplace door swung open and a draught of fresher air wafted down over them, cutting through the musky reek. With a snarl, Django turned toward it, bounded over Becca and past Rafael, and shot out into the den.

Becca heard the impact of the dog knocking someone to the floor, a man yelling. She kicked off of the stone stairs toward the melee. But when she emerged from the fireplace, she realized with horror that she also knew the man who had broken down the door.

Agent Brooks was shielding his face with his arms, kicking at the frenzied dog. Blood ran down one of his hands, across his wrist, staining the white cuff of his shirt. Becca put her palm between Rafael's shoulder blades and shoved him toward the kitchen, toward the door to the backyard. He went with a quick glance over his shoulder to make sure she was following but the sight of the attack had stopped her in her tracks.

"DJANGO! NO! NOOO!"

The dog released his grip and the agent seized the opportunity to draw his gun. Rafael was tugging Becca's arm now, wrenching her into the kitchen as she screamed, *"No! Stop!"* but whether at the dog or the man, not even she knew. Rafael was dragging her, and she couldn't hold her ground against him. He threw open the door to the night. Cool air rushed in and chilled the sweat on her brow.

A single shot roared from the gun.

The black-robed body of Darius Marlowe staggered into view and fell to the floor as Django bolted from the gunshot and launched through the open doorway, over the back steps, onto the leaf-strewn ground.

Becca followed into the darkness of the backyard, realizing only after it was too late that she had dropped the heavy book on the kitchen floor when the gun went off.

Whatever secrets the *Mortiferum Indicium* held were lost to her.

Chapter 19

Brooks nearly tripped over the book when he reached the back door. He kicked it across the linoleum and shouldered through the storm door, gun raised, sweeping the dark yard. Philips and the graffiti artist had already disappeared into the trees—he could hear the jingling of the dog's collar fading on the wind.

He bounced on the balls of his feet, resisting the temptation to run after them. It wouldn't be hard to catch up, but what then?

Darius Marlowe was bleeding out on the floor inside and any accomplices he had were likely spilling out of the basement and stepping over the body to reach the front door right now while Brooks was chasing kids caught in the crossfire.

Fuck it.

He circled around the house and found no activity on the street. The jeep he'd checked the plates on when he arrived was still there, dark and vacant. The door he'd kicked in hung motionless.

He trotted up the stairs, set his back against the house, then swung around through the entrance in firing position.

Despite whatever magic had been on display at Copley Square, Darius Marlowe's blood was red. It pooled around him on the floor, soaking his splayed robes.

Brooks dropped to his knees, set his gun on the floor, and took his phone from his belt. He hit the speed dial with one hand while applying pressure on Marlowe's stomach wound through a fistful of bunched up black wool with the other. His own wounds from the dog bites added to the mess, but he barely felt them through the adrenaline.

Marlowe's eyes were fixed on the ceiling, glassy and dim.

Brooks hoped the book he'd kicked aside in the kitchen held some answers.

Getting any out of Marlowe was a diminishing proposition.

Chapter 20

Becca was having trouble coaxing Django onto the boat. The poor boy just didn't trust the water or the way the thirty-foot passenger craft was rocking and swaying in the lapping waves of the river as she shifted her weight and reached out to scoop him up in her arms. He reared back at the gesture, and she sighed. "Come *on*, Django. It's okay. Trust me." She feared she might have to set his trust for her back a few clicks by climbing up onto the quay and tossing him into the damned thing.

Rafael's ass was poking out of the tiny cabin, his boxers almost entirely free of his jeans as he struggled with the wires behind the instrument panel. The light of the headlamp occasionally sparked out of the cabin, as did curses and grunts.

"You sure you know what you're doing?" she said to his butt. "You're not gonna get electrocuted on me are you?"

The light flashed in her face now, and she could imagine that the scorn he was directing at her was even fiercer than that blinding glare. She shielded her eyes with her hand. "Jesus, keep it down, Raf. Someone will notice if you wave it around."

The light swept back into the little cubby, and she heard his muffled, affronted voice, "I grew up on the water, Becca. The first thing my father taught me after *futebol* and fishing was how to hotwire a boat. Only problem on this bitch is getting into the box without tools. Just be thankful the battery was left on board, and pray there's enough gas in the tank."

When Brooks had failed to give chase in the aftermath of the shooting, they had stopped running, crept up Hangman's Hill and stalked across the cemetery, crouching amid the leaning headstones. The hill offered a clear view of the Aylesbury Pike, the road they had taken into town and the main route from which they could expect State Police and military vehicles to enter Arkham if the full weight of the authorities descended upon them. But the road was quiet.

They'd scurried down the embankment and across River Street before the next set of approaching headlights could limn their silhouettes: man, woman, and dog disappearing like ghosts into the mist-shrouded docks where fishing boats and pleasure craft bobbed gently in a row of slips. The tide was low, the ramp to the floating docks now a steep incline; and descending below street level with the slimy timbers towering above their heads, they gained a sense of protective cover, while relinquishing the security of hard ground and passing into the unsettling embrace of the maritime realm to which most of the town's macabre legends could trace their origins.

Becca sighed with relief at the sound of the outboard engine coughing and sputtering to life, roaring, and finally purring under Rafael's deft touch.

He directed Becca to untie the ropes from the cleats, but Django was still on the dock, whimpering. "He'll come," Rafael said. "He won't be parted from you." And sure enough, as the little boat began to drift out from the mooring slip, the dog leapt after it, landing first on the engine compartment, then hopping to the fiberglass floor at Becca's feet.

They trolled into the dark currents, skirting the rocky hulk of Themystos Island, where Becca shuddered at the sight of the standing stones amid the crooked, skeletal trees. Rafael kept the lights off until they had cleared the bridges, and Django peered up into the darkness of the stone arches as they passed under. Becca could faintly descry bats hanging from the dripping bricks as they floated through the echoing vaults. She felt better when the embrace of the rocky channel fell away at the widening mouth of the Miskatonic, and they passed into open water beneath the dull gray glow of suburban midnight.

They followed the coast south past Beverly and Salem, Rafael doing a remarkable job of navigating the great rocks with only a few buoys and no chart to guide him. In the deep night, under a scattering of stars, he climbed onto the bow and, with a few long wind-up swings, cast the anchor onto the beach of a small, seemingly deserted island off the point of Marblehead. Had they known for certain that they had arrived at Tinkers Island, where several small camp shacks sat vacant for the season, they might have ventured off of the boat and forced their way into one for the night, but having made it this far with no sign of pursuit from sea or air, they were reluctant to test their luck with any exploration.

The cabin of the little vessel was small and spare, and the sea air was cold, but the cushions at least were soft, and they settled in to sleep as the boat rocked gently on the surf.

Rafael found a not-too-musty blanket stowed in a compartment under one of the seats and draped it over Becca's legs. She located the cabin light and switched it on, and the tiny space soon felt cozy. The boat was clean and well cared for, and in spite of the end of the world likely happening around them, she felt guilty about stealing it. Django was curled up on the cushions with his head on her belly, already snoozing. When Rafael tossed the blanket over her, she looked up and asked, "Is it okay to have this light on for a little while or will it drain the battery? I could use the headlamp to read."

"It's okay for now, but if you're up long, you should switch over. Do you think there's anything in that journal that will help?"

She had only scratched the surface, and many of the entries were too fragmentary and self-referential to make much sense. But it was all she had to work with. "Hard to say. I think she could sense things were coming to a crisis right before she died. But most of what I've read so far is a bit guarded and cryptic. I wish we'd had more time in the house. If I could have found older journals I might have a better chance of making some sense of it. And that book I dropped..." She scratched her arm.

"Are you sure it was important?"

Becca nodded, pressed the heel of her hand to her eye socket. "I think most of these notes make reference to it, and she was the translator, so there's a lot she took for granted that she wouldn't spell out in a journal. I don't know...I've only skimmed it, but some of it reads enough like rough sketches for a book that I might be able to glean *something* from it."

"Well, I'll let you read. I'm gonna put the canvas on this thing so we don't freeze to death. Hopefully it'll hold in enough body heat to get us through the night."

He looked genuinely worried about the temperature drop on the water in the small hours before dawn. At least there wasn't any wind. She patted the sleeping dog's flank and said, "Django will keep us warm."

Rafael uttered a rueful laugh. "Keep *you* warm, maybe. I ain't gonna fit in here with the two of you, but the seats fold down like cots."

Becca twisted her hair around her forefinger and bit her lip.

"All right, you study hard," Rafael said. His face disappeared from the cabin door.

Becca soon heard him climbing around on the bow above her, snapping down the cover and stretching it out. The boat rocked as he shifted his weight, and she tried to concentrate on the journal, but found herself thinking of the kiss she had planted on him before venturing through a doorway not much bigger than the one to the cabin she now lay in. She'd surprised herself with the gesture, had been thinking something at the time about how he'd earned it. But she knew now that to view it that way was to avoid the truth—she had wanted it for herself, that kiss. For luck, desire, and for the possibility that she might not get another chance if bad things happened down in the dark. Now she was surprised at herself for dwelling on it when there was so much happening, so much at stake. The threat had awakened a long-dormant vitality in her. Looking back on the past week, she saw that fight-or-flight adrenaline had carried her through, and she realized now that they really *could* flee, could point the boat north and head for Nova Scotia, leaving the beleaguered city behind. It was tempting.

And yet she couldn't do it. She had a role to play before this was all over. Catherine had left her the scarab. And had she seen fear in the dark man's reaction to it? If so, she needed to know why, needed to know what Catherine had been embroiled in in her final days. It wasn't rational, but she felt that she owed it to her grandmother to at least try to understand. When she finally put her finger on the feeling, she recognized it for what it was: a sense of duty. Not to her city or country, but to the woman who had raised her.

No one had *asked* her to do anything. She'd been born into a fucked-up family with a history of insanity, and now that madness was made manifest, unleashed on an unwitting world. Her genes had been entangled in this story since before she was even born. And she might be the last one left who could determine how it ended.

Tell me a story, Gran. Make me a myth.

Soon she was immersed in her grandmother's voice, and all amorous thoughts faded as she was drawn into the web of the great scholar's efforts to decode the histories of the artifacts she had tracked down, obtained, and experimented with: the obsidian mirror, the golden scarab, and the book that joined them, the *Mortiferum Indicium.*

The title, as translated by Catherine, was, *The Deadly Talisman.* At first Becca thought the book itself was the talisman referenced, but the more she read, the more apparent it became that the tome, a holy book of the Starry Wisdom Church, was focused on the identification and history of a weapon devised by a wandering sage, an artifact which posed a threat to the cult of the Black Pharaoh because of its power to banish their dark gods, a jewel Becca recognized with a jolt as the scarab she now wore around her neck, known for generations as The Fire of Cairo.

That title was a misnomer, acquired during centuries when the scarab was lost and rumored to be somewhere in Cairo, the last place it was known to have been used, during the reign of Ramses the Great. Its true place of origin was Amarna, or Akhetaton of old, the city of Aten, the sun god, and his greatest worshipper, the pharaoh Akenaten—a heretic who abandoned the capital city of Thebes to establish his throne among the open-air temples he had erected for the worship of the solar disc, sole object of his adoration.

His monotheistic zeal aroused the ire of the priest class and fractured the kingdom. And when a dark conjurer arose, offering to strike him down, it seemed to many that no price was too great. The conjurer was known as a mere scribe when he gathered the priesthood in secret to demonstrate his hidden power. When they had witnessed his abilities, they entrusted him with the oldest treasure from the deepest vault of Egypt, a jewel wrought in the furnaces of Yuggoth and passed through the temples of Valusia, Lemuria, and Khem: The Shining Trapezohedron. The scribe took this mighty treasure in payment, and fulfilled his oath to bring down the pharaoh of the sun.

In the thirteenth year of Akhenaten's reign, a plague of black airs dripped from the sky like ink and his city was stricken. His mother, Queen Tiye, three of his daughters, and his wife, Nefertiti, were dead within a few years, followed by the king himself. But his son, Tutankhamen, was spared long enough to take the throne under the tutelage of many councilors, including one wise sage who would soon supplant him, a priest who would rule in the wake of the boy-king's assassination. He would be known (until his name was stricken from all public monuments) as Nephren-ka. The Black Pharaoh. He of the gifted tongue, who was finally banished by a wandering sage from the east bearing a golden scarab set with a fiery gem.

Some scholars speculated that this wanderer had known Akhenaten in his youth, or that contact with such a nomad hailing from a cult of the Far East may have been what inspired the rising pharaoh's devotion to the sun god. Whether or not this is true, it is agreed that the mysterious figure, flitting like a phantom through the scrolls of the New Kingdom, possessed not only great metal- and gem-craft, but also a mantra which he used to set the ruby ablaze and the beetle to flight. His name is unrecorded, but the mantra survived, preserved in a book hidden by the Black Brotherhood: *The Mortiferum Indicium.*

The cult of the Black Pharaoh also preserved an obsidian disk, upon which Nephren-ka exhaled his dying breath. But the Shining Trapezohedron, dark counterpart to the red stone that would be known as the Fire of Cairo, was lost to the ages, until rediscovered by an archaeologist and New England Freemason by the name of Enoch Bowen in 1843.

Most historians credited Bowen with founding the Starry Wisdom Church in Rhode Island in the mid 1800s, but Catherine's theory was that a secret faction within the Egyptian Rite of Freemasonry had developed the cult at the dawn of the American Revolution, and that only after the Trapezohedron was discovered did they go above ground as an openly practicing religious sect.

At this point in the journal, what had begun as a historical treatise started to devolve into equations of Hebrew and Greek Gematria, charts of constellations and geo-coordinates, and records of experiments, including meticulous documentation of weather, moon phases, and tides, occluded by an alphabet soup of acronyms that only Catherine, or perhaps a scholar of ceremonial magic, could decipher.

One of the late entries from July of 2019 had the tone of an exuberant epiphany:

7/16
I knew the Black Brotherhood had steered Solomon's Lodge to erect an obelisk on blood-anointed ground for the rites of Nephren-Ka, but now, having seen it with my own eyes, I know how they arranged for the transmission of dark rays from the Shining Trapezohedron. They must have the mirror rods in their keeping for use in the days when the old chants will be restored, when our world and the Other are aligned. But the architect must have known that his creation could be subverted. He coded a tribute to the sun, the Greater Light, in the number of steps in the ascending spiral: 294!

Did he know that the Fire of Cairo could be used instead of the dark jewel? If true, then the tide may yet be turned by the providence that brought it into my keeping in Syria all those years ago, long before I knew what it was. That it should have found its way to a young graduate student who would bring it half way around the world to Miskatonic, to Massachusetts, the exact location where it would be needed most…. It forces me to consider the influence of an unseen and benevolent hand.

And yet I fear that I will never learn where Peter hid the stone. I failed him. It seems strange now to contemplate this black mirror as if it were a telephone I could pick up and, dialing the right number, try to make amends. I've never believed in the charlatans who claim to offer contact with the dead, but if ever there was a time when the fate of humankind depended on such a thing, it is now.

Dare I call forth my long-dead husband from the depths? Dare I face him one last time in this life?

Becca woke with Rafael's hand in her own. The boat rocked like a cradle, and Django snored in the well between them. Rafael was curled on his side, his left hand tucked under his chest in what looked like an effort to keep it warm. He had taken the journal away and turned off the light while she slept and had draped the one blanket over her shoulders, leaving himself uncovered but at least holed up in the cabin with her where the closed door did more than the canvas to contain their collective heat.

Becca was hovering somewhere in the liminal state between waking and dream when she slid closer to him, threw the blanket over his shoulder, and wrapped her arm around him. Rafael stirred. She wondered groggily if he had been awake the whole time, listening for helicopters. She tucked her head under his chin and breathed into the hollow of his neck.

His skin felt cold, but in the little tent created by the blanket, her breath was trapped and warmed her face, his chest. He squeezed her fingers in his. She burrowed her head down into his chest and felt his heart beat against her cheek. A quick, pounding tempo. She kissed his jawline and felt his hand close around the nape of her neck, then trace her vertebrae down to her hips and ass. She turned her face up and kissed him, taking his full bottom lip between hers. And then they were rolling and writhing in the rising heat between them, and the boat rocked on waves born within its hull as the stars faded at the rumor of dawn.

* * *

They watched the sunrise, a bright, burnished spot on a sheet of dull aluminum, behind the Graves Lighthouse off the port bow on approach to the mouth of Boston Harbor. They were hungry and craving caffeine but cold enough to feel painfully awake, and desperate to get off the water. Django, smelling land and probably the fumes of breakfast wafting from some waterfront restaurant, was pacing the boat, whining. Becca sat in the passenger seat with the blanket wrapped around her shoulders, scrolling through photos in her camera, when Rafael, at the wheel, pointed at the shore.

"Look," he said, "You recognize it? Four Point Channel is just past those bridges. I could almost drop you at your doorstep."

Becca scanned the waterfront, saw no overt police presence, but said, "Don't." Her gaze drifted skyward to the black orb floating high above the city. It hurt to look at it for more than a second, almost like staring at the sun, but different. It caused a throbbing ache in her left eye, and a tingling in her fingertips on that side. She wondered if some deep part of her right frontal lobe was being taxed, like an underused muscle suddenly forced into heavy lifting.

Rafael steered the boat to starboard. The great arch of the Boston Harbor Hotel loomed beyond the prow. "How about there? We can dock at the marina on the wharf."

"Okay."

"Get ready to tie up fast and run before the harbor master grabs us."

"Would they know if the boat's been reported stolen?"

"Nah, the owner probably doesn't even know yet, but we got no reservation and no way to pay for docking. You want to have your bag packed when I bring us in."

"Okay. Try not to scratch up the boat. I'd like it to be returned the same as we found it."

Rafael smiled at her. "Aye, Captain."

"What?"

"Not too many people would worry about scratching up a boat while trying to stop the apocalypse."

Becca stretched out her foot and kicked his calf gently. Rafael tipped his chin toward Django. "Don't forget leash laws, while you're at it."

"He'll follow us," Becca said, and stowed the camera on top of the Moleskine journal in her bag.

The blackness from the orb swirled down in rills that reminded her of ink twisting in gray water, converging on a point north of the city.

"Raf, slow down for a second so we can talk before we land."

He pulled back on the throttle until the boat was idling in neutral, drifting northeast. The harbor was sparsely trafficked in the early hours of a weekday, in the wake of martial law. Becca pointed at the black sun, and traced her finger along the oily streak to the horizon. "Do you see that?"

He squinted. "See what?"

"You'd know if you saw it."

"What do *you* see?"

She touched the spot where the scarab was under her shirt. "It looks like a negative exposure of the sun in the sky, and it's been putting out smoky...roots or something. It's hard to describe. But one of them touched the reflecting pool at the Christian Science Center when I was there, and it drew something out of the water. A monster."

"You saw this with your own eyes. A *monster*."

Becca stared at the sky. Rafael put his hand on the small of her back and she felt a tingle run up and down her spine.

They were drifting, but the landing was still far off. "I saw the homeless man from the mill come out of a whirlpool right behind the thing. Like he stepped into a parallel world at the mill and came out of it in the reflecting pool when another portal opened up." She pointed at the horizon to the north, to the thing he couldn't see and the charcoal trails that scored the sky beyond the peninsula of the North End. "It's getting worse, whatever it is. Something's going to happen over there."

Rafael followed her gaze. "Can other people see it too? There's a lot of cars on the bridges, planes in the sky. It doesn't look like a city in lockdown."

"I was thinking the same, and I don't get it. It's not over."

"Did the journal shed any light on what this is? You say something's going to happen over there, but do you know what?"

"I can't say for sure that I understand it. It seems like if Gran meant for me to understand, she would have been more direct, would have spelled it out. She left me the scarab, but that was in a will written before she fully understood it."

"And she didn't leave you the journal."

"Exactly. I don't think she knew she was going to die. And her last notes tell about how she thought she could contact my grandfather." Becca looped a finger under the chain around her neck and slipped the scarab pendant over the black fabric of her thermal shirt. The metal gleamed even in the ashen light that hung over the city. "She needed him to tell her where he hid the jewel that's missing from this."

"Your grandfather? The one who was in the asylum?"

"Yeah. He did something with the stone, prevented some breach from the other side while he was locked up there. I think she may have even had him committed in the first place so he could do it. He hid the jewel somewhere in the asylum. Gran never knew where, but I think I might. It's a long shot, but when I was looking through the pictures in my camera, I saw something....

"I need to go back. If we find that ruby, we might be able to stop this. I think the scarab was *made* to stop this, over three thousand years ago."

Rafael raised his hand and tentatively touched the scarab with the tip of his middle finger, as if he half expected an electric shock. "It doesn't look that old. Wouldn't it be more worn?"

"I know. It looks like gold, but I don't know if the metal is even of this Earth. And you probably thought I was crazy enough back when I was just a depressed, artsy chick."

He smiled. "You say the pendant was made to stop this. How about you? Were *you* made to stop this?

It seemed impossible that anything so grandiose should fall to her. If she'd been asked just a few weeks ago whether the human race was worth saving, she would have expressed doubts; and if anyone had told her that *she* would be elected to dig the means of salvation out of the clay of ancient history, she would have laughed.

"If there's a God, he has some sense of humor, picking a girl who has trouble getting out of bed on a good day."

"You believe in God?"

"Not really. So much horror in the world...what good is a god who doesn't intervene? Do you?"

He nodded. "So do those brineheads. Many gods, and you've *seen* theirs. Don't you want one on your side?"

She sighed. "I don't think those are gods. Maybe they're just our nasty neighbors, aliens from another plane of our own planet. They see us the way most people see animals."

"Food."

"Yeah."

"You think they're more evolved than us? More intelligent?"

"I don't know."

"*Some* humans have compassion for animals. You do."

"I don't think those creatures know what compassion is. Or self-sacrifice. Maybe those are the things that make humans more evolved, the things that *defy* natural selection. Maybe that's why we're worth saving.

He pulled her close. "So we're going to Allston when we hit dry land? To the asylum?"

She turned away from the terrible sky and searched his eyes. They looked deep in the morning light. "You don't have to come with me. You might be safe from *some* things just because you can't see them or share space with them, but that won't keep you from getting stabbed by a cultist or shot by a jittery cop when the shit hits the fan."

"You're not going anywhere without me. I've got your back. Don't you know that by now?"

She studied his face. It was a new thing for someone to tell her unequivocally that she wouldn't be abandoned. "Sometimes you have to alter the focus to see what's right in front of you," she said with a wry smile.

"What?"

"My mentor told me that shortly before he handed me over to SPECTRA."

"Yeah, well if you want to rock the quotes, Helen Keller said, 'Walking with a friend in the dark is better than walking alone in the light.'"

She studied his face, so serious, and laughed.

They were drifting sideways on a current that had driven them perilously close to a barge. Rafael engaged the throttle, and the nose of the little boat rose up as the prop dug into the water. He steered clear of the rusty behemoth and aimed for the dome that marked the marina. Shouting over the engine noise, he said, "You ready to run for the street?"

Becca plucked a length of nylon rope out of a side compartment. "Yeah. Bring it in."

Rafael killed the engine and let the boat glide up to the dock. He had jumped out and tied the front rope to a post before Becca could even find one for the stern. She scooped up Django in her arms, tossed him onto the dock, and climbed out after him. A man in a polo shirt and windbreaker was walking toward them across the grass, but they didn't wait around to find out if he was the Harbor Master, a marina worker, or just another sailor. As soon as they reached the end of the dock, they broke away from the marina and hurried through an alley to the street.

In under a minute they were doing their best to blend into the early morning urban foot traffic—office workers with their coffee cups and briefcases. It clearly wasn't the right hour of the day for a pair of ragged bohemians to be up and out, let alone in this part of town. Becca kept her hood up in case her photo was still circulating, and passing a newspaper-vending box, she shot a glance at the front pages.

She wasn't on them, but a headshot of Darius Marlowe filled the front cover of the *Herald*, beneath the headlines:

DEAD, NOT DREAMING!
TERROR CULT LEADER
SHOT BY FEDERAL AGENT

She grabbed Rafael's arm. "Brooks killed him," she said. "At Gran's house. He shot him dead."

"Keep walking," Rafael said. "People are looking at us."

"They must have caught or killed the other cult members, too, or the city wouldn't be back to business." She stopped walking and wheeled on him. "Maybe they aren't looking for us anymore."

"You think it's over?"

She wanted to believe it was, but one glance at the sky told her otherwise.

Chapter 21

Brooks was being briefed by one of the translators when his phone buzzed with a summons to the interrogation. The translator was a heavyset young guy with a thick, black beard, a member of the team Brooks thought of as the *Necronomajohns*. They huddled around their own tables in the cafeteria and talked in a bizarre jargon no one else understood. He'd often tried to tell himself that they were no different from your garden variety IT geeks, but the way they never quite made eye contact *was* different somehow.

Their fascination with the most obscure footnotes of occult lore seemed to have given their eyes a bulbous look, like fish that never saw sunlight. And he had the distinct impression that if any of them were ever invited out for a beer with the field agents, they'd die of the bends upon entering the bar, their blood carbonated by rapid ascension into the upper regions of shallow small talk and sexual banter.

Brooks gently scratched his wrist where the dog bites itched like a bastard under the bandage. Thank God he was up to date on tetanus. He looked at the phone screen in his hand: the text summoning him to room 217 had to be an error. That was a conference room, the kind used for light interrogation. It was not the kind of setting required for the job at hand. For that you wanted a concrete floor with a tap and a drain and some chains anchored to the ceiling.

"I'm sorry...uh...." He tipped a pointing finger at the man's chest.

"Kenneth," the burly bearded guy reminded him.

"Sorry, Kenneth, I'm being paged. Give me that last bit again in layman's terms. Sum it up for me like I'm an idiot who hasn't read his Agrippa."

Kenneth laughed. It sounded forced. He smelled like pepperoni. "Okay. The book is called the Deadly Amulet. It's about two powerful gems that are polar opposites: one is the Shining Trapezohedron, which enables cultists to draw their dark messenger Nyarlathotep from another dimension into this world. The other became known as the Fire of Cairo, a ruby-red stone set in a golden scarab and endowed with the power to dispel the creatures of darkness. But neither one would have *much* power unless the two worlds—the two dimensions, that is—could be brought into alignment so that fissures would open between them. And no one has been able to make that happen since about 1300 BC in Egypt, when the pharaoh Nephren-ka was the last person with the genetic gift for chanting the right overtones. Some books say he was an incarnation of Nyarlathotep. You still with me?"

"Yeah. What about this Saint Jeremy?"

"Right. Allston Asylum, 2007. Well, no one can prove that he really caused a dimensional breach, but the staff and inmate accounts do seem to describe that phenomenon. And him using a birdbath for the manifestation, like they say he did, makes sense because once the overtone chant fractures the façade of three-dimensional space-time, reflective surfaces in the vicinity become portals. *If* Jeremy really succeeded in a partial manifestation, then he had to have been a freak of evolution, an anomaly."

"What do you mean *anomaly*?"

"Well, how many people are born with perfect pitch? Not many, but some, right? Now how many are born with not only that, but a set of pipes like Mariah Carey? *Very* rare. She's an anomaly. But to be born with a larynx that can naturally produce *this* language? We're talking about odds so long that it probably only comes along once in a millennium."

"Unless you're a genetic engineer with a 3D printer."

"Like Marlowe. Yeah."

"But assuming for a moment that Jeremy had that gift…what stopped his monster from coming through? What stopped all of this from happening twelve years ago?"

Kenneth tilted his palms up and reclined in his leather office chair. "Beats me. Maybe his voice box was only *mostly* right for the chanting, but not perfect like the pharaoh's, so he birthed an abortion."

Brooks' phone buzzed again. He nodded. "Gotta go. Thanks."

He turned away from the cluttered desktop and gazed over the glass partitions dividing the lab into cubicles. In some, there were chalk circles on the floor. Others were adorned with byzantine mandalas and divine names scrawled in red and blue sharpie across the glass. It reminded him of biohazard zones in private-sector labs he had visited; only here the precautionary devices were spiritual. He still had trouble accepting what was happening, but every time he passed a window to the outside world, the pulsing abomination in the sky drove the reality home. He was momentarily distracted by a grotesquery glimpsed through the double panes of a locked case (something that resembled a brain tattooed with arcane sigils), when a tall, thin geek with a blond goatee and black-framed glasses bumped into him. The kid looked like he'd run the entire corridor and all of the stairs. He was trying to catch his breath and holding a printout in both hands, the paper wrinkling under the sweaty pads of his tight-clenching fingers. "Agent Brooks…."

"Yeah?"

"We cracked it." The guy huffed and heaved.

"Cracked what?"

"The astrological diagram at the end of the *Mortiferum*. It points to a time when the worlds align, a specific date and time when the membrane is thinnest and the stars are right for widening the breach to let them in. It's called the *Red Equinox*: the autumn equinox of the year in which the Black Pharaoh awakens.

This year. *This* week. Monday, September 23rd, at 3:50 AM, to be exact."

"You're sure?"

"Triple checked."

The phone in his hand was buzzing again and a pair of armed security police was striding down the corridor, their eyes fixed intently on his, the bizarre trappings of the lab doing nothing to diminish their focus despite the transparency of the place.

"Agent Jason Brooks," the one on the left with an iron-gray crew cut and eyes to match said, "we have orders to escort you to room 217 for the interrogation."

"What, is Northrup worried I won't show?"

"You haven't responded to his texts, sir. Please come along."

* * *

The small theater was dimly lit to reduce reflections on the one-way glass. The two security officers closed the door behind Brooks and stood in parade rest, flanking the only exit. Of the four men already in the room, he recognized two: Northrup and Hanson, the SPECTRA director and Limbus spook respectively. A third was dressed in the uniform of a Navy admiral, but with no nametag amid the medals and regalia. The fourth was young, scruffy, and apparently important enough to dress casually in a plaid shirt and jeans. At least the jeans weren't ripped.

Beyond the glass he saw that the conference table and chairs had been removed from the adjacent room. A large plastic tarp had been spread out on the floor to cover most of the carpet. Three objects rested on the tarp. Brooks had expected these, but somehow seeing them sitting there looking so ordinary made the whole scenario feel more real, and for a fleeting moment he wished he had shot Darius Marlowe in the chest or head and not in the gut.

Until he remembered the carnage on the train and the screams that he couldn't differentiate between men, women, and children because most voices sounded surprisingly similar in the upper register of excruciating pain.

Northrup stabbed a finger at a folding chair that had been placed in front of the rows of theater seating. "Sit, Brooks."

Brooks walked down the carpeted slope, sat, and leaned forward, hands cupped on his thighs. "What is this?"

"We'd like to interview you before we interview your prisoner."

Brooks laughed. "Guess I should be happy I'm on this side of the glass."

For a few long seconds he thought no one was going to speak. Finally Northrup said, "You're a hero, Brooks. You caught the bad guy, and your country is grateful for your service. Thanks to the photos we've leaked, everybody thinks you killed him, too, which I'm sure makes you even more popular than we'd all be if Mr. Marlowe had to go through that due-process bullshit before Boston could have the pleasure of seeing him on ice. So relax. You're going to be on all of the Sunday morning shows. You're not here to be punished, even though you broke protocol by pursuing Rebecca Philips without a TAC team."

Brooks stared at the backlit silhouettes of the men seated before him. "But it's not over," he said. "Right? Not everyone can see what's going on in the sky, but the ones who can probably have a fucking Facebook group by now."

"Actually, no. While you were off leash on the North Shore, we rounded them all up. Well, we're pretty sure we got at least ninety percent of them. The one silver lining of terror events happening in public places is that you have a lot of surveillance cams to feed into the facial recognition software. And your Facebook joke isn't that far off, either. People do most of their talking online these days, so that helped us track them down. You and Philips may be the only two people with EDEP still walking free." Northrup let the statement hang in the air for a moment. Brooks didn't know the latest acronym, but the unspoken accusation was clear enough: *You lied to us about your exposure.*

"EDEP?"

The skinny guy who looked like a young George Lucas said, "Extra-Dimensional Entity Perception. Hearing the chant causes a modulation of consciousness—"

"It's what enables you to still see that black shit in the sky," Northrup interrupted.

Brooks scoffed. "Ninety percent, huh? What about the other ten?"

"A few people who see strange things is a psychiatric problem, not a national security issue."

"And you think you can just disappear a whole group of civilians without their friends and families noticing?"

"Who said anything about disappearing anyone? They're being treated for PTSD on the house. You gotta love government health care." Brooks couldn't quite make out Northrup's face, but he knew the smile the man was wearing right now, had seen it enough times to know how smug it would look.

"Where are they, the witnesses?"

"In this facility," Northrup said. "And they'll be right as rain when we send them home. No black rays in the sky to trouble them. No tentacles writhing in their peripheral vision."

"How?"

Dick Hanson spoke for the first time since Brooks had entered the room. "We call it Nepenthe. It's a Limbus product. One injection and the nightmares go away. We've prepared a dose for you, James. If you have any questions or concerns, I'm sure Gary here can address them. He developed it."

The guy in the plaid shirt, Gary, leaned into the light, his hairy forearms resting on his knees. Brooks could see the capped syringe curled casually in the fingers of his right hand. The silhouettes of the guards at the door shifted almost imperceptibly.

Brooks sat up straighter in his chair. "Turning a blind eye to what's happening won't make it go away. Is that really your solution?"

"My understanding," Northrup said, "is that this is one case when *If I can't see you, you can't see me* is actually true. These invading entities need us to share the same plane of perception with them to do us harm."

"For now," Gary said, and Brooks was pretty sure Hanson shot his pet genius a corrective glance.

"What if the cult sets off more of these...whatever they are...*harmonic bombs?*" Brooks said. "What if when you think it's over and loosen up security, they find away to do it over the PA at Fenway Park? Are you going to try to round up thirty thousand people for mass vaccinations? Or will you just crop dust the city with aerosolized Nepenthe? I'm sure you won't get any resistance to that in a state where you've had to beg parents to get an MMR shot for their toddlers. And what does he mean, 'for now'? This breach is headed toward a critical mass, isn't it? After that, it won't matter if you heard the chant or not—everyone will see them among us. The Book Breakers downstairs think it will happen on the equinox. Am I right? *Gary?*"

Gary looked uncomfortable. Brooks was sure he could wrestle the syringe away from him as long as the two guards didn't have his arms pinned behind his back. But what was he about to fight for, anyway? The ability to be seen and devoured by monsters? No, it was the right to see things as they really were and have a chance of stopping it without fighting blind.

"You need me to be able to see them," he said to Northrup. "You need at least one agent who can tell you what's really happening."

Now Northrup leaned into a dim pool of light. "Why did you let her get away? Twice."

"There were more urgent priorities. She didn't represent a threat. I still don't think she's a threat."

"Then why has she been in the middle of this from the start?"

"Judging by what we found at her grandmother's house, I'd say she was born into it. She might even have pieces of the puzzle that can help us, but I doubt she knows exactly what they are and how to use them."

"You're talking about the scarab," Gary said. "The book is all about it. The guys downstairs think it could be a weapon."

"Do you think she knows how to use it?" Northrup asked Brooks.

"I don't know. Maybe. Who knows what her grandmother told her?"

"Really? Who knows? I think maybe your wife knows. Should we bring her in?"

"She's not my wife anymore and she doesn't know shit."

Of course they had pulled Becca Philips' medical records and knew that Nina was her shrink. But they hadn't come to him with the information until now. How long had they known? Was this some kind of test?

"Don't think we won't use her if we need her to establish trust with the girl."

"*Use* her?" Brooks laughed. "You don't know Nina."

Northrup said, "If Rebecca Philips knows how to stop this and has a device in her possession to do so, then why is she running from *us?*"

"Uh, maybe because we've been locking her up, hunting her down? I get the impression she has some trust issues." He turned his head away from them and stared pointedly through the window into the adjacent room, where the waterboarding equipment waited. "Problem with authority, I guess."

Northrup nodded at one of the guards, who in turn opened the door and signaled someone in the hall. A moment later two more black-clad security contractors led Darius Marlowe into the room beyond the glass. A third man, with wavy blond hair, a weathered face, and a sporty white neoprene shirt entered the room behind them, his body language casual, almost lazy as he leaned against the wall and waited for the guards to strap Marlowe's ankles and arms to the board.

Marlowe's black robe had been replaced with a navy blue smock and matching linen pants. He didn't struggle, only stared blankly at the ceiling, his mind fixed in another zone entirely, as if he could see the black orb, the promise of salvation, through the ceiling and roof of the building.

Brooks stood, but the guards in the theater didn't make any move toward him. Somehow, with no verbal command from Northrup, the focus had shifted away from inoculating him with Nepenthe. For now, anyway. Northrup turned in his chair to face the glass. The two guards flanking Marlowe squatted and angled the bottom of the board so that the prisoner's feet rose above his head. The microphones were live in the room, fed to speakers in the theater, and Brooks could hear every rustle of the plywood on the plastic tarp.

"Everybody thinks he's dead," Brooks said, looking at Northrup's transparent reflection in the glass. "Is that because he soon will be?"

"Pronouncing him dead was a calculated risk: the fastest way to flush Philips out of hiding. If martial law were still in effect we'd have no chance of finding her. But with normal transit up and running, she gets signals that we no longer care about her, and she's likely to return to familiar places."

"But you can never let it get out that I didn't kill him at the scene."

"True. Darius Marlowe has passed beyond the realm of due process."

The man in the neoprene shirt bowed over Marlowe's inverted head, set his hands on his knees, and, staring into the prisoner's eyes, said, "There was a tall man at the Mapparium and reflecting pool. People heard him chanting when the shit hit the fan. Same songs you like to play on your boom box. He goes by many names, but I believe you know him as Nereus Charobim. He's your mentor, your connection. He provided you with housing, money, materials, and information to execute your plot. Where is he now, Darius? You're going to tell me the truth within fifteen seconds of getting the water, that's just a statistical fact, something I'm sure you can appreciate as an MIT guy. So why not cut the extreme suffering out of the equation and tell me now? Everyone thinks you're dead anyway. No one's ever going to know how long you lasted. They already think you're a martyr."

Marlowe gave no sign of having heard the speech, none that Brooks could discern from the other side of the glass. The interrogator took a small, dark-green towel from beside the water pitcher on the floor and draped it over Marlowe's face, tucking the sides behind his head. He picked up the pitcher, and, holding Marlowe's chest down with his left hand, poured the water in a long, slow stream over the towel. The shrouded head jerked from side to side reflexively, then settled, as if bracing against the inescapable flow. It lasted mere seconds, but to Brooks it felt like an eternity. He had read about the gag reflex, the body's panicked certainty that it was drowning, the burning in the lungs, and again, he wished he'd aimed higher in Arkham.

The interrogator removed the wet towel. Marlowe spluttered and coughed, the wheezing through his nose loud and distorted in the theater speakers.

"Same question, Darius. Where is he? Where is Charobim?"

"I don't know."

"Then how do you get in touch with him?"

"I used to need a consecrated mirror." Marlowe drew ragged breaths, winced at the pain they brought to the bandaged wound in his diaphragm. He pushed through it, *wanting* to speak. "But now his presence is palpable. I can find him in any mirror." He turned his face toward the one-way glass and stared straight at Brooks, a grim smile lighting his waxy face. Brooks recoiled from it in revulsion.

"Whatever sixth sense you turned on in people, we're shutting it down, Darius." The interrogator said. "We have a drug that shuts it off." He took a syringe from his pocket and held it close to Marlowe's eyes. "I'll give it to you. Maybe that'd be worse than the water, huh? Losing your ability to see, hear, and touch your precious gods. And you're never going to get your hands on the technology again, so...your prayers will be as good as Pig Latin. You'll have as much chance of evoking Cthulhu as the Flying Spaghetti Monster. It's over, Darius. Your part in this is finished. Tell me where to find Charobim."

Marlowe stared at the needle. It was still capped with orange plastic.

"He will arise on the blood-soaked earth when the stars are right. He will appear in his guise as the Haunter of the Dark. He will inhabit the stone and usher in the new aeon at the Red Equinox, and you are powerless to stop it!"

The board had been tilted so that Brooks could see Marlowe gloating through his bloodshot eyes and quivering lips. "You want to know where he is? I've *seen* his safe house...a palace of black crystal on the shores of the Cerenarian Sea. I have crossed over and back again from that nightside realm, and I no longer need science to evoke my gods, to draw them forth from the spaces between worlds. I *invoke* them to inhabit my own flesh and blood. No drug will purge the blessed brine from my blood. And all your torture games will only empower—"

The interrogator wrapped the wet towel over Marlowe's face, cutting off the mad diatribe. He began to pour again. This time there was no struggle. The towel went concave at the location of the mouth, as Marlowe seemed to suck it in, inhaling the water. Then the shape under the towel began to change. Something was writhing under it. Marlowe's forearms, the only exposed flesh on his body, turned a grayish-green hue. His muscles went taut and seemed to inflate. The straps snapped, and the guards scrambled to seize his ankles.

Brooks was on his feet. He could hear the guards behind him rushing out of the theater to provide backup. He sensed the other men in the room also standing, moving closer to the glass, transfixed. Marlowe reached up and swiped the wet towel from his face, revealing a squirming nest of tentacles with a chattering, many-layered beak at the center. The guards were scurrying across the floor to get away from it. One kicked the water can and spilled it. The creature seized the interrogator by the hair with a clawed hand and yanked the screaming man's face into its own, as if for a kiss. The tentacles wrapped around the back of the interrogator's head. Blood sprayed from the gaps in the sinewy embrace.

The two guards from the theater burst into the room, guns raised. The first squeezed off three shots, two of which penetrated the Marlowe creature's shoulder, causing ripples but no damage. The gray flesh sprouted puckered orifices, which spat the lead out onto the floor.

The creature dropped the interrogator's limp body and approached the glass. Brooks sensed his superiors retreating to the rear of the theater.

When it spoke, in a mockery of human speech, the words seemed to bubble from a deep well of putrid mucous. Brooks could only make sense of the mangled words coming from the overhead speakers because they were already familiar to him. They were from a poem that had haunted his memory ever since he'd first encountered its beautiful, harrowing nonsense in a high-school anthology. "Weave a circle round him thrice and cross your heart with holy dread, for he on honeydew hath fed and drunk the milk of Paradise."

It walked toward the mirrored glass, crouched, swung its elongated arms back, then dove and disappeared, leaving the glass intact and the men behind it shielding their eyes against the impact.

Chapter 22

Becca waited at a coffee shop down the street from Rafael's apartment while he went to retrieve what they needed. She wasn't sure if he was being tracked by SPECTRA, wasn't even sure if *she* was anymore, but it seemed prudent to assume that she was, despite what she read in the newspapers while she waited.

She was the only patron seated on the outdoor patio, and the server had even brought her a bowl of fresh water for Django. Thankfully, the girl didn't seem to recognize her. Becca's innocence wasn't front-page news; it was tucked in after the details of the slaying of Darius Marlowe and the PTSD treatment being offered to witnesses of the attacks. There, on page seven of *The Boston Globe*, was a small black-and-white headshot and a headline that said almost as much as the article:

Photographer Cleared of Suspicion

Apparently she'd been brushed under the media carpet. The mayor had stated in a press conference that she had only been a person of interest because authorities believed she might have captured photos of the cultists.

She found it odd that neither paper mentioned the address where Marlowe was shot and killed, nor that she had once lived there. Most puzzling of all: they could have publicized that she was missing and possibly dead, Marlowe's final victim, but hadn't. Under the auspices of concern for her well-being, they could have put out a call for tips from anyone who knew her whereabouts. Instead, they were going out of their way to sell the narrative that the city was now safe, even for the briefly notorious Rebecca Philips.

She drank her tea, and her eyes drifted to the black orb in the northern sky. She wondered what had happened to all of those PTSD cases who knew what she knew—that this was anything but over. She tugged her jacket sleeve over her bandaged wrist, and wished she had a baseball cap to cover her eyes. She felt exposed sitting so close to the street, but the foot traffic was light, Django seemed happy, and it was better than haunting an alley between buildings while Rafael fetched supplies. The candid art photography she favored had always brought with it a certain secret-agent sensibility, and she had learned long ago that sometimes the best way to hide was to appear engaged in ordinary activity in plain sight. Of course, it was likely that any agents following her were doing the same, and she found her eyes returning to the parked cars in the gas station on the corner and the blank windows brooding above her in the apartment towers across the street.

Django growled, stood erect, and tugged at the leash. Before she could do more than tighten her grip and whirl around, a man in several layers of ragged clothes, a dirty Red Sox cap, and sunglasses appeared out of nowhere and slid into the seat opposite hers at the small metal table.

"It's me, Becca."

"*Jeez*, Raf. I didn't recognize you. That's good. Were you followed, you think?"

"Don't think so."

"How about your apartment, was it ransacked?"

"Not obviously, but I'd probably never know if they didn't want me to. I shoulda put a piece of scotch tape on the door when I left or some crafty spy shit like that, right?"

Becca tried to smile. "You make a scarily good homeless guy." She couldn't help thinking of Moe Ramirez, and a shadow passed over her heart, an uncomfortable reminder of why she was doing this: to rectify things for the dead.

Rafael watched the street as he spoke. "Got that laptop you wanted in the bag and my Bowie knife strapped to my leg."

Becca glanced under the table. He picked up a battered canvas shopping bag and set it beside her boot. She looked at him with a raised eyebrow. "Bowie knife? If I'm right, you only need a screw driver or a putty knife."

"I usually have it on me for urbex outings; you just didn't know it because I never had to save you from a gang of skinheads."

With the sunglasses hiding his eyes, she couldn't tell if he was serious. "Well, don't go poking any federal agents. You're not spending the rest of your life in prison on my account."

"Girl, I was ready to do that the minute I picked you up in Dave's jeep. Aiding and abetting a fugitive? Sure beats my usual trespassing."

She gave his hand a squeeze. "I don't know if you smell bad enough to pass for a vagabond. Maybe."

"Should I piss myself? Let's do this before people start wondering what the hot chick is doing talking to the dirtbag."

She took the laptop from the bag and set it on the aluminum mesh tabletop. It was an old Dell with a lot of peeling stickers on it. She pulled the Wi-Fi card out before flipping the lid up. A moment later she had removed the SD card from her camera and inserted it into a slot.

Of the twenty or so pictures she had taken at the asylum, only one partially captured what she was looking for, and viewing it on her camera's LCD hadn't revealed enough detail for her to be certain. Now she pulled up the image and zoomed in.

It was a shot of the birdbath in the courtyard where they had encountered the reverend from the Starry Wisdom Church performing his prayers and prostrations. Beyond the black cloth of his frock coat in the foreground, the glass mosaic adorning the concrete basin was in focus enough to reveal one place where the pattern was off. Most of the shards of glass were triangular, but one piece was round and surrounded by just enough triangular blank space to suggest that the original fragment had been removed and this misfit set in its place. It was almost the right size, and the color, although rendered as a shade of gray in the infrared photo, was close enough to the surrounding pieces that unless you were looking for it, you wouldn't notice the substitution.

It might have been red.

Becca touched the pendant through her shirt and turned the laptop to show Rafael the screen.

"You see it? The round piece. That has to be it, that's the ruby."

"I wonder what kind of putty or glue your grandfather had access to."

"We'll find out soon enough."

"I'll find out. You're laying low in case the place is being watched."

"I'll stay close. And if we don't see anyone, I'm coming with you."

"Not a good idea. Too many places in there for agents or cultists to hide. I'm gonna get in and get out."

"I hope it's still there, Raf. God, I hope nobody found it."

"It stayed hidden this long. That's a lot of years. Why do you think he put it there? In the open?"

"I'm not sure. If he buried it or hid it in a totally secret place, no one would ever have a chance of finding it. The doctors were reading his letters. He knew that Catherine, who gave it to him in the first place, would recognize it if she was looking for it, but without the scarab, no one else would know what it was. Only she never made it back there to look for it. Instead she tried to contact him beyond the grave to ask him where he hid it."

"Seriously?"

"She used that black mirror. But I don't think she found her husband on the other side."

"What *did* she find?"

"The black man in the red robe. I think she woke him up. I think she caused the very thing she wanted to prevent."

"And now you plan to finish it for her?"

"I need to make it right, Raf. It was clever of my Grandpa to hide a shiny red thing in the one place where it wouldn't stand out, where it would blend in with all the other colored glass. But there might be more to it than that. Something happened at the birdbath. Another inmate, a member of the Starry Wisdom Church, evoked something from the water. It set the whole institution into a panic. From what I can tell from the journal, it sounds like Peter banished it with the gem. But I don't know if setting it in the fountain was part of the process, or just an afterthought."

"Lucky thing they didn't break that birdbath up with a sledge hammer and cart it away."

"Yeah. I like to think there was a protective force at work, that maybe I was meant to find it."

"A little faith couldn't hurt."

"Well, I don't have much. But Raf...I feel like I should be the one to take it out. Who knows if removing it will...*unleash* something. I can't put you up against the risk."

He looked at the sky, took her hand and said, "I can't see the things you can. I haven't been exposed, right? That part of my brain isn't turned on, so I'm not vulnerable like you. It's better if I do it. Safer. Besides, you don't have a swanky disguise."

She smiled; it felt faint and must have looked it too.

He squeezed her hand again. "Don't worry. In half an hour, we'll have what we need and you'll be on to telling me all about the next way we get to risk our lives. You *do* have a plan for that right?" He grinned at her and closed the laptop.

"I'm afraid I don't really. I'm still trying to decipher Catherine's notes, but whatever is happening, it's reaching critical mass, and I think if we follow the black trails to where they touch down north of the city, we'll be in the right place to make a difference. Maybe even at the right time."

"So you'll know it when you see it?"

"Hope so. But the notes don't even sound like she's talking about Boston. More like Egypt or Jerusalem. There are all these references to an obelisk and Solomon's masons and I don't know. I don't get it."

Rafael's eyes widened and his brow furrowed with an epiphany. "That's the Bunker Hill Monument."

"*Holy shit*...an obelisk."

"North of the city. Built by Masons."

Becca's hand trembled as she removed her camera card from the computer and reinserted the Wi-Fi card.

"Wait, I thought you were afraid of being tracked," Rafael said.

"They can't see my photos, those are on the card. The risk of this machine being traced to you in the next five minutes is probably small, and I have to know, I have to check it out and see if something jumps out at me, something that could help."

She selected the café's free hotspot, went to Wikipedia, and pulled up the Bunker Hill Monument.

"Granite obelisk erected between 1827 and 1834 in Charlestown to commemorate the Battle of Bunker Hill...Actually on Breed's Hill where the misnamed battle took place...There was something in the journal about blood-soaked ground, this has to be it.... The first monument at the site was created by King Solomon's Lodge of Masons in 1794... Final monument was based on a design by architect Solomon Willard...Capstone laid on July 23, 1842...Wait a minute, wait...a...minute." Becca pulled the journal from her bag and flipped to a page she had marked with the fabric bookmark.

"This is it, Raf. Two hundred ninety-four steps to the top. That's what Catherine was speculating about in all of these calculations of Hebrew words from the Bible." Her heart sped up as she went on, jabbing a finger at the page, "Genesis 1:16 refers to the 'Greater Light' that God set in the sky: the sun! And the words 'Greater Light' equal 294. The mason who designed the obelisk was making a reference to the sun, the power of light. And according to her notes there was a dark faction of Masons in Boston who later formed the Starry Wisdom Church, who intended for the obelisk to be an instrument of dark forces when the stars were right and some gem of power was found."

"Gem of power. You mean the ruby? The scarab?"

"I don't know. That doesn't seem right. The Fire of Cairo was made to banish darkness. This sounds like they were searching for a stone that was its opposite. An evil stone."

"Well let's hope they have more trouble finding their stone than we had finding ours."

"If they don't already have it."

"Come on, shut that thing down and let's go."

* * *

The hike to Allston took most of the afternoon, but they couldn't ride the T with Django. Rafael had brought along a baseball cap for Becca to cover her face. She didn't seem to attract any obvious attention, probably because most eyes tended to linger on his ratty getup. The sky maintained its iron-gray austerity throughout the day, and when they reached the hole in the slouching chain link fence that hemmed in the asylum, the sun was dissolving in an acid bath of pollution-laced clouds on the western horizon. They were both sweating from the climb—Rafael more so for the heavy layers of clothes. Only Django still seemed as alert and energized as ever.

Huddled in the shelter of the tree line where the evening shadows gathered in wide pools, they could see no cars parked in front of the crumbling stone gates on the street. Rafael had done a quick reconnaissance of the parking lot beyond the chained off entrance.

"Empty," he said when he returned, "But that don't mean there's no agents, cops, or cultists in the building. You should stay here like we planned."

"I don't have a good feeling about letting you do this, Raf. It feels like it should be me."

"I'll be back in five."

She shook her head, then swept her eyes across the sprawling ruins of the asylum. Rafael, sensing that she was gathering her thoughts, waited for her to speak.

"I used to be afraid of this place, you know."

"Seriously? Then why'd you keep coming back?"

She swallowed. "Maybe I thought I could get a handle on it, get some power over the fear by photographing it. Don't get me wrong, it's fucking creepy, but I think what scared me was how it reminded me of my grandfather, like a *warning* sign, a warning of what could happen to me because it ran in my family."

"Insanity?"

She nodded.

"You said it *used to* scare you. Not anymore?"

"I'm starting to see it as a place where he did a really brave thing. But Gran left the beetle to me. I should be the one to do this, to make it whole."

Rafael smiled. Damn, the boy was pretty when he smiled. "Becca, you've done a lot of brave things lately. It's hard to believe you're the same person. Let me do this one thing for you. You can't help shit if they jump you and throw you in a van. I'm fast, and I'll be outta there before they know it's me. All right?"

"At least take Django with you."

Rafael shook his head. "Defeats the purpose. How many squatters have a dog on a leash? And you've been seen with him. I'll be right back."

He turned to go, and she reached out and grabbed his sleeve, pulled him back. She went up on her tiptoes and kissed him deeply, let go of his sleeve reluctantly.

Django was whining and straining at the leash, anxious to keep their little pack together, anxious for her to follow Rafael as he ducked through the hole in the fence and shambled up the scraggly, balding slope toward the ivy-draped brick edifice with its shattered windows.

Becca massaged the dog's scruff and tried to soothe him. "Shhh…. Quiet, boy. He'll be okay. He'll be right back." And she knew the reassurance was more for herself than for Django.

Clouds passed. She fought the urge to step out of the shelter of the trees and the weed-woven fence and approach the ruined building for a better vantage point.

The grounds were cloaked in an unsettling silence. With each car that passed, she tuned her ear to the engine noise, listening for any change of pitch that might indicate someone slowing to a stop. But none did.

And then, amid the rustle of leaves in the evening breeze, she heard a whisper. Her name. There was no mistaking it.

She squinted into the deeper shadows of the nearby patch of woods where only a neglected shed lay between the abandoned asylum and the nearest house.

"Rafael?" Could he have circled around behind her somehow after spotting a threat? Was it *him* coaxing her away from the scene as quietly as he could? And did he have the ruby already?

Django barked at the woods, and she yanked on the leash, crouched down, and cupped her hand over his muzzle. He growled.

Holding the leash close to the collar, she took two slow steps toward the trees, as if stealth would help, as if whoever was there hadn't already spied her and called her by name, as if the tall grass underfoot were a wood-plank floor that might creak if she stepped too fast, too hard.

The whisper came again. Her name, just her name, toneless. And she took another step. She could see a shadow at the corner of the shed, a human silhouette, and a chill passed through her at the sight despite its androgynous anonymity. Her body was screaming at her to turn and run from it, but her memory found it somehow familiar, and all she knew was that it wasn't Rafael, and Django didn't like the scent of it.

*   *   *

Rafael stepped through the brick frame, where the metal doors had long ago been removed, and onto a bed of cinders. He saw the fallen oak tree still leaning against the building, its crown disappearing through the window it had shattered when it went down, and he remembered taking Becca to the ECT room to show it to her because he knew she would want to photograph it. How many days ago had that been? Twelve? It felt like months, and it struck him as strange that this place should look so much the same when so much had happened since. He saw the fountain, too, in the center of the courtyard. The westering sun glanced off of the few unbroken windows high above and cast a pallid sheen down on the filmy gray, leaf-strewn rainwater gathered in the basin.

He circled around it, scanning the mosaic for the misfit part, silently praying *(Let it be, let it be, let it be)* that the gem was still there, where they had seen it in the photo. He looked up at the windows, but saw no motion in them, no sign of sentries on the rooftop, where for all he knew there could be a helicopter perched beyond his line of sight. Or maybe they *were* alone here. Maybe Becca *could* have come with him—

And there it was; a small red stone gleaming like a droplet of blood amid the shards of colored glass.

He wanted to be her hero, to deliver the jewel, but now that he was here, he hesitated, knowing that once she had it, she wouldn't be able to turn back. Her course would be set, and she would be marching into deeper danger.

He almost wished that SPECTRA agents would rappel down from the roof into the courtyard with guns drawn and take the choice away from him, bring her someplace safe. The past few days had divided his desires for her: he could see how this crazy quest he barely understood was invigorating her, pushing her past her limits, and giving her a purpose he wanted to help her fulfill. But it went against his every instinct to help her keep risking her life.

She had asked him once, on a bad day early in their friendship, why he wanted to hang around with someone like her, someone so moody and fucked up, and he had told her that her moods were like the weather: sure, there were stormy days, but they passed. He didn't hold her nature against her and wasn't a fair-weather friend. Now that she was engaging with life on a scale he'd never seen before, he found her more attractive than ever; but he feared it was too much too soon, and the cost might be too high for her.

Rafael knelt and pressed a fingertip against the gem. It appeared to be set in a wad of dried bubble gum that had hardened over a decade ago. "Please let it protect her," he muttered. He tried to dig the stone out of the gum with his fingernails, but they were too short. He took the Bowie knife from under his weather-stained trench coat, unsheathed the blade, and gingerly pried at the stone.

A high-pitched whine penetrated his consciousness. Still holding the knife, he rose from his haunches and looked around. The surface of the water in the bath was vibrating as if an electrical current passed through it.

He stared into the mucky basin where years of leaves had decayed under years of rains. Something moved in the bottom. The water could be no more than six inches, but it seemed to absorb long rays of silver light from the breaking clouds; *too* long, as if stretching them down fathoms, miles, leagues.

The rays rotated as he watched, hypnotized by their motion. He knew he should pry the stone free and get out of the courtyard, go see if Becca was okay, but that imperative seemed faint and muted by wooly layers in his head, because this water, this silver mirror, was so fascinating, so odd…and now something seemed to be surfacing in it.

Rafael squatted, his left hand gripping the basin rim, and with the knife in his right, he pried the gemstone loose and watched it drop to the dirt at his feet.

* * *

Becca saw the face of the figure beside the shed. She didn't know she'd been holding her breath until she let it rush out. It was Neil. But the sense of safety that came with recognition was quickly diminished when more recent memories clamored in, reminders of betrayal, and her footsteps faltered.

Neil, whom she called Uncle, had handed her over to SPECTRA when she'd sent him the photos. If he was here, then the agents might be here with him, using him as a lure to draw her over.

She took a step backward, shaking her head. She pulled the leash to turn Django around. But Neil was stepping toward her now, emerging from the shadows. He looked haggard. There were blue shadows under his eyes. She supposed she probably looked equally worn, with her nest of unkempt hair and rumpled clothes, but she'd been on the run. Seeing the toll stress had taken on him gave her a sickly tingle of petty satisfaction. She hoped he'd lost sleep over her these past few days.

"What are you doing here? Who are you with?"

"Becca, we need to talk. You don't have to do this alone."

"You're going to help me now? It's a little late for that."

"I'm sorry they grabbed you. I thought they'd understand that you were just in the right place at the right time to catch these things on film. I thought my vouching for you...I didn't even think I needed to vouch for you, I just... It never crossed my mind that they would lock you up."

"How did you find me?" She was still walking backward, pulling on the leash, and Django was reading her body language, her stress, smelling the fear pheromones spicing her sweat, and sensing the tension in her grip on the leash, in her voice. He bared his teeth, and Neil stopped advancing with his palms turned out, less than five feet away.

"Some of your pictures were taken here. And it's not like I don't know the significance of the place, the family history. I thought you'd come back."

"*Why* would I come back here? Why would you think that with everything that's happened since?"

"I saw the stone, Becca. In the photo, in the birdbath. That's why you're here, isn't it?"

Heat flashed across her face, like a slap. Her eyes and nostrils flared, and she whisper-shouted, "*Who else knows?*" She wheeled around and scanned the tree line, the street, the windows above.

"Becca, calm down," he said, his hand hovering parallel to the ground between them.

"No. I won't. Answer me. Who's here with you?"

He shot a glance at the street. "Someone you know. Someone you trust, in that dark red car."

"Someone I trust like I trusted you? *Who?*"

"Nina, your therapist."

Becca reeled. What the fuck was going on here, an apocalyptic episode of *This Is Your Life?*

"Nina? How? How did you even find her? I've never told you my therapist's name."

"I can explain everything after you get in the car."

"Not gonna happen."

"Becca, listen to me. We will keep them from putting you in a cell. We will keep them from injecting you with a drug that will make you blind to what's going on. But you have to trust us. All we want to do is protect you, keep you free to do what you have to do."

"And what's that, Neil? Just what do you think I have to do?"

He looked at the ground between them. When his eyes came up to meet hers again she saw the fear in them. "Do you have the stone?"

"Neil you're freaking me out. How do you know about it? And no, I don't have it…. *Wait,* I called Nina before I went to Arkham. Is that how that agent found us there?"

"Listen to me, Becca. There are a lot of connections around you. Some of them may be…*fate,* for lack of a better word, or synchronicity, but it's not a conspiracy. There *are* conspiracies at work, but I swear to you I'm not part of one. And I don't believe she is either. Her ex-husband is the agent assigned to you, Jason Brooks, but listen, *listen, please.*" He was talking fast now, his placating hand trembling. He was afraid she was going to turn tail and run and he'd never see her again. It was written all over his face. And why shouldn't she?

"Brooks thinks there's a cultist on the inside at SPECTRA, or some other agency they're working with, LIMNUS or something. They had Darius Marlowe, the cult leader—they had him in custody yesterday and they were interrogating him, but someone set it up so there was salt water and a giant mirror in the room, and he used those to transform into something monstrous, and he got out. He slipped into that other dimension, the one showing through in your photos, and now he could be anywhere."

"Okay, now I know you're lying because Marlowe is dead. I saw Brooks shoot him, it's in the news."

"Don't believe the news, Becca. They had to restore order to round up the witnesses and flush you out. They know you have pieces of the puzzle. Brooks has other pieces from the book you dropped in Arkham. That's why he sent us to find you. To tell you it's not over, to tell you that the Starry Wisdom cult may have infiltrated the government. He wants to help you put the pieces together and end this. If you don't have the stone, just get it and let's get out of here."

Becca didn't know what to believe. She felt like she'd been clinging to a piece of driftwood in a maelstrom of paranoia, the waters rushing around her laden with the shards of her broken sanity, and now Neil was tossing planks pierced with rusty nails into the whirlpool with her as the wind picked up. She wanted him to go away and let her think, wanted to hide in the shed, shut down and sleep, make it all go away. She no longer wanted the responsibility of knowing that something she had only the barest intuitive grasp on might save the city.

Fuck the city, she thought. Fuck the human race and the Hummer it rode in on. What was she supposed to do, anyway—kill a horde of sea monsters with a blast of radiation from a nuclear scarab? Wipe out a race of ancient intelligent, godlike creatures that had walked the earth before mankind and had now come back to reclaim it after he'd failed as a steward? She wasn't sure she could, or even should stop it.

Who was she really helping? Who could she really trust?

And then she heard a layered siren, like a scream and a whistle rising together. But Django had heard it first and he was off—lunging over the fallen door of the asylum after Rafael before she could tighten her grip on the vanishing leash. She pinned her panicked gaze on Neil's face long enough to see if he had knowledge of this new turn, but he looked as bewildered as she felt.

Heart pounding, she turned to run, but he grabbed her by the wrist.

* * *

Rafael held the ruby in his fist. It was such a small thing, but it seemed to hum with power, charging the air around him and making his body buzz from his dreadlocks to his toenails. Something was uncoiling in the impossible depths of the basin, surfacing. His consciousness was also surfacing at the prompting of the dog by his side, nudging him, whimpering.

A human hand splashed out of the water and grabbed his wrist, jerking him toward the bath. He had time to think that the concrete bowl was too shallow, the pedestal too narrow to hold a man. Then the Ju-Jitsu he'd learned as a child kicked in, and he pressed the thumb of his left hand into the webbing between thumb and forefinger of the dripping gray hand and twisted his wrist out of its grasp while squeezing the pressure point. The fingers unclenched, but before he could step back a bouquet of tentacles lashed out of the water with astonishing speed and twined around the back of his head, wrenching him forward. He felt his ribs crack as his chest slammed into the concrete, and then his head was submerged, screaming bubbles, inhaling foul water, drowning.

He could dimly hear the frantic barking of the dog, then felt its teeth pulling at the leg of his jeans, ripping the fabric, and pulling him back in a tug-o-war against the muscular grip of the tentacles. But Django wasn't strong enough, was losing, and Rafael's eyes were locked on the chittering beak of a beast that could not exist; and the dimming of his consciousness as his brain cells were starved of oxygen was a mercy, but the searing in his lungs as capillaries burst was an anguish beyond any pain he had ever known.

The dog let go of his leg, and his face lurched toward that horrid orifice where a black tongue rolled and uncoiled into his own mouth, filling him with rot and revulsion, making him bite down and push away from the birdbath with his left hand. In his right, he still gripped the stone, determined to the last not to drop it, and then he felt the paws on his back: Django climbing and launching over him. The tentacles released him and thrashed like dying snakes in the dog's jaws.

Black blood in the water.

Black novas blooming in his head, like what Becca said she saw in the sky. Sweet Becca, whom he would die for…and he was doing it right now.

* * *

Becca struggled to break free of Neil's grip, anger rising and flushing her face. "Let me go!" To her surprise he did, and she stumbled and fell on her ass on the grassy slope.

She scrambled to her feet and started to run toward the courtyard, but the sounds rising around her came into focus and slowed her step. The rising whistle and scream had ceased or been masked by Django's frantic barking, the drone of a helicopter, and tires screeching as cars she couldn't see raced to the front gate.

Neil was yelling at her to come back, to get in the car or they'd catch her, and he was right. *Damn him*, he was right, but she had to help Raf, had to see if he was hurt, had to know he was okay.

"You can't reach him now. If you want to get out of here you have to get in the car. Get in the car, Becca, or you can't help anyone."

She wanted to run to the courtyard. Every instinct in her was screaming for her to do it, but she knew he was right. They'd grab her before she got there and throw her into a car or a helicopter, and that would be the end of it. They'd take the journal and the scarab, and….

"The stone," she said, "they'll take the stone."

"It's too late. Get in the car. Maybe Brooks can get it from inside SPECTRA, but you have to come now. I can't be seen here, Becca, and neither can Nina."

She saw real desperation in his eyes. Enough to make her finally believe him. He was here to keep her free, to make up for his mistake.

But Rafael and Django....

She took a step toward the car and felt like a coward, felt like she was abandoning the first person she'd ever loved who hadn't abandoned her.

Black smoke streamed into the courtyard from the orb, twisting in the air on whatever ethereal currents it responded to, but not stirring or scattering at all in the turbulence of the helicopter landing in the courtyard. Who had sent SPECTRA here if not Brooks? Who else could monitor the sky? Were they still using witnesses for it or had all of those people been "cured"? She couldn't leave Raf, but she couldn't spend the equinox in a cell either. What good was the little bit of hard-won knowledge and power she possessed if she was locked away by a cult-infiltrated covert agency?

Neil was already climbing into the front passenger seat. Nina's sharp eyes stared out of the driver's side mirror. As soon as he closed his door, they would be gone.

Becca ran down the hill, pulled the rear door open, and threw herself onto the leather bench seat. The car started to move before she could get a grip on the door handle to close it, her army bag still dangling in the gap. The door bobbed against the bag strap as she pulled it in, and then she saw Django bounding down the slope toward the street.

"Stop!" she shouted at Nina, but the car kept rolling, picking up speed.

"Stop, it's my dog!"

Django ran after the car. Nina hit the brake and Becca fell into the foot well. She kicked the swinging door open and Django jumped into the car, tail swishing and smacking back and forth between the seats. Becca pulled herself up and pulled the door shut as the car accelerated. Django toppled onto her as Nina took a hard turn. And then they were cruising down the hill under the pulsing yellow light of the streetlamps, Becca stroking Django's fur, which was wet and brackish, but he didn't shake off in the car, only whimpered and rubbed his cold, damp nose into the palm of her hand.

The dog opened his mouth and dropped a gobbet of blood…no, a gleaming red gem into the palm of her hand.

Chapter 23

The night sky churned in a roiling black vortex above the granite obelisk on the crown of Breed's Hill. The monument, two hundred and twenty-one feet of towering white stone, was lit by stands of high-powered halogen lights around the base, like radiant, upturned trees. Six black-robed figures climbed the hill unseen at 3 AM and gathered at the spiked iron fence around the base of the obelisk. The trees bordering the hill were mostly barren, their leaves scattered on ground which had two-and-a-half centuries ago absorbed the blood of the fallen at the Battle of Bunker Hill.

A mound of overturned dirt marked a spot not far from the top of the hill where the earth had been broken with a small spade, now cast aside on the grass, clods of dirt still clinging to the blade. The cloaked assembly paused to gaze at the small hole as they passed. Beyond the statue of William Prescott brandishing a sword, the city stretched: towers throwing light at the low cloud cover, the darker thunderheads sweeping inland with lightning in their hearts, and the white cables of the Zakim Bridge fanning down from arches tipped with obelisks that echoed the monument.

The houses surrounding the hill were dark and quiet at this deep hour, the gray façade of Charlestown High School across the street from the monument as lifeless as a mausoleum. But the squat stone lodge adjacent to the obelisk, its entrance adorned with Ionic pillars, its flat roof topped with banks of upturned lights, was occupied.

The brethren had assembled at the appointed time, less than an hour before the equinox. One of the six now knocked on the iron door: 1-3-1. The door swung open and Cyril ushered them in. Beyond him, beneath a marble statue of Joseph Warren flanked with flags, lay a National Park Services ranger: a ginger-haired young man in a gray-and-green uniform, curled in a fetal position, his wrists and ankles bound in black duct tape, his eyes wide above a gag of the same.

"He's here," Cyril said, his eyes alight with boyish glee as he led the brothers and sisters into the echoing, candle-lit chamber and closed the door behind them. "Darius has come back to us, and he's...look, he's *magnificent*." He waved his hand at a cloaked shape huddled in the corner, a shape crowned with undulating appendages where its head should have been, a shape which cast a shadow-dance of writhing gray snakes across the pale wall, white Doric pillars, and marble wainscoting.

The figure rose, and the crawling shadows retracted and resolved into the shape of a man.

A wooden box with brass bands and hinges lay on the floor amid crumbs of dirt. Cold purple light seeped from the cracks in its rotting lid and ill-fitting joints.

* * *

"He's here." Neil held the curtain aside with a finger. They were at Nina's brownstone, Becca sitting on the couch nursing a cup of hot tea that was doing more to warm her hands than her belly, Django curled at her feet, and Nina leaning against the island counter in the kitchen, smoking a cigarette to calm her nerves.

Becca got up, pulled her coat on, picked up her army bag, and walked to the head of the stairs, Django at her heels. Nina extinguished her cigarette under a thin stream of water from the tap, and stepped around to touch Becca's arm. "Good luck," she said, obviously self-conscious about the whole situation.

Becca knew that the number of boundaries they had breached in the past few hours was staggering. After eighteen months of professional distance, here she was in her shrink's kitchen, about to get in a car with the woman's ex-husband to fulfill a quest that should have them all committed for schizophrenic hallucinations and delusions of grandeur. It felt weird on a grand scale, but it somehow felt weirder to be wished luck by the one person who knew best just how unequipped she was to save anyone, including herself.

Nina seemed to sense Becca's fear and the source of it: not the tangible darkness out there in the night, but the personal darkness inside that made her feel too weak to make a difference. The therapist straightened her posture, drew a deep breath, and patted the collar of Becca's coat. Becca felt herself straightening her own spine as their eyes met.

"Whatever it is you have to do tonight, just remember that *you* were meant to do it," Nina said. "You're here because of how you see the world, and you'll know what to do when the time comes."

Becca looked at Neil. He looked as terrified as she felt.

"See you later, kiddo," he said with a bloodless smile.

She nodded and hurried down the stairs, Django shadowing her out the door and into the back seat of the idling black car.

Brooks met her eyes in the rear view mirror. "How you feeling? Ready?"

Becca dipped a finger under the neckline of her shirt, found the chain, and pulled the scarab out. It gleamed in the glow of the dome light, the red gem, the Fire of Cairo, restored in the round bezel between the beetle's pincers. "Yeah," she said, "ready." She closed the door, the light went out, and the car pulled away.

* * *

Darius Marlowe carried the dirt-caked wooden box, the box that held the Shining Trapezohedron, out of the lodge, across the metal grate bounded by spiked iron fencing, and into the base of the monument. The door in the sheer granite façade was ajar, having never been locked for the night. White light spilled into the entrance from the high-powered lamps surrounding the obelisk. The light was hostile to Nyarlathotep in his truest form as the Haunter of the Dark, but Cyril had figured out how to cut the power when the time came. For now, illumination was needed for the preparations.

Inside the monument, the winding stair marched upward to the left, spiraling around a central circular shaft, a newel, that had once housed an elevator to the observation deck at the top. The elevator, a basket on a cable connected to the steam engine used to raise the granite blocks during construction, had been abandoned and dismantled in 1844, after the first year of service, the shaft covered with an iron grate at the top. At the bottom, the entrance to the newel was shuttered with a gate through which visitors could see a replica of the first temporary monument erected on the site before the obelisk's construction; a marble Tuscan-style memorial pillar topped with an urn filial and fronted with a brass plaque.

Darius had used his newfound changeling abilities to great effect on the ranger, terrifying him into divulging the locations of all keys and security features. The chain had been removed from the gate, which now stood ajar. He stepped into the base of the shaft, laid a hand on the marble pillar, and looked up. A hinged metal lid above the pillar lay open in a half-moon shape. Beyond it the dark shaft yawned, a quarter mile of cold stone ascending to the observation chamber at the peak. Darius drew a deep breath of the cool, damp air, and smiled. The chain Cyril had removed from the gate was coiled on the floor beside a popped padlock. Soon they would use the chain to bind the ranger to the base of the marble pillar, a sacrifice to the Haunter of the Dark.

Darius left the newel and ascended the stone steps, cradling the box against his belly, in the crook of his arm, like a baby. It was a long, dark climb, but with the iron handrail for a guide one didn't need to see to follow the tight, winding spiral up and up and up. At intervals the white light from the halogen floods outside spilled in through narrow ventilation slits too small to be called windows. Otherwise, the stairs were lit only by the sparse violet light spilling from the cracks in the box he carried. The original, ornately-engraved brass box had been lost after the fall of the Free-Will Church, when the stone had been cast into the Narragansett Bay, and simpler housing had been fashioned for the artifact after a dive team hired by a wealthy benefactor retrieved it in the years when the church was operating underground.

At length he came to the small observation chamber and found his brothers busy with the preparations. They had hauled tools in burlap sacks up the 294 steps, had cast their robes from their sweat-slicked backs, and now resembled ordinary workmen in jeans, removing the Plexiglas panes from the square windows that gave a sprawling view of Charlestown, and Boston beyond, and the menacing thunderheads majestically under-lit by urban light pollution.

Two of the brothers stacked the Plexiglas against the wall while another pair removed segments of elaborately engraved brass poles from a bag, and set about screwing them together. These wands—among the oldest relics in the church treasury—had long been an enigma to Reverend Proctor and his predecessors, but Darius, under the tutelage of Nereus Charobim, had learned their purpose. The Black Brotherhood, the left-hand inner order of high-ranking Masons who had subtly guided the construction of the obelisk, had equipped the structure with mounting hardware for these ancient tools. The rods were in fact ocular wands with crystal cores designed to channel dark rays from a power source mounted on a tripod at the center of the chamber, direct them out the windows at the cardinal points, and angle them upward from mirrored tips to converge on the pyramidion capstone. All four windows had originally been fitted with pairs of iron rings for the exoteric purpose of holding flagpoles in the early days of the monument when four American flags had been draped from them. The flags had been retired when the Plexiglas panes were installed for safety reasons, but the mounting rings remained in place.

Now, with the panes removed, the Brothers extended the brass rods through the windows and fitted them into the rings. Darius inspected their work, setting his eye to the base of each staff in turn, and peering through the crystal cores like periscopes, rotating each until all four mirrored tips were focused on the apex of the capstone. The Brothers gave him a wide berth in the small stone chamber, then donned their cloaks and descended the stairs one-by-one as he dismissed them.

Alone at the top of the obelisk, Darius transformed, his sinuous appendages blooming and writhing from his human shape. He bent to the floor, gripped the bars of the round iron grate with curled fingers and tentacles, and lifted it from the newel. He set it on the floor with a rolling clang, and gazed into the pitch-black shaft.

One of the Brothers had assembled the brass tripod and leaned it against the wall. He now spread its legs apart and placed it over the hole.

Violet light played over the walls from the cracks in the box, as if the stone inside sensed that its time was nigh. He lifted the latch, raised the lid, and the exquisite non-Euclidian angles of the Shining Trapezohedron dazzled his mind and heart. It was a fist-sized crystal of marbled blood; it was all sin and song; it was his own heart in mineral form, and the heart of his dark and terrible god.

He took it in his trembling fingers and set it atop the tripod. He heard the faint strains of a chant on the hill below as the adorants began their circumambulations around the great stone spire on the blood-rich mound. And closer, the inchoate grunts and gag-muted cries of the ranger at the bottom of the well, the chiming of the chains like temple bells as Cyril bound the man to the marble pillar.

Darius checked his watch and waited, reveling in the sublime anticipation of the moment, the breath before the plunge. Sweet ribbons of incense wafted up from the black hole at his feet, curled around the glowing stone, and teasing his alien olfactory glands, lit up his mind like a plasma globe.

* * *

The black car shot down Storrow Drive beside the river. The road was empty at 3:23 AM. Becca could only make out vague impressions of the black orb and its tendrils in the darkness to the north, faint stains on the billowing curtains of night. A storm was moving in, and no stars shone. She kept looking at the rearview mirror, trying to catch Brooks' eyes and read something there. He wasn't a big talker, his brow grim and focused. But she needed to know something Nina and Neil couldn't tell her, and needed to know if his answer was truth or lie, so she held the question, suffering under the weight of it, saving it for when they were out of the car and standing face to face, when she could read more than his isolated eyes.

"How do you know your people aren't tracking us?" She asked.

"I don't. But I know how it's done, so I'm pretty sure they're not."

"Your wife says you think there's a cultist on the inside."

"She's not my wife. And yes, I do."

"So...why did she dump you?"

Becca was pretty sure his deepening crow's feet were connected to a smile.

"How do you know I didn't dump her? Maybe I got tired of being analyzed."

"You don't want to talk about it, just tell me to fuck off."

"Did *she* say she dumped me?"

"She's not allowed to talk about her personal life."

He laughed. "It was a lot of things...but mostly my gambling habit."

"Did you quit?"

"I'm taking a gamble on you right now."

"*Touché.*"

"Pretty sure you're taking one on me too."

"That's just because I need a ride to Bunker Hill and I don't have cab fare."

* * *

From the window Darius could see the Black Pharaoh climbing the stairs to the crown of the hill. The brethren were positioned at the quarters, tracing sigils in the air with daggers, intoning the sacred names, and re-consecrating the hallowed ground.

Darius wished he could witness the sacrifice of the ranger, but it would take too long to descend the stairs and he didn't want to miss the moment when his master arrived at the top of the shaft—well-fed, restored to his true form, and reunited with the holy stone that was once his home.

Darius had prepared the way, had restored the black speech, rent the veil between worlds. He had reclaimed the Shining Trapezohedron from the earth and set it in its rightful place as intended by the church founders. And now he would bear witness, stationed at the left hand of the master when the stars were right, when that which was below joined that which was above.

The floodlights went out. Cyril had cut the breakers to make the obelisk safe for Charobim in his form as the Haunter of the Dark. Darius took a cautious step toward the gaping hole, dragging his shoe to avoid stepping into the void. Dropping to one knee, he pressed his hands against the cold stone floor and tilted his head to the open shaft.

There was a charged silence as the ranger chained in the bottom of the well beheld the coming of Nyarlathotep.

Then the screaming and rattling resumed with fresh intensity, rising through a series of crescendos and peaking when the gag was shredded along with the face it bound, and the chasm echoed with the wet slap of meat and blood and alien anatomy, followed mere heartbeats later by the slither and scurry of myriad appendages, feelers, and folded wings, climbing the stone shaft.

* * *

Brooks parked on Monument Square. The dashboard clock read 3:40. No sooner had they climbed out of the car than the floodlights on the monument went dark. Brooks had a flashlight at the ready in one hand and the *Mortiferum Indicium* in the other. He put the barrel of the flashlight in his mouth and flipped to a page marked by a Post-It strip.

"Here," he said, jabbing a finger at the page as if it wasn't a rare grimoire but a phone book and he wanted Becca to memorize the number of the power he needed her to dial on her scarab. "A guy I trust told me this is the mantra you need to activate the beetle."

"A guy you trust?"

"I trust his knowledge, anyway. Can you pronounce it? Memorize it?"

She silently read the line beside his finger and nodded, unable to speak, her breath caught in her throat.

He closed the book with a snap and tossed it onto the car seat, shut the door and locked it. Django was already padding across the street when she seized Brooks' arm and turned him around, forcing him to look her in the eye. He was taller, but she was close, and the light from a colonial-style street lamp was still shining in the absence of the monument floods. It was enough to lend his face a thin, parchment-tinted glow.

"Tell me what happened to Rafael at the asylum. Is he okay? Do they have him in custody?"

The hesitation was all she needed to confirm her worst fears. He might have lied to her easily in the car's mirror, but face-to-face she could see the conflict fluttering through his jaw and brow. He was sizing her up, deciding which would make her more able to act here and now—the truth or a lie. She knew then that he favored games of chance, wasn't a card player. The calculation only delayed him for a half second, but by the time he opened his mouth to answer the question, he had seen the change wash over her face, the welling up and caving in, and he knew that she knew the truth and all that was left was to try to salvage her or take the scarab and go on without her.

"Rebecca," he said gently, and laid a hand on her forearm, "He didn't die in vain if we end this here. He's the reason you have the ruby, he gave it to the dog…."

"No…*no, no, no. Please….*"

He pointed up the hill at the dark spire. "Whoever, *whatever* is up there is responsible for Rafael's death."

"Oh God. It's my fault, I sent him there, oh *fuck*, Jesus fuck…."

She was buckled over, her wrists pressed against her stomach, her hair draped over her face, when it started to rain. Something was pressing against her folded arms, something hard and leathery burrowing between her arms and belly. Brooks was giving it to her, trying to make her take it. She looked down through the curtain of hair and saw a leather-sheathed Bowie knife.

Rafael's knife that he had used to pry the stone from the birdbath.

"Take it," he said.

Becca curled her fingers around the handle, and was surprised to find that it gave her strength. Hot tears were running down her face, cold rain down her hair. She drew a deep, steadying breath and looked at the sky above the monument. The orb was pulsing against the darkness now. It resembled a purple-tinted negative exposure, darkly radiant, with all tendrils converging in a dome over the hill, the higher lines jumping to ride the lower to earth like loose electricity seeking ground. More purple light flickered from the window at the peak, where something like a brass pipe protruded from the window.

Brooks had stowed his torch and was checking his gun in the half-light when a scream ripped the night. He jogged up the stone steps to the crest of the hill.

Becca followed on his heels.

Two figures in black robes blocked the path to the monument, one brandishing a dagger. Brooks raised his gun, pointed it in the face of the armed one, and drove the pair back onto the grass. Django appeared at the edge of the path, his hackles raised, a low growl issuing from his chest. The coward dropped the dagger and raised his hands, and Becca took the opportunity to run for the ramp that led through the short iron fence into the monument. She knew Brooks wouldn't fire unless he absolutely had to, wouldn't want to telegraph their arrival, but she also knew the cultists wouldn't be cowed for long. They had strength of numbers. She needed to make every second that he could hold them off count.

The gate hung ajar, and, reaching the end of the ramp, she stepped into the darkness of the vestibule. She smelled iron and incense and knew that the iron wasn't from all that metalwork but from the blood she could feel sticking to the soles of her boots. There was a horrible sound of something crawling, slither-shuffling high above in the core of the great structure.

She felt blindly in the dark until her hand found a railing, her foot a step. She was on the winding stair with only one way to go now, and up she went, quiet at first, but soon climbing with as much abandon as her stamina would allow, her steps echoing in the spiral vault above, and another sound, a subsonic rumble issuing from the damp granite, always to her right as she wound around the core.

She stopped climbing at one of the steel diamond mesh ventilation grates that let on to the central shaft, and listened to the horrid sound, the slither and slap of something monstrous. It made her flesh crawl, and there was a moment when it seemed she wouldn't be able to force her feet to take another step. On the street outside she had broken down in front of Brooks after keeping up a tough act since their initial encounter in the interrogation room. Now she was alone in the dark with no one to back her up, not even Django.

"What I came here pretending to be, I am becoming," she whispered.

On she climbed. At intervals she passed slots in the outer wall through which the cold wind rushed into the stairway. She glimpsed the city lights in the distance, and, invigorated by light and air she pushed harder, huffing and pulling on the iron rail, rising and turning toward the peak, rising and turning.

A gunshot crackled outside, followed quickly by another. She thought she heard shouting under the hiss of her own labored breathing. She wished she had counted the steps from the bottom, but knew she wouldn't have been able to maintain the necessary concentration. On she climbed until she detected a faint, cold light above.

She paused to catch her breath, touched the scarab at her breast, and stealthily ascended the remaining steps.

There was an iron balustrade guarding the stairwell to keep tourists from toppling down if they misstepped walking around the observation deck. Becca crouched low when she reached it, clutching Rafael's knife in her right hand, the sheath discarded on the step below her. Waves of violet radiance, energized like laser light, ebbed and flowed across the walls and ceiling. A tall figure stood near the top of the stairs, gazing in awe at something in the center of the room. Perched on the stairs, with a hand touching the floor, she crept forward and peered around the metal plate.

A creature lay sprawled on the lip of the pit, streamers of disintegrating matter issuing from its leathery wings, twitching tentacles, and three-lobed burning eye, and pouring up into a redblack stone mounted on a tripod over the void. Whatever it was, it was transforming into energy and flowing into the faceted crystal, which in turn emanated beams of purple light to the four compass points where they were channeled through the brass rods mounted in the windows.

Becca was almost at the man's feet, and her eyes followed the cut of his robe up to his face, painted in rapture and ambient radiation: Darius Marlowe. Was *he* Rafael's killer? She didn't know, but what did it matter whether Marlowe himself had done the deed at the asylum? He was the one who had started all of this, the one who had unleashed dark forces on innocents all over the city, so yes, he was ultimately responsible for Rafael. Becca bit her cheek at the sight of him and tasted her own blood through clenched teeth.

She heard another gunshot, and now through the windows the shouts of men mingled with Django's snarling and snapping on the hill below.

At the sound of the gunshot Darius spun around to face the stairs, but before he could see her, Becca launched off the top step and drove her shoulder into his gut, slamming him into the curved granite wall. His face blurred on impact, tentacles blossoming, mouth mutating, involuntarily flickering in and out of the terrestrial dimension. She brought the Bowie knife up in an arc, the blade jutting out the bottom of her closed fist, lopped one tentacle off and scored a deep groove across another. Then they were gone again, and Darius was howling, raising his hands to grasp at the air in front of him.

He brought his knee up and kicked her away. For a dizzying moment she teetered on the brink of the void, then regained her balance. She lunged forward, stabbing at him, and he rolled away from the blade, fumbling in his robe for his own weapon.

Becca kicked the tripod and watched the brass legs clatter down the shaft, but the dark crystal didn't go with it; instead it hovered above the chasm, suspended by the beams it cast through the rods in the windows.

Darius had drawn his dagger—a long, curved, obsidian blade etched with runes. He took a deep breath and on the outflow morphed fully into his nightside form, the tentacles sprouting again, one of them gushing black fluid, the fingers gripping the dagger hilt springing yellow talons. Then, relishing the hunt and seeming to drink in the hot waves of primal fear she radiated as her last vestiges of sanity crumbled, he stalked her around the circle.

The knife fell from Becca's trembling hand.

Tentacles sprang from the creature's shoulders. In an instant two had coiled around Becca's legs, wrenching her into the air, swinging her around, and dangling her over the black hole beside the hovering stone. She forced her gaze from its dark radiance, following one of the beams through a window to the sky beyond. She sensed some seismic shift in the colossal clouds that had gathered around the monument, could imagine how the violet light reflected upward from the tips of the rods was feeding the black sun at the heart of the vortex, the tumorous portal between worlds dilating like an eye; and she felt every inch of the white obelisk bathing in the negative photons raining from that malevolent pole star.

The scarab dangled in her hair from the chain around her neck. The chain slipped, almost caught in her lips, then grazed her nose and fell away. She watched in horror as the talisman vanished down the tunnel, a glint of gold like a falling star consumed by shadow.

Without thinking she moaned the syllables that were already on her lips, calling after the talisman down the echoing shaft.

"Yehi Aour!"

For a terrifying, brief eternity nothing happened. Then a red flame shone, a burning coal in the well below her. The blood had rushed to her head, and she was imagining how it would burst like a paint balloon when the Marlowe-creature dropped her all two hundred feet. But then the beetle buzzed past her in a redgold flash, mechanical wings fluttering, the Fire of Cairo blazing in its pincers, blinding the creature, sending it flailing backward and pulling her up out of the hole. The tentacles uncoiled and dissolved in the corrosive light, and, free of them, Becca fell, caught the edge of the well with her fingers.

The scarab hovered in the air at the center of the room, shedding its dazzling light, filling the chamber with a blinding, white, arctic noon. The other gem, the dirty thing with the dark light, the inverse light of an alien hell, was blasted to shards, blown through the windows. In the aftershock of the white flare, the rays from the scarab blazed redgold, streamed to the four quarters through the brass rods in the windows, reflected up at the apex of the obelisk, and pierced the nucleus of Azothoth, the writhing black orb at the heart of the whirling cloud.

Dangling from the lip of the chasm, Becca shed a tear at the brightness and beauty of it.

Gunshots compressed the air in the chamber, and she almost let go.

Marlowe jerked back and rolled along the wall, leaving a smear of inky blood in his wake before toppling into the shaft. The body, which had resolved back into wiry human form, bumped against Becca on the way down. She let out a cry as she swung to the side, shifting her weight as best she could without letting go. Seconds later she heard the distant thunder and splash when Marlowe hit the metal lid at the bottom, and then Brooks had seized her wrist and was pulling her up, the scarab still floating between them, flooding the room with light, blasting everything into stark contrast.

Becca got her knee up onto the floor and rolled away from the hole, which had terrified her more than the creature. She shuffled her feet, sliding on her butt until her back was against the wall. The light was fading now, as if it were being absorbed into the red gem. Fading and dimming to an orange glow that reminded her so much of steel in a forge that she almost flinched when the beetle fluttered toward her and dropped into her upturned hand. But it was cool to the touch.

The chamber fell into shadow again as the fire in the ruby faded.

Brooks slid down the wall to sit beside her in the dark at the top of the white stone spire as the first faint suggestion of a sunrise touched the sky on the morning of September 23rd.

Chapter 24

What had begun for Becca Philips with a burial, ended with a scattering of ashes.

In the days following the events at the monument, she returned to her warehouse loft and spent most of her time napping with Django, in bed or on the futon. SPECTRA had returned her computer equipment, but she had no desire to look at photos. It was weeks before she had any inclination to pick up a camera.

She had sat for a short debriefing at Government Center on September 23rd; short because Brooks made them stop and release her when it became obvious to him that the questions were causing her too much anxiety. She was sleep-deprived and hungry and didn't understand what had happened to her, he argued. To her surprise and relief, they listened to him. She caught a look in his eyes that told her he was equally surprised. *Hero*, he kept calling her, and they either believed him or had reason to fear publicity problems, because as they put her in a cab, they told her she would have to come back in a few days for another interview, but that call never came.

When she finally picked up her camera again, it was to revisit the abandoned buildings and out-of-service train tunnels that Rafael had emblazoned with his graffiti art. He had never found a conventional niche at the Museum School, and these crumbling, moldy walls had remained the canvas he was most comfortable with. Becca felt it was her duty to preserve them in her own way. She didn't bring the IR modified Nikon, but rather a normal digital SLR to capture his work in all of its shocking color.

It turned out to be a bigger job than she first anticipated because she felt compelled to shoot each mural from multiple angles, with close ups and panoramic shots, and in as many different states of light as she could manage. Most of the buildings had sections of collapsed roofing where sunlight or moonlight could find a way through. She also took to carrying high-powered, portable lighting, fitting Django with a set of saddlebags to help ease the burden of gear. The two of them would sit in dank places, eating a picnic lunch and waiting for clouds to shift.

There were fewer clouds over Boston in those first weeks of November, which was odd for the month but seemed to feel right to everyone on the street. Like a cleansing after long suffering. Whether those crisp, sunny days had been bought by sacrifice or were a gift of grace, only a few people knew. And none more than her.

And so she waited for clouds. Waited for them to cover the sun and smooth the sharp highlights on the painted bricks. Waited for them to pass through her heart. But they never did.

The new photos eventually forced her back to the computer and back to her archives. Her journal of the expeditions she had taken with Rafael didn't provide enough information to pinpoint the weather and time of day when he had painted many of his pieces, and she wanted to photograph each in the closest approximation of the light he had seen as she could manage. The photos she had taken of him working helped her to puzzle it out, and the project occupied her mind and hands and kept her from thinking too much about what might lie behind the walls, or the sky.

Some nights she woke in the deep hours with the fierce imperative burning in her mind that she should destroy every infrared photo she had taken during the crisis and triple-wipe the hard drives. But she couldn't erase her own memory, so why bother with the computer's? Even the thought of letting the cursor arrow hover over those folders chilled her. What if she was tempted to open one? What if she opened them all? And what if she saw things in those photos that she hadn't seen before?

As winter came on with the first flurries, she wore the beetle always and everywhere. Sleeping. Showering. And it troubled her that now, after the monsters had been banished, she was more afraid of them than she had been during that season when they had walked the streets of the city. But there hadn't been time for fear then, and things you could see would always be less dreadful than those you couldn't.

She haunted the abandoned places through November, until she could no longer deny that she had all the photos she was going to get and was only lingering to feel close to him, and then she realized how little was left for her in Boston. The prospect of trying to hold her sanity together long enough to finish her degree while her peers—people who listened to Emo and hadn't lived through hell on earth—critiqued her work...there wasn't enough Klonopin in the world to get her through that.

She hadn't seen Nina since the equinox, either. Every time she scrolled past the name in the contacts list on her phone, she felt weird. The relationship had changed, and there was no going back.

By Thanksgiving she was thinking of getting away for a while, and then Brooks called and gave her the excuse she needed and the destination to go with it.

"How would you like to do a job for me? It includes airfare to a sunnier clime."

"Is this a SPECTRA gig?"

"Sort of." He paused. "I'll understand if it would be upsetting for you, but...I figured it might give you a chance to do something you'd want to do anyway. Also, way I see it, we kind of owe it to you."

"Okay, out with it already."

"We've been back and forth with Rafael's mother, Estela, in Brazil. Apparently he once told her that he wanted to be cremated. She was against it, would have preferred burial, but not enough to refuse his wishes. The US government is treating him like a fallen hero of a covert war, and we've offered to take care of the cremation here in Boston. We would have flown her up for it, but she doesn't want to come. She only asks that his ashes be taken to Brazil so she can scatter them where he wanted. I'm not trusting an airline with this, and I'm sure as hell not handing it off to FedEx. I thought maybe you could deliver him personally."

She couldn't speak for a good minute after that, but the sniffling must have kept Brooks on the line, let him know she hadn't hung up on him. Finally, she said yes, she would go, if he would take care of her dog while she was away. He told her it was a deal.

* * *

Becca didn't know how to talk to Rafael's mother on the phone. Even after all that she had been through, the thought of telling a woman she'd never met that she was responsible for her son's death terrified her more than anything. She hated phones. Having a conversation about anything of significance without eye contact, facial cues, body language…it unnerved her and always had. She could have turned down Brooks' offer, could have stayed out of it entirely, but she knew she needed to go. Not just to be there when the ashes were scattered, but to face Rafael's family, to own up to her role in his death and try to explain what he had died for, if that was at all possible, which she doubted. They would likely send her away, cursing and screaming at the Insane American, the art-school slut who must be a delusional drug addict. And she was loath to admit it, but she actually felt better knowing that Brooks had her back. Estela had been in communication with SPECTRA, had already heard some version of the story that lauded Rafael as the hero he was, and had processed it. The woman knew that a friend of Rafael would be sent by the US Government to deliver the urn, and Becca hoped that counted for something.

So she was grateful for the opportunity, but when she met Brooks at the crematorium in Andover, she found that she had little to say to him. Small talk seemed impossible after what they'd been through, and any talk in the presence of Rafael's body would have been irreverent anyway. She watched the box roll into the flame chamber in silence, and touched the stone in the scarab at her breast while he burned.

In the parking lot Brooks asked her if she wanted to get coffee, and she accepted. At a nearby café, it felt a little less weird that they weren't discussing Rafael. Becca wrote directions for Django's care and feeding on a pad she kept in her camera bag, tore the sheet off and handed it to him.

"That's some dog, you got, Becca. Braver than most people."

"I think most dogs are," she said. "They rise to the occasion and put on a tough act no matter what. But yeah, he's a keeper."

The silence spun out.

Becca thought about the other occasion they had spent together, in and around a helicopter in Back Bay when the fabric of reality was fraying around them for the first time, and she realized they had nothing normal to talk about whatsoever.

"How's Tom?" she asked, "That guy in the helicopter you took along for a set of eyes. You keep tabs on him?"

Brooks nodded, fiddled with his watchband. "Yeah, we check up on everybody. He's good. The drug therapy…Nepenthe, it seems to have worked. None of them remember what they saw, and no one has claimed hallucinations or nightmares in the follow-ups." He stared at the scarab as he spoke, and she knew he wondered if no one saw anything because of the drug treatment, or because she had banished the darkness with magic she herself still didn't quite understand.

"He's uh, he's going to be a father, Tom. He and his wife are expecting in April. He seems to be looking forward. I'd tell him that you asked after him, but I doubt he'd remember who you are."

Becca squeezed a lemon wedge into her tea. "Do you think I should have had a dose? They wanted me to, didn't they?"

Brooks looked out the window. "Yeah, they thought wiping your drive might be a good safety measure."

"But you intervened." It wasn't a question.

He sighed, stared at his car on the street, where the cedar box containing Rafael's ashes lay in repose behind tinted glass. "When you lose a friend who died a hero, you should get to remember why. Not to mention remembering what *you* did for everybody."

"You calling me a hero?"

"Somebody has to. Not like you're gonna be on CNN."

"Thank God."

"Do *you* ever think you should have had a dose? You ever want to forget?"

"Yes and no. I want to forget a lot of it, but not all of it. If I'm going to be haunted by it at all, I want to understand at least as much as I do. So I guess I'm stuck with it."

"What about the others? Does Tom seem haunted by it at all, even in a vague way?"

"Hard to say. I didn't know any of these people before they were witnesses, so maybe he was a little off to begin with, right? Lot of people have some depression, or sorrow in their past. I don't know, I couldn't say. Not like the world was a perfect place before the monsters broke through."

* * *

According to Estela Moreno, her son wanted to be scattered at Iguazu Falls, a UNESCO World Heritage site and one of the New Seven Wonders of the Natural World. Situated deep in the rainforest on the tri-border of Paraguay, Argentina, and Brazil, the falls were a major tourist attraction with an airport just thirty miles away. SPECTRA offered to fly Becca direct to Foz do Iguaçu International on a private jet, but she politely declined, insisting instead on a flight to the sprawling metropolis of São Paulo, Rafael's hometown.

She wanted to meet his mother at her home so that the poor woman could decide for herself whether to send her away or invite her on the pilgrimage. It would be a sixteen-hour bus ride from the city to the falls, and that felt right to Becca. Flying in seemed too easy. She wanted a journey. If Estela allowed her to come along, the ride would give them time to get to know each other. And if she were turned away at the door after presenting the cedar box, at least she would leave having seen where he came from.

In the end, her anxiety was unfounded. One look in the woman's eyes—Rafael's eyes—told her that she was a welcome guest, and a wish that she had secretly held close was granted in the days that followed when Rafael's older brother Diego took her on a tour of his earliest paintings, hidden in alleys and behind the buildings of the dirty city.

Becca photographed them all.

São Paulo was much bigger than Boston, but the paintings made her feel strangely at home. The Frias de Oliveira Bridge reminded her of the Zakim in Boston, and the whole trip started to feel like a dream, as if her waking life, her familiar environs had subtly shifted into a parallel world, in which some things were the same, and some were alien, and even those that were the same were somehow alien, and then the appointed day came when it was time to take the bus to the jungle.

She was grateful for the change.

She had tried to talk to Estela about Rafael's death, but the language barrier made it difficult, and the woman seemed to need little in the way of explanation. She had understood the word *hero* and that seemed to be enough. On the third day, while they ate lunch together in the kitchen, she asked Becca, "You love him, *meo menino?* He love you?"

"Yes," Becca replied. And that had been enough. Estela took her hand, and squeezed it, and they shared the tears. "We go together," Estela said. "You, me, and Diego. We go Iguazu together."

"Thank you. *Obrigado.*"

* * *

On January 28th snow was falling on Boston, but at Iguazu Falls, summer was just beginning. Becca Philips stood at the edge of a wooden platform overlooking Devil's Throat, a semi-circle of terraced waterfalls, and the sound of crashing water was a white noise to wash all other echoes from her mind.

Thousands of butterflies, red and black, yellow and blue, dressed in endless variations of markings, hovered around her in the mist, alighted on the railings, and fluttered amid the ash when Estela poured it out into the chasm. For a moment Becca couldn't tell the difference between ash and mist as he fell.

She resisted the urge to take her camera from her bag. It was too easy to make life smaller by placing a lens between its vastness and her eye. In this moment she wanted no distance, wanted memories, not photos.

She breathed the ionized air deep into her lungs. Looking up and down the towers of thundering water, she knew she had never felt so small in the face of the power of nature. Not even in that red September she would never forget.

The sun flared off the stone that hung from her neck, and Diego leaned in close to be heard over the roar of the falls, and he recited the legend of their origin into her ear.

"They say that the river was the domain of a great serpent god named Mboi. And the local tribes would gather once each year to appease him by sacrificing a maiden to the waters. But one year the chieftain's daughter, Naipí was chosen, and a boy named Tarobá, who loved her, was heart-stricken and tried to persuade them to let her go. But even the chief would not defy the fearsome serpent, and they said it must be done.

"So the night before the sacrifice, Tarobá freed her and spirited her away in a canoe. But Mboi was enraged, and, pursuing the lovers, he raised his giant body high into the sky and crashed into the riverbed, cleaving the earth, and creating the falls.

"The Guaraní say that Tarobá became a palm tree standing on these cliffs above the falls, and Naipí became a rock below the gulf, and there they remain, separated forever, while Mboi watches them from a cave.

"But on sunny days, like this one, a rainbow bridges the distance, connecting them once again."

Becca cast her gaze over the falls, over the iridescence of the rainbows and the butterflies, the vast swathes of lush green jungle, and thought about how it would be summer here for months, and the water on the coast would be blue, and even when winter came, the days would be long. She wondered if Brooks could call in another favor and have Django put on one of those private jets. After all, the dog was a hero. When the house in Arkham sold, her uncle would send her enough to live on for a while, and maybe by then she'd have sold something to *National Geographic*. A girl could dream, anyway.

Boarding the bus back to São Paulo, Becca noticed the driver fiddling with the antenna on a transistor radio. The box hummed and crackled, blasted a vulgar buzz as the aluminum rod searched the sky for the right frequencies. At last a signal came through— faint and fuzzy at first, then clear and bright. It was the guitar intro to "Here Comes the Sun" by The Beatles.

Chapter 25

Brooks sent the dog to Brazil and moved on to getting caught up in the lives of new strangers, most of them hapless witnesses to the strange sciences that threatened civilization periodically while the sane people of the world carried on in blissful ignorance of the shadows beyond the cold light of the collective digital campfire. But he smiled whenever he received a postcard from Becca, and he kept tabs on the Harvard, Copley, and Back Bay witnesses— especially Tom, because Becca had taken an interest in him and if she asked about him again Brooks didn't want her to think he didn't care.

Tom and his wife Susan's baby arrived two weeks early, on March 30th: a healthy boy weighing in at 6.8 pounds, 19 inches. They named him Noah.

Brooks called ahead and dropped by their condo three weeks later with a basket of food for the sleep-deprived couple. They seemed happy, and Tom had gotten used to Agent Brooks as a fixture in his life, albeit a rare one, even if he couldn't quite remember exactly what they had done together and understood that he probably never would.

Brooks made himself scarcer after the baby came, but he still called every five or six months. On one such call, around the holidays, Tom mentioned that Noah had spoken his first word: *banana*.

Brooks could hear the pride in the man's voice. "*Mama* or *Dada* would have been nice, but those could be gibberish. *Banana* is a real word. I mean it was clear as day."

"That's great," Brooks said. "First word. He'll be crawling before you know it."

"Oh man, yeah, that'll be chaos. Yeah, before *banana* it was *all* gibberish. The sounds babies make…it almost sounds like a language sometimes. Makes you wonder what he thinks he's saying."

Brooks felt a chill, like a trickle of icy water had been poured down the collar of his shirt. He licked his suddenly dry lips and asked, "What kind of sounds?"

"Just sounds I didn't even know humans could make, you know? Like…I don't know if I could even remember an example well enough to mimic it. Some of it repeats though. Like…Oh, yeah: *Cthulhu R'lyeh Wgah'nagl fhtagn.* That's a piece of something he says a lot. Funny, huh?

"You still there, Jason?"

Brooks still held the phone, but he had half forgotten it as he walked to the window and looked out over the icy, gray city, wondering how many other babies had been born to people whose ears had been infected with those infernal harmonics. He was looking at the silver line of a contrail and the shadow it cast against the burnished gunmetal cloud cover, and thinking about what might lie in wait behind the sky.

ACKNOWLEDGEMENTS

Over the past couple of years, I've been lucky to have the support of some amazing friends and allies on this writing adventure. I'd especially like to thank Jeff Miller and Jill Sweeney-Bosa. Jeff's story insights and artwork have often helped me to clarify my creative direction, while Jill has been a phenomenal help as a beta reader, publicist, and event planner, making every book a celebration. I love you both and don't know what I'd do without you. Thanks also to Sue Little and Dan Chartrand, proprietors of my favorite indie book stores—Jabberwocky and Water Street— and to Christopher C. Payne at JournalStone for once again giving me the opportunity to do this thing I love and for blessing me with a great editor in Dr. Michael Collings. Thanks to National Park Services Ranger Eric Hanson Plass for answering my questions about the Bunker Hill Monument on a January day when the steps were too icy for climbing. But don't blame him for my addition of flagpole mounts in all four windows even though these days the monument only has them in two. Just think of my Boston as a hub slightly out of alignment with history. Early readers who improved the book and to whom I owe much gratitude include Brett J. Talley, Chuck Killorin (who also rocked the cover this time), Robert Falzano, S.T. Joshi, Vincenzo Bilof, and my first and last manuscript reader, my wife, Jen, who helps to keep the chaos at bay.

DOUGLAS WYNNE is the author of two previous novels: *The Devil of Echo Lake* and *Steel Breeze*. He lives in Massachusetts with his wife and son and a houseful of animals just a stone's throw from H.P. Lovecraft's fictional town of Arkham. You can find him on the web at www.dougwynne.com

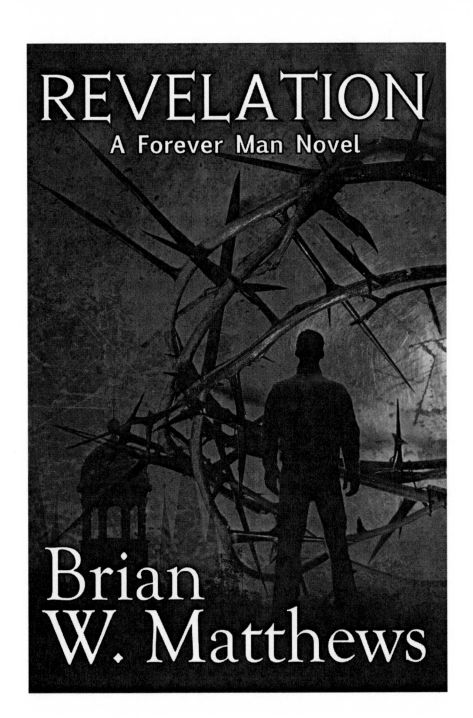

REVELATION

A Forever Man Novel

Brian
W. Matthews

OUT OF TUNE

CHRISTOPHER GOLDEN

DAVID LISS

DEL HOWISON

GARY BRAUNBECK

GREGORY FROST

JACK KETCHUM

JEFF STRAND

NANCY KEIM-COMLEY

KEITH R. A. DeCANDIDO

KELLEY ARMSTRONG

NANCY HOLDER

SEANAN McGUIRE

SIMON R. GREEN

LISA MORTON

JEFFREY MARIOTTE

MARSHEILA ROCKWELL

EDITED BY

JONATHAN MABERRY

NEW YORK TIMES BESTSELLER

CPSIA information can be obtained at www.ICGtesting.com
Printed in the USA
LVOW11s1911181016

509270LV00003B/579/P